S H T U M

A Novel

J E M L E S T E R

The Overlook Press
New York, NY

This edition first published in hardcover in the United States in 2017 by
The Overlook Press, Peter Mayer Publishers, Inc.

141 Wooster Street
New York, NY 10012
www.overlookpress.com

For bulk and special sales, please contact sales@overlookny.com,
or write us at the above address

Library of Congress Cataloging-in-Publication Data
Names: Lester, Jem, author.
Title: Shtum : a novel / Jem Lester.
Description: New York, NY : Overlook Press, 2017.
Identifiers: LCCN 2017002703 (print) | LCCN 2017007027 (ebook) | ISBN
9781468314724 (hardcover) | ISBN 9781468314717
Subjects: LCSH: Parents of autistic children--Fiction. | Fathers and
sons--Fiction. | Autistic youth--Fiction. | Domestic fiction. | GSAFD:
Black humor (Literature)
Classification: LCC PR6112.E775 S55 2017 (print) | LCC PR6112.E775
(ebook) |
DDC 823/.92--dc23
LC record available at https://lccn.loc.gov/2017002703

Manufactured in the United States of America
1   3   5   7   9   8   6   4   2
978-1-4683-1472-4

In memory of Stuart and Sharon Lester

SHTUM

Wynchgate Children's Services
The Civic Centre
Brown Street
London N24 3EA

18 January 2011

Dear Mr and Mrs Jewell
Re: Jonah Jewell D.O.B. 11 May 2000

Having discussed your request for the SEN Complex Needs
panel to consider placing Jonah in a specialist residential
school for children with autism, it is the panel's overwhelming
conclusion that Jonah's educational and social needs would be
appropriately met by his remaining in borough.

It is the Council's policy to educate its children in
borough wherever possible, using a multi-agency approach to
support them both in the home and in an educational setting.

All garnered reports suggest that Jonah is making
appropriate progress at Roysten Gate and that he is extremely
well supported by a loving family. The panel has therefore
recommended that Jonah's transition to the newly enhanced
Maureen Mitchell Secondary School should proceed in
September 2011.

Yours sincerely
Adele Latchford
Director of Children's Services

cc.
Claire McDonald, Speech Therapist
Anita Kaur, Educational Psychologist
Jennifer Porter, Headteacher, Roysten Gate School
Emilio De Rossi, Consultant Paediatrician
Mary Carey, Social Worker

Groundhog

Emma waits in the kitchen because the smell makes her gag. So the day unravels like every other: bath running, Jonah standing half-sodden while I open the windows, remove the bedsheets and spray the mattress cover with disinfectant. The sheets I ball together with his reeking pyjamas. The aromatic nappy and soiled wipes get tied in a plastic bag, and in he hops – the bubble-covered water turning to consommé on contact. I clean him vigorously, showering off the stubborn bits, and dry him with *his* navy towel – any other provokes a tantrum. Dressed, I shoo him along the corridor for breakfast. That's our division of labour – she deals with what goes in and I deal with what comes out.

The letter lies open on the table, evidently scrunched then patted down. We don't talk for ten minutes at least – any less and it'll be my fault. I've learnt to play the long game. Finally, I pick it up and read – it holds no surprises, but I still feel indignant, 'Well, that's it then.'

'Optimistic as ever.'

'They're bloody Orwellian. What is *appropriate*? Do you think they believe their own Newspeak?'

Sitting at the dining-room table with my head in my hands has become my breakfast yoga hold – the *why me?* position.

This minor swapping of self-pity has taken no more than a minute, but in that time our son has slid from view.

'Where is he? Jonah? Weren't you watching him, Ben?'

'I've been talking to you,' I say, making for the kitchen – which, unless supervised, is Jonah's morning workout. He isn't there but the evidence is, an empty tub of Cornish Vanilla. There's ice cream on the black gloss units, stainless steel fridge, marble floor tiles and – as I turn back to the kitchen door – also in his shoulder-length hair, all over his face and his blue school tracksuit. 'Oh you shitbag, Jonah – Emma, he needs showering and changing.'

We watch the minibus take him off with guilt-ridden relief.

Emma cries. 'I can't do this.'

Her sobbing turns my knuckles white.

I choose the wrong words with aplomb. 'Don't be so melo-dramatic.'

'Shut up, Ben. What bright idea do you have? Hold the panel hostage with your father's old Luger until they give in?'

'Like Bonnie and Clyde?'

The image makes her giggle. It neutralises the acid in my stomach. We've been here many times in the past eighteen months, but the life-saving humour has darkened to pitch and we can't really see each other. So she talks, a lot. Repetitively – a mantra of misery.

'I just keep remembering those words coming from his mouth: bubble, door, Dada, Mumma – why did he stop? Last night I dreamt he walked into the lounge and started talking to me and the strange thing is that it was *his* voice – I'm sure

4

of it. When I woke up I was convinced it was true and then I heard you in the bathroom, cleaning him up, and I felt sick with disappointment. Has that happened to you?'

'Sometimes.'

But it hasn't.

She studies the letter again while I finish my coffee. I watch her eyes tilt skyward and her fingers run through her chestnut hair, the spotlights highlighting a strand of grey. Her lips mouth words as she shakes her head and then her voice rises to a whisper as she repeats the phrase: *loving family, loving family, loving family*.

'They're perverse. This whole thing is upside down. We're being punished because we love and care for him and he's not as good at autism as he could be.'

'He'll never play autism for England.'

'It's like they're persecuting us for not being completely destroyed by the situation. Things aren't bad enough, yet. He doesn't need to wear a crash helmet or headphones and we aren't crack addicts.'

'Yet.'

It is truly a system to behold, a cost/benefit analysis without the human element.

I say, 'Maybe I'll have a nervous breakdown, you could grope a client and get disbarred, then we'd be poor and insane – that would boost our case? And if the worse came to the worst we could always split up, they love a single parent.' I laugh to myself at the craziness of it all.

I look at her, but she isn't looking at me and she isn't laughing. She grabs her briefcase and heads off.

'See you later,' I say to the closing door.

*

I'm at the warehouse by eleven – where hundreds of plates sit waiting to be washed, caked in the remnants of celebratory food that has gone hard and rank over the weekend. This is my daily rhythm: tables, chairs, crockery, cutlery and glasses – sent out for hire in pristine condition, picked up in chaos, washed, wrapped and sent out again. It's a living for the sick of life.

'I'm going to lunch.' Valentine, who, at well over six feet with his massive shoulders, looks like a West Indies fast bowler, doesn't look up from his glass polishing. 'I'm going to lunch.'

'Heard you,' he says. 'Got your phone? I'm not answering it.'

'I'll only be an hour.'

'Uh-huh.'

'Back by twelve.'

'Right.'

'Leave it to go to answerphone.'

'Okay.'

'If my dad comes in, tell him I'm on a delivery.'

'Okay.'

I swipe twenty quid from the cashbox and head through the next-door printers to the high road. Vinod blocks my way.

'Need to talk to you about the rent.'

'Have a meeting. Twelve?'

'You said that yesterday.'

I push past him and dive through the front door.

'Six hundred and twenty pounds, Ben.'

'No problem.' But it is.

'Morning, Ben.'

'Andrea.'

'Guinness?'

'Please, darling.'

She talks and pours. 'How the flats going, love?' Permed brunette Andrea has the height of a supermodel and the voice and Adam's apple of a prizefighter.

'Still waiting for the bloody council to sort the planning permission out. Bastards.'

'Bastards. Still, suppose it gives you time to work on your house?'

'Sure,' I say, settling on to a stool at the snug's horseshoe bar. 'Bloody planning.'

This is my alter ego, relayed to the other members of the Professional Drinkers Club – all tradesmen, all Irish – in an effort to fit in. So, it's early and I'm happily alone in the snug with a pint of Guinness, drowning my angst. I like the wood panelling, sticky floors and Irish company. I love that they think I'm one of them. It happened by accident, but I didn't correct them and now I wax lyrical on everything from plastering to the Pope. It feels good being Catholic for a couple of hours a day, I like to try it on for size. It certainly beats the ignominy of hiring out catering equipment and I love the anonymity. It wasn't easy, I had to earn this seat – five months in the public bar before I plucked up the courage to join them. I'm just beginning my second pint, when my mobile wriggles on the bar top like an upturned woodlouse. JONAH: SCHOOL.

'He's fine.' Jonah is grinning, looking over my shoulder toward the car park without blinking. His eyelashes could catch dragon-flies. 'Are you sure he was sick?'

'Mr Jewell, it was a projectile.'

'But he's clean as a whistle?'

'Yes, but Miss Glen needs a dry cleaner.'

I resist offering to pay.

'It's the coughing that triggers it, he's not ill. Seriously, look at him.'

Jonah is jumping up and down at the door, following the manic formation flight of an advance group of starlings.

'I'm sorry, Mr Jewell. He has to stay off school for forty-eight hours following a sickness episode – it's borough policy.'

'Brilliant. What am I supposed to do about work?'

'I'm truly sorry. Could his mother not look after him?'

She's new, Maria. Only joined at Christmas. I don't know how she copes. She is pale-skinned, red-haired and willowy – very attractive in an ethereal way – but no physical match for Jonah and his gang of unpredictable classmates.

'Friday, then?'

'Yes, Friday, as long as he isn't sick again,' she says.

'And what about Cherrytree?' The play scheme that he visits twice a week after school and on Sundays – a blissful day free from nappies. She grimaces.

'I'll let them know Jonah won't be coming.'

Sentenced. No parole. 'Okay, come on, Jonah.' I reach for his hand, but he jerks it away, so I follow his skipping form to the car – dividing the coming two days into hours and minutes and seconds – and clench my fists in my pockets.

'No I can't, Ben. I'm in court both days.'

'But you know Thursday and Friday are my busiest days. Can't we at least do one each?'

The pause and heavy sigh is the answer. She pushes some rocket leaves around her plate with a fork.

'What about your dad?'

'You know we haven't spoken since Yom Kippur in September.'

'You're both so childish. What you have to understand is . . .'

Here we go.

'. . . that if I miss court, someone stays on remand; if you stay at home, someone may not get their fish forks. Do you want me to phone him, he'd love to see Jonah?'

'No. Have you finished?' I ask, taking her plate. But she has me and she knows it and I can't face her now, so instead I begin the washing-up – my rage as hot as the gushing water.

'I'm going to check on Jonah. Meet you in the lounge?'

She's back in seconds.

'He's wide awake and the room stinks.'

'So change him.'

'Ben . . .'

'Tell you what, I'll do it, shall I?'

He's not a baby any more, physically, anyway. As the years have passed I've watched other people's kids developing quickly, dreading the inevitable day when – like a burn-up at the traffic lights – my son remains in neutral as they roar off into the distance. Month by month the chance of hearing words again grew fainter. Now he's ten, statistically those words will never escape. His mind is like a dictionary with the pages glued together. I kiss his forehead and pull the duvet up to his chin. I don't know if he sleeps at night, but as long as he's quiet I can live with it. The trouble is he rarely is.

Before I join Emma, I quietly dispatch the remaining half bottle of wine and return the empty bottle to the fridge.

'Is he all right?' She's curled up on the sofa. 'Are we all right?'

'I'd say we're all about the same, aren't we? Sleepwalking?'

'Suppose a shag's out of the question?' she asks.

I laugh, flute-like and nervy, and file it in the drawer marked 'rhetorical'. It's been months and her half-suggestions and hints

9

leave stab wounds all over me. It's not that she's lost her attraction for me; it's the possible result. The silent knowledge of her desire to extend our family, her outward broodiness in baby company. This has yet to become a full-blown crevasse between us, yet the cracks are appearing. Maybe if Jonah had been born second... She unfolds herself from the sofa, walks down the hall and into the bathroom. It's the fourth time this evening, five minutes of sanctuary, I suppose.

'Could you get me another glass of wine?' she asks when she comes back.

'It's finished.'

'No, there was at least half left.' She stares into my eyes.

'What?'

'You know what.'

'Suddenly I can't have a glass of wine after dinner?'

'It's what you seem to be unable to do after your glass of wine and your brandy or scotch. Don't think I don't realise why you're always suggesting I go to bed early. I'm not stupid, Ben.'

I'm not good at being caught, humiliated. It invokes silence, heavy with unwashed linen. We both know it's my method of avoidance, but I don't know if she suspects that her wriggling bottom – pushed into my groin in the early hours of the morning – feels like an attempted rape. There is nothing carefree about sex any more and a thick blue line appearing on a stick of piss-washed plastic may be her foremost desire, but it just might finish me off for good. It's easier to fall back on a drink problem than admit I don't share her wish. So occasionally I succumb, praying that my sperm have zero sense of direction and the motility of a sloth – they are, after all, mine.

She goes to open another bottle and pours herself a glass.

'Ben, I spoke to a colleague today.'

'Oh, yes.'

'She specialises in educational tribunals.'

'And?'

'As it stands, she doesn't fancy our chances.'

'And that fabulous piece of insight is worth?'

She digs me in the ribs. 'She said *as it stands*.'

'And how does it stand?'

'Us. Together. With the resources we have.'

'I thought this whole thing is about Jonah?'

'It is about Jonah. I showed her the letter; we discussed other cases – successful cases. There were commonalities, certain things that would help him.'

'Such as?'

'This morning's conversation. Splitting up. They love a single parent, remember?'

'That was a joke, Emma, and not a good one.'

'Do you hear me laughing?'

'You're serious? Pretending to split up?'

'It would be for Jonah.'

'Just for him?'

'Yes. But don't tell me you think I'm loving life at the moment.'

'And you've noticed me tap dancing in between arse-wiping?'

'It wouldn't be real, Ben, just a temporary arrangement until the tribunal is over.'

'That could be months. You're being absurd. How would you cope with Jonah and work by yourself? And where would you move to in this charade? Next door? Wouldn't it look a little suspicious?'

'I agree, it would. But single fathers are one of the commonalities I mentioned. Ben, for this to work, Jonah needs to be with you.'

'Just hold on a second, I don't remember agreeing to the first part, the splitting up, let alone the idea that I could cope with him by myself. Emma, the two of us can barely cope together. To be frank, I'm not interested in either suggestion.'

She groans. 'But it would help our case.'

'Jonah's case, you mean? Get the lawyers and judge to live with him, he'll convince them inside an hour.'

As if to hammer home the point, Jonah has rejoined us,

'Go back to bed, Jonah,' I say. But my tone must have given away my irritation and he's jumping so hard that the floor is shaking. Emma approaches him, calling his name softly, but as she closes in, he forces one hand into his mouth and smacks his head with the other, violently.

'Emma, keep away,' I say as he swipes an empty wine glass off the table. It thuds on to the carpet and he kicks it. I throw my arms around him, but he slips my grasp and buries his teeth into my shoulder with force. I have to slap him on the head to get him to release me and it forces the tears from him. Emma moves in to console him and lead him back to bed. She kneels on the floor before him and grazes his chin with the gentlest of kisses. Jonah falls forward until their foreheads touch. I leave them like that and go in search of antiseptic cream.

It's half an hour before Emma returns, pale and yawning. She falls heavily on to the sofa beside me. 'Are you okay?' she asks.

'Yeah, just another souvenir. You'd better take a picture, I suppose.'

She goes to our bedroom to grab the camera and takes half a dozen snaps of my red and punctured shoulder. One more for the album of cuts and bruises, smashed glasses, plates and picture frames – the supporting evidence of Jonah's aggression and unpredictability, saved for a hoped-for tribunal – his anti-matter CV. She hands me a glass of wine.

'I'm not doing it, Emma.'

'There is another solution,' she says.

'What, a straightjacket?'

'To you living here by yourself with Jonah.'

'I've already told you, Emma, that's not going to happen.'

'Ben, do you think you can survive this for another year, two, three, ten? I don't think I can. Not to mention poor Jonah. He needs more than we can give him, more than is on offer at Maureen Mitchell. He needs and deserves better than this. He needs to be given the chance at a little dignity. He needs a residential placement, Ben, he needs the consistency, it may be his only chance.'

I drain my glass.

'Ben,' she continues, 'we have to do whatever it takes, however painful it is in the short term. We have to do it for Jonah.'

'So what's this other solution?' I ask. Already feeling my need to please her overwhelming my sense of self-preservation.

Jewell
14 Oakfield Avenue
London N10 4RG

23 January 2011

Dear Ms Latchford

Re: Jonah Jewell – change in domestic circumstances

Unfortunately, Jonah's mother and I have separated and
Jonah's care is now solely my responsibility. It has been
decided that Mrs Jewell will remain in the family home, while
Jonah and I will move in with my elderly father at the above
address.

As you will no doubt understand, this is a less than ideal
situation – especially for Jonah – and I would be grateful if I
could meet with you at your earliest convenience to discuss
any help that may be available.

Yours sincerely
Ben Jewell

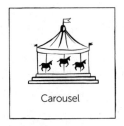

Carousel

'So. I'm honoured.'

Jonah pushes past his grandfather and, like a guided missile, heads directly for the kitchen.

'Coming in?'

'Just a couple of months,' I say, 'like I told you on the phone.'

'So.' He opens the door wide and invites me in with a sweep of his arm. 'What did you do?'

'Nothing.'

'Let her go without a fight then?'

He turns and glides down the dim hallway. His wiry frame may have receded from its five-feet-eleven-inch zenith, but it remains erect and there is threat in the way he holds himself.

'JJ? Are you in my cupboards, already?'

There is rustling and the crack of MDF against wood – Jonah is scavenging.

'What have you found? So! You like bagels, eh?'

Jonah sprints past me into the lounge as I reach the kitchen and he claims the brown chenille sofa like an invading colonial power, a bagel lodged between his jaws.

'JJ, you can't eat it plain. Let me put some salmon in it...'

'He doesn't eat salmon.'

'This he's told you?'

The same old carousel. 'I've tried, he spits it out.'

'This salmon? It's from a delicatessen, or from a supermarket?'

'Neither, Alaska.'

'Always so clever. I'll make him a salmon bagel.'

His accent is no longer strong, but has a noticeable, lilting rise at the end of questions that has always hit me as disdain. It's time to retreat.

'I can't stay, I've got a load of things still to pack and bring from the flat. Can you look after Jonah, just for a bit?'

He shrugs. 'You'll be back when?'

I check my watch. 'Two-ish?'

'It's already midday. Get back by four. We'll go walking, maybe see Maurice.'

'You sure?'

He holds his hands to his chest – palms up. 'What can happen?'

I'm about to list the possible outcomes but he's gone. I hear him humming from the kitchen. He's enjoying this. I'm crying inside and desperate for a drink and my father is in his element. I check my watch: every minute I lose to his bagel-making is robbing me of some much-needed solitude. Finally, the perfect salmon bagel is ready and is being delivered to the lounge. Jonah is halfway through his first and flicks it nonchalantly behind the sofa as the second arrives. From the safety of the hallway I watch as his tongue makes contact with the smoked salmon. And now he's eating it. Little bastard.

'Florsheim's Deli, Temple Fortune. There, something else for your menu, eh, JJ?'

Jonah doesn't flinch as his cheek is pinched. I'd swear he is staring right at me. But I know better.

'His bag's by the door,' I call. 'Dad?'

'Four. Not before, we won't be here.'

Three hours and twenty-two minutes at home. I'll pack up in an hour, but I must sit down first. I want a drink, something to eat, but a disarming thought floats into my head: maybe I could stay the night? It could be a date – we could try proper sex and sleep through the night without the threat of interruption. But no, Emma will worry about Jonah, she'll worry about my dad. Still, the idea of a secret liaison seems to flick my libido switch.

I turn the TV on and the sofa devours me. I'm panicked by the notion of not seeing her for weeks, of being ignored, and – despite all evidence to the contrary – the efficiency with which this status quo has been engineered. I want to cry. Instead, I drink and pass out. In my stupor I hear chickens, cows, the triple-whistle of a shepherd. Some Wordsworth gives way to a chanting football crowd, the rising pitch of celebration, a gunshot, the clack, clack, clack of manual typewriter keys, more gunfire, the rousing, sweet scream of a boy soprano.

My right arm is dead beneath my chin and glistens with saliva illuminated by the cathode glare of the TV. The walls repaint themselves green, then red, then blue and back to green. The sound is muffled by darkness. Darkness. I begin to make loose connections, but they're transitory, almost imperceptible – like Jonah's presence. Darkness. Dribbling. Dead limbs. Daylight. No daylight. Shit.

I jump to my feet and invite the vertigo. Fall to my knees and scrabble for my watch on the floor. Hold its face to the light of the TV screen. Eighteen-fifteen. Shit, shit, shit. Should I phone? I stumble like a drunkard to the front door. Double back to the kitchen to slug from last night's wine. Light a cigarette. Slug again. Glug. Drain the bottle. Shuffle the deck and deal my thoughts to the left, to the right. Pull them together. Shuffle again. Spread the pack. Demon thoughts are alcohol soluble. Additional vodka clears the remaining dregs. I grab my car keys from the table.

The front door is open. Does he think it's the 1950s? The single bare bulb burns circles into my vision, so I feel my way inside the house. The Van Gogh 'Sunflowers' block-print swings like a pendulum as I make contact with it and dust flies off like a Saharan sandstorm. The wrought-iron and glass telephone table eats a chunk of my shin as I try to blink away the floating white spots from my cornea. Who else but my father would swaddle an Edwardian terrace in brown and orange? The last remaining vestige of seventies minimalism in Muswell Hill.

'Hello. Dad? Jonah?' The kitchen light is off. The lounge glows halogen from the peeping-tom streetlight. From the Bakelite radio the clipped tones of Radio 4 caress the ancient oak-hewn furniture. The ugly, obese dresser and dining suite, dark as ebony – its Marmite-varnished surface saved from scarring by crocheted doilies – dominates so completely that in the gloom it embodies some ancient gargoyle, a Golem carved by a wizened shtetl mystic bent on vengeance and vigilantism. I turn the light on and the radio off.

'Hello.'

'Up here.'

'Where?'

'Here. Bathroom.'

He sits on a plastic garden chair next to the bath, massaging Jonah's head with a green sliver of soap.

'So when did he get hair down there?'

'You didn't have to bath him.'

'We had an accident.'

'Wasn't he wearing a nappy? I left you the bag.'

'We were in the garden, so why should he always have to suffer the discomfort?'

'And I suppose crapping in his pants is comfortable?'

'He was just wet. I rinsed his trousers and put them on the radiator. They should almost be dry – it's been three hours.'

'Look, I'm sorry I'm so late ...'

'Did I say anything?'

'Not in so many words, no.'

'Not in any words ...'

Jonah starts laughing and stuffs his mouth with foam.

'You have bubble bath?'

'Washing-up liquid.'

'Jesus, Dad. He can't eat that.' I move sharply to scoop the bubbles from Jonah's mouth. 'It's full of detergent and other shit, he'll be ill.'

Jonah reacts by sliding back and forth – the laughter stops. Waves of brackish water break over the bath and seek gaps between the lino and the skirting. I put my hand on his shoulder but he swipes it off and bites down hard on his own hand. My scalp is prickling. Singing calms him down – singing and dancing.

'Bu-de-bu-de-bum, bu-de-bu-de-bum, boo-di-boo-di-boo.' Dad's hands are raised above his head screwing in two imaginary light bulbs. Jonah is still splashing, but his face has relaxed, reverted to angelic. He makes rhythmic, guttural noises in time with his splashing and his eyes – shining – seem to be locked on to my father's.

'Going to make myself a coffee,' I say, leaving.

The ancient kettle dances a jig on the hob as the water becomes steam and billows towards the whistling spout. The coffee, when I finally locate it in an unmarked earthenware container, looks archaeological and tastes as though it accompanied Dad from Budapest. I hear them pad down the stairs, Dad chatting to Jonah and answering for him as well. I stand in the kitchen sipping my coffee and hear Jonah chuckle. I am flooded with jealousy, not towards my father but towards Jonah. I enter the lounge like an intruder.

Do they look alike? It's hard to tell with Jonah's heavy-metal hair. Do *we* look alike? I study them as they sit close on the sofa, examining the refracting light from Dad's prize crystal paperweight.

'JJ, let us look at this closely. Now, what happens is this: the light that we think is white is actually made up of lots of different colours. How many? Well, I don't know exactly but if we look really carefully, we can see them coming out of the crystal. Look, here.'

Dad holds the crystal in front of Jonah's face and twists it gently from side to side. At certain angles, a rainbow forms on his cheek. He reaches toward the crystal with his thumb and forefinger so, so slowly, like he's pulling a thread through the eye of a needle, and gently plucks it from Dad's hand. He doesn't blink. Not just now – as he examines the miracle of splitting wavelengths – but ever. At least, I don't think I've ever seen him blink. Even when I've tried to catch him – by clapping close to his face or clicking my fingers – he stares straight through. No reflex action, or just no fear? It comforts me to imagine the latter.

'Have I ever told you about this magic crystal before, JJ? No? Well, it's been in the family for over a hundred years. It is made of Bohemia Glass, very famous and beautiful glass.'

I carefully place my coffee mug on a doily. I've never heard the paperweight's history before, just assumed – as with the rest of the tat in this musty house – it was bought on a whim and for too much money in some East London 'antique' shop.

'Dad, it's well past his bedtime.'

'He's happy, leave him be.'

'You want to deal with the fallout?' The oversleeping, over-full nappy and shit-smeared walls.

'He doesn't look tired, Benjamin. Anyway, you are not my lodgers, you are my family, so I will put him to bed.'

'He needs his medication . . .'

'Then maybe you should have arrived at four as I asked instead of spending the afternoon in the pub. He wants to hear the rest of the story.'

'He doesn't give a shit about the story, Dad. He just wants to twiddle the crystal.'

'And how would you know?'

'How would you?'

I sit in the lounge flicking channels, trying to time the changes to one a second. I check my phone for the umpteenth time, then attack his ancient whisky, stealthily, placing it back in the cabinet, silently, with the label pointing out. Old habits die hard. I amble around the room. Nothing of me has invaded this space – except in the ancient carpet stains and cigarette burns. To be fair, it is completely unadorned. With the exception of

Jonah's last school photo sitting on top of the television and the crystal paperweight keeping it company, it is barren. If we were Catholic, it would host an open casket perfectly, although the wake would have to be elsewhere. My dad has read thousands of books but refuses to keep a single volume; his music comes from the radio, his food from containers. Everything seems set up for a quick getaway, but he hasn't been anywhere in years.

I used to believe that this austerity was a guilt hangover from the rabid socialism of his younger self, but the colour scheme is more fascist tyrant than Trotsky. If you look 'through the keyhole' here, all you are likely to discover is the pain of being poked in the eye with a pencil. Through my musings, I've missed Dad standing at the door.

'He's asleep. Now, have you eaten? You haven't, have you?'

'I'm fine, just sort yourself out.'

'Not hungry? What, did you have one of those doner kebobs?'

'Kebabs.'

'Tsch. It's all shit. You'll have a piece of fish.'

'Don't want a piece of fish.'

'You'll have it.'

I'm too tired to argue and thankful for the food, to be honest. He flits around the kitchen like a nectar-guided bee, opening foil here, plastic pots there, until a chipped dinner plate arrives – a scale exhibit of a Chelsea Flower Show garden.

'Florsheim's. Eat,' he announces, poking his fork in my direction, losing two cubes of beetroot on to his grey-stubbled chin.

We eat, silently. We always ate silently, mealtimes could not have resembled a traditional Jewish family meal any less – and I'm surprisingly intrigued.

'Dad, why did we never talk during mealtimes?'

'Shush. I'm eating.'

We do the washing-up his way, in a single sink-full of dirtying water. I get to dry with a formerly white tea towel and stack the dishes in wallpaper-lined cupboards.

'How's Maurice?' I try.

'Maurice is Maurice. He doesn't change.'

I haven't seen Maurice for a couple of years. Apparently he is the first person Dad met on his journey alone from Hungary. Stopping in Maurice's native Holland to recover, they stayed ten years before coming to London. Now Dad's eyelids rise like theatre curtains and out comes the reminiscence. I've heard it all before, how Maurice ran errands for the working girls of Amsterdam before they arrived in England, how he helped Maurice start his *shmutter* business.

'You know, at least I had shoes when we left. Maurice? All he had were a couple of red tulips and a dose of the clap. Those tulips he gave to your Auntie Lilly, the girl he eventually married.'

'And the clap. Who did he give that to? Apart from Auntie Lilly.'

My dad is the only person I know who smiles with a down-turned mouth – he'd look more human standing on his head.

'Now, that, you would have to ask Maurice. Tea?'

'I've brought some proper coffee.'

'You'll have to make it yourself, so you can make me a cup of tea at the same time. I'll be in the lounge.'

The light is off but the lounge is illuminated by the changing camera positions of a *Newsnight* special report.

'Turn the sound up if you want? I don't mind,' I say.

'No, it's his voice, the sarcasm, him.' He points. 'Paxman. Reminds me of your mother, keeps me awake half the night.'

'You're mad.'

'Am I?' he spits back. 'You are sitting here at the age of thirty-seven watching Paxman with your father in silence. You want me to turn it up or you want to sleep?'

'Don't pull any punches, please.'

He shrugs.

'Anyway, we've only separated.'

'Separated? Yes, like oil and water.'

I can feel the lie churning up my dinner. How many times will I have to lie to him? To everyone else that trusts me? If we admit to the deceit, we'll be criticised, or laughed at. I already feel too displaced to bear any scrutiny.

'More like the two Germanies. We were meant to be together and we will be again soon.'

'Believe me, they too would have been better off divorcing. And anyway, using that analogy, you would have definitely been the East to her West.'

'You think it's permanent, don't you? Since when were you such an expert on marriage? How many years ago was it that Mum left you? Twenty-five?' He doesn't take the bait.

'I am just saying that you are too much of an idealist. Things happen, Ben, things change. People change. It's best to be prepared.'

'What are you saying, Dad?'

He doesn't reply. Jonah stands in the doorway clutching three slices of bread with a beseeching grin on his face. Dad beckons him in.

'Come, JJ, sit here with me and watch your grandma on the television.'

Jonah skips to the sofa and sits, unable to believe his luck, and my father pulls him to his hip.

'Go to bed, Ben, you look tired. Leave him with me, we'll be fine.'

'Sure?'

'Go, before I change my mind.'

Even though the sound remains down, I can't sleep. It's not easy, sleeping in your childhood bedroom for the first time in almost twenty years; examining the half-removed stickers by the light of a streetlamp through curtains that never quite close or reach the sill. The mattress feels thin and the bed narrow and the sheets restrictive, tucked in as they are, army style. But most significantly, I am by myself in this single bed, which almost physically hurts.

I like being a husband, was desperate to be a father. I lived a fairy-tale life in my head before I even met Emma and the fairy tale became real for two years. Then Jonah was born and it was fluffy clouds and sleepless nights. But as he reached three, the fairy tale revealed itself an imposter – the red hood fell away to show the Big Bad Wolf of autism.

Lying here, this Sunday night, I feel cast adrift. There is insanity in this situation; even though it's a charade, the fear is three-dimensional, lapping against the sides of the bed, undermining my stability. I have lost my compass in the haste of the move, my head spins, so I sit on the edge of the bed and stare at the Lowry print, counting matchstick dogs. In the bedside drawer I discover an old Bush transistor radio, still tuned to Capital Radio, as I'd left it decades ago. I plug it in and turn it on, half expecting songs from the seventies and eighties, to drag out a bit of melancholy in this evening of oddities – but all I get is hip hop. It takes me twenty minutes to dial a decent signal for Radio 4 and three seconds to dial my home number.

'This is horrible,' I tell her. 'What are you doing right now?'

'Just got in, ordered an Indian.' She sounds drowsy, a little slurred.

'Bit late, isn't it?'

'It's only ten, Ben. How's Jonah?'

'Eating smoked salmon.'

I hear the entry phone buzz.

'Need to go, that's my curry.'

'Speak tomorrow?'

'Ben, I can't cope with going over it every night. Look. I'll phone you. I'm being sent to Hong Kong in a couple of days, anyway. There's a chance I may have to stay for a month.'

'A month! When were you planning on telling me?'

'Look, they only told me today.' I hear her sigh. 'Ben, you're going to have to handle this, okay? You need to do the school visits, deal with the local authority, sort out the barrister. It's all in the file – you'll have to read it all.'

'You know I can't bear to read about Jonah.'

'You can't remain above this, Ben. This is not blissful and you cannot maintain the ignorance. You can't just be his good-time dad.'

That stings me. 'Okay, okay. Where do I find this file?'

'I put it in the boot of your car. You have your father and we can talk about it by email. It's not so terrible. Give Jonah a hug for me.'

And she's gone.

I'm marooned, confused, disorientated. A month? She's away regularly with work, but now? The timing stinks. I could be round there in ten minutes, but instead, I pad gently down the stairs and take the ancient bottle of whisky back to bed for company. Within minutes I hear the whumping of my father and son.

They are at the top of the stairs and Dad's still talking, talking his bollocks to the only person who'll listen to him. Poor Jonah.

'JJ, did you enjoy yourself today? Were they nice to you at your play club? There are some things I need to talk to you about, but you must promise not to repeat anything I say. These things will be our secret, just you and I – here, give me your hand, we must shake on it. Good boy, where to begin? Your geography's not so good, I think, so let me just explain a bit about our family.

'My grandfather, that's your great-great-grandfather, JJ, was an important man. He was an educated man, a man of wisdom, but a man of few words. Rather like you, my little JJ, yes. He lived in a village, in Hungary, not far from the town of Balaton, on the shore of a beautiful lake. Our whole family lived there in peace for many generations. Anyway, Josip was a man of principle – rather like your father, JJ – and as a merchant he had many dealings with the local count, Szelezny – a decent-enough man, if a bit of a Jew-hater.

'I was born in Budapest – it's two cities actually: Buda and Pest, divided by the River Danube but united by a great bridge. Well, JJ, the Friedmans – that was our name back then – were not unhappy there. We were a good family, a big family, your great-grandfather – my father – Louis, was a physician. That's a doctor, and he had many patients and we lived well.'

Friedman? Our name changed? In a rage, I jump from my own bedroom to Jonah's. Only the sight of Jonah stops me from flying at my father.

'Can we help you?' my father asks, looking me up and down. Then he continues as if I wasn't there.

'Your father was born here, he's English, but he was the first of our family to be born here – you are the second. I don't know if you know this, but we are Jews – not an easy thing to be, but a good thing to be.'

I slink away trying to work out how to confront him about this without killing him. Am I just some form of psychological experiment – withdraw all stimuli and see just how crazy you can make me? Why has he never told me this? Of course, I've asked about our family many times, but he just dismisses my questions with a flick of his left hand and four words: 'gassed by the Nazis'. It's as if he gets pleasure from having me floating around like an unanchored dinghy.

When I was thirty, I spent months searching genealogy sites, Holocaust databases and historical accounts, yet found nothing. Now I understand why, because I had the wrong bloody name. As far as I knew until this evening, Georg Jewell just appeared out of thin air, or was crafted from clay like the Golem, and, by extension, so was I.

I can't face asking again, only to hear him evade my questions. I'd like to force it out of him with Sodium Pentothal and some gardening shears. I bury my face in the pillow. Let him tell his parables to Jonah and I'll drink his whisky until I pass out.

'What day is it?' I croak.

'Monday, here.'

He passes me a cup of coffee. There's milk in it and it's horrible. I hadn't passed out until four and I woke up in a panic, but Jonah is miraculously ready apart from his sweatshirt, which is back-to-front.

'Thank you, Dad.'

The phone goes and Dad rushes to answer it, turning his back on me. I hear a muffled conversation and he returns with a jotted note.

'Jonah's school wants to see you at noon.'

'I forgot,' I groan. 'The transition meeting. Was that them on the phone?'

'No. You want to send him away?'

'Was that Emma? Why didn't you pass me the phone?'

'It was just a message. So you want to send him away to school?'

'We'll talk about it later, I need a shower.'

'Answer me, Ben.'

'Later, Dad.'

He shouts at me as I mount the stairs. 'Emma won't be there, so I'll come with you.'

I put my head round the banister. 'No.'

'Yes.'

'No, Dad, I'll talk you through it later.'

'This car is a disgrace.'

'It's a working vehicle.'

'Why would you need a working vehicle?'

He kicks his feet around the footwell; envelopes and empty cigarette packets fly up.

'Stop it, please.' He takes off his seatbelt and bends to pick up a sheet of paper. I glance across – it's a bank statement. 'If you don't drop that now, I'm stopping the car and you can walk home.'

He releases the statement with a flourish and it floats back to the floor.

'Put your bloody seatbelt back on and when we get there, say nothing.'

He mimes a zip across his lips.

*

I am desperate to see Jonah in class, to witness the experts work their apparent miracles, but if he sees me, he'll be distracted and it's better if we both wait in the family room for Mrs Porter, the head teacher. We sit in silence, lukewarm drinks perched on our knees and the supposed evidence of Jonah's progress before us in his recent school reports.

Mrs Porter bursts in followed by Jonah's class teacher, Maria, and a large blonde minute-taker.

'Sorreee, Ben.'

I smile at her and greet Maria with a wave. The three sit opposite us.

'So how do you think Jonah is doing?' asks Mrs Porter.

'That's what we're here for, you to tell us, so tell us.' I look at Dad, firing little incendiaries of indignation at him.

Dad shrugs.

Mrs Porter says: 'I'm sorry, who are you?'

'Georg – Jonah's grandfather.'

'Well, as you know, we're here to discuss Jonah's transition to secondary school at the end of this academic year.'

'Which secondary school?' he keeps on.

Mrs Porter glances at me, I nod.

'Well, the borough's provision is growing all the time with a number of mainstream secondaries either already having integral units or opening them in September. However, given Jonah's obvious limitations I think we would all agree as was stated in the borough's letter that Maureen Mitchell School is the preferred option for Jonah.'

Dad says, 'He's going to Maureen Mitchell then.' We all look at him. 'That's it,' he says.

'No he's not,' I say.

'Ben,' Mrs Porter says, 'Maureen Mitchell has been completely restructured in the last three years and it's now the borough's specialist autistic secondary provision. We have been working very closely with them and they will be using identical methods to us so it is, in effect, a new facility but an extension of here.'

Dad is smiling, his hands folded contentedly across his stomach.

'Would you say, Mrs Porter, that Maureen Mitchell is as good as Royston Glen?' I ask.

Mrs Porter hesitates. 'Well, of course it will take a little time for them to get up to speed. Roysten Glen has been operating for eighteen years now – but, with our help, Maureen Mitchell will avoid all the mistakes we had to make.'

'So, if I'm correct, what you are saying is that Maureen Mitchell isn't currently as good as here and will take some time to achieve that level, yes?'

'Inevitably, I suppose that's true, yes.'

'And it may take a couple of years?'

'Realistically, I suppose. But rest assured we are consulting with them on a regular basis.'

'Oh good, good – *consultation*. And do you think Jonah can afford to wait another two years for this new "school" to sort itself out?'

'Well, I...'

'Well let me put it another way. How long has Jonah been here?'

'Six years.'

'And when he arrived he was in nappies and as he's about to leave he's still in nappies. So after six years of the best specialist education the borough can provide, my beautiful son still cannot use a toilet. So tell me, Jenny, just what is this new, cobbled-together excuse for a provision going to do for my son when in six years you couldn't get him to piss on a toilet.' Mrs Porter looks indignant, while Maria seems crestfallen and I'm now full of shame. I like Maria; she cares about Jonah.

'But you know how different all these children are...'

'I don't care, Mrs Porter. We're talking about *my* son.'

I scan down Jonah's annual report, the paper shaking.

'Literacy, Numeracy, Science, Religious Education, Geography, History,' I quote: '"This term, Jonah has really enjoyed learning about the Victorians." That's remarkable,' I say, addressing Maria. 'Dad was only telling me the other evening how he'd had a most enlightening chat with Jonah about the iniquities of the workhouse system. Jonah thinks it served them right for being poor.'

'No, I wasn't,' he says.

'Shut up!'

Mrs Porter manages hurt and sympathetic in the same cock-headed grin.

'I'm sorry, Mrs Porter, Maria, he's been happy here but he's made no progress and this is his last chance for a bit of personal dignity. I want him to go to Highgrove Manor – it's a residential school. Check the website, you'll understand why. I love the way you have cared for my son, but understand, if he was "normal" and couldn't read a word at the end of primary school, wouldn't everyone be up in arms?'

'Ben, we all admire your devotion to Jonah's future, especially given the recent change in your home circumstances, but we truly believe – as do social services – that it would be detrimental to remove Jonah from the community...'

Dad nods his approval.

'A community of one...' I say.

'A community he has grown up in and Maureen Mitchell will

be an outstanding school, I can assure you. Have you visited it yet?'

I grudgingly accept that I haven't.

'Maria, could you get Ben a brochure?'

Maria disappears for a minute or two, while Dad and I play 'nasty-look tennis'. She returns clutching a folder and joins Dad and me as we head out the main door toward the car park.

'Mr Jewell?'

Both of us look up.

'Ben, could I speak to you for a moment?'

I hand Dad the car keys and he strides off, in a temper. Maria and I sit down on a bench by a small, oval patch of lawn with shrubs.

'I'm really going to miss Jonah,' she says, staring at her shoes. 'He's so, so lovely.'

'He certainly is,' I say.

'Often, I wonder how my kids would be if they didn't have autism, because their personalities still shine through, despite all the tics and obsessions and difficulties. Don't you find that?'

'Yes, I do, but I've always wondered if anyone else did or could.'

'One just has to look a little bit harder. I mean, Jonah...' She stops, draws breath and looks up at me as if checking for permission to continue.

'Please go on,' I oblige.

Her voice rises and her eyes smile. 'Well, Jonah I imagine ambling across the campus of some university, his crazy hair blown around by the wind, a very pretty, petite, long-haired girl chatting animatedly by his side. He is studying philosophy, or English, is regularly late for morning lectures and has a talent for making people laugh. Does that sound about right to you?'

33

I turn away, not wanting her to catch the sadness in my eyes. Maria has just sketched out a perfect portrait of me as a twenty-year-old. She sees me in Jonah. It has never once occurred to me that such an inheritance could take place, as if autism breaks the chains of DNA as well as hearts. Maria's insight, her care for Jonah, has opened my eyes. He's not just my autistic son, he's my *son*.

'Ben, have I upset you?'

Her hand is on my shoulder. 'Not at all,' I say, reaching back to take her hand. 'It's just a little melancholy, that's all.'

We sit with our own thoughts for a minute or two. I can't get the image of the student Jonah out of my head.

'Ben, look, I really think Jonah deserves and needs everything you're trying to win for him. I would really like to help if I can.'

'Maria, that's a very uplifting thing to hear, but it will put you in a difficult position, won't it?'

She nods in acknowledgement. 'My phone number and email are on a piece of paper in the school brochure.' She passes it over to me. 'Really, if you need anything, help with Jonah, anything...' She bites her lip. 'I know that things are difficult for you and Jonah at the moment, so please don't hesitate, okay?'

'Thank you,' I whisper.

I walk back to the car, clutching the glossy folder like a parking ticket. Dad mutters under his breath as I get in. The inside of the car windows steam up the moment I close the door.

'Bravo,' he says.

'Could you possibly just shut up – for ever?'

The next ten minutes, sat in traffic, are spent in silence, but I can sense his itching tongue. Finally, he has to scratch.

'Who hatched the plan?'

'What are you talking about?'

'This business, this sending-away business.'

I actually try to pull my own hair out. Then light a cigarette.

'Are you trying to give me cancer? Put that out and answer my question, Benjamin.'

'No.'

'I have a right to know. I'm his grandfather.'

'Where do I start?'

'You can start by explaining why I haven't seen you since Yom Kippur and all of a sudden it's okay for me to be your landlord?'

I turn the engine off again. 'God, you're just so obtuse!'

'From you, obtuse?' he says, poking the finger. 'I made something of myself without all the advantages I gave you—'

'Yes, you spent your life washing other people's shit off crockery. Splendid.'

That's busted the anger and replaced it with shame. 'Sorry, that was uncalled for.'

His face has softened. 'Maybe, but there is no lie in it. It's not what you do, Ben, it's why you do it. So, you're unhappy running the business?'

'You've noticed?'

'I don't need sarcasm when I try talking to you like an adult,' he says.

'Dad, I *am* an adult.'

And here is the point at which it always breaks down. I say the word, but do I believe it? Am I an adult? Do I want to be? I feel like a child that is desperate to join his older sibling's party. Like the fourteen-year-old who got turned away from the X-rated film when all his peers got in. I look around at my friends, at Emma, and I'm bemused. How do they know what to do? How to act?

I half turn to him. 'Dad, why do I always feel as if I have to ask your permission to do anything? I even feel as though it's your money in my pocket, or Emma's money.'

'Benjamin, when you asked me to stop coming to the warehouse, did I not stop?'

'Not until Christmas, no. And before that, your weekly visits, Dad, looking over my shoulder, telling Valentine what to do, tutting, checking the deliveries.'

'But do I say anything?'

'You don't need to say anything.'

'And do you like it more, when I'm not there?'

'I hate it less.'

'Ben, the business is not my son; you are. But even if I give you permission to stop being a victim, would you?'

Bastard. 'Now you're my therapist.'

'And I don't charge. But how is any of this Jonah's fault? Why should you deprive us of seeing each other? To punish us? Why?'

I look at the pedals and shake my head. 'Yom Kippur, Dad.'

'Yes, I remember it, so what?'

'You turned on the business mobile.'

'What use is it off?'

'You answered it, you promised on my behalf, you made me leave my family at four in the afternoon on Yom Kippur – to deliver ten fucking tea plates to Knightsbridge. Why is my time so cheap? That bloody mobile phone is like an instrument of torture. Why do you always send me off like the hired help?'

'What? I should have phoned Valentine and ruined *his* day? And for this you punish me? So, again I ask, what's all this rubbish about sending Jonah away?'

*

Where on earth will I find some tranquillity? I sit on the closed toilet, smoking and drinking from a quarter of vodka, trying to read *Heart of Darkness*, but it's a bit light for my current tastes. Through the plasterboard wall I feel the whump, whump, whump of the industrial dishwasher's spinning rotor arm and hear the almost metallic notes of Valentine loading and unloading dinner plates. The sickly-sweet smell of two-day-old curry hangs in the air like a heat haze. I've turned the warehouse phone off.

The cubicle door flies open, almost removing my nose.

Johnny looks me up and down. 'Didn't anyone tell you it's better to drop your trousers before you take a shit?'

'What the fuck are you doing here?'

'Valentine's cursing you rotten. I'd be scared if I were you.'

'What are you doing here, Johnny?' I say, closing my book, sliding the vodka into my pocket and dropping my cigarette on the floor.

'I was worried about you. You haven't been returning my calls, you rude bastard.'

'I've had a bit of domestic trouble,' I say.

'I know.'

'You know?'

'What can I tell you? Girls talk.'

We leave the toilet and I peer round the door to check on Valentine.

He spots me. 'What you doin'?'

'Just popping out with Johnny for a bit. Business talk.'

'What about the washin'-up? Can't do it all by myself, you know.'

'I'll only be an hour.'

'Said that yesterday, never saw you again,' Valentine says.

'Take your lunch now too, then.'

'Ain't hungry, it's only eleven.'

'Well . . . just do what you can. Bye.'

Johnny is grinning. 'You could do with some management training.'

'I could do with a pint. Come on.'

'You're being very furtive,' Johnny says.

'Sure you don't want a pint?' I ask.

'No, bit early for me. Anyway, what's going on, Ben?'

'You probably know more than me.'

'Well, I know you're at your dad's and Emma's going away . . .'

I wince.

'What's happened?'

'It'll be fine, Johnny. She's just going away for work.'

He gives me a sideways glance.

I drop my face to the glass of my pint and draw some Guinness into my mouth. Maybe I should confide in him? But he has a way of skewering my stupidity. Over the thirty-plus years I've known him, he's never put a foot wrong – well, almost never. I am his foil and his vicarious escape.

Only once have I been able to save him the way that he regularly bails me out. He wasn't always so good with money. When we were sixteen I took a beating on his behalf over a poker debt he failed to pay. His parents would have killed him if they'd known how much he gambled; what he'd stolen and sold as a result. Whereas Dad accepted my excuse of a mugging and handed me a bottle of Dettol for my cuts.

'And what has Amanda told you?' Johnny's wife and Emma are best friends.

'Just that Emma's exhausted, confused and at the end of her

rope with you. Doesn't sound like it'll all be fine, Ben. Why are you smiling?'

I hadn't realised I was. But the thought of the shared secret of this conspiracy, of Emma's apparent performance, somehow turns me on. Like, I guess, an affair would feel. The frisson of risk and excitement. And now I'm nervous that I may already have said too much, been too upbeat. I indicate to Andrea that I need another pint.

'What do you expect me to say?' I offer.

'I just want you to know that I'm here for you, all right?'

And now the guilt of deceit. 'Look, Johnny . . . the thing is . . .'

'What?'

'It's not real.'

'What are you talking about, Ben?'

'The separation. We're only doing it to help our tribunal case.'

'It's all an act?' I nod. Johnny's eyes look at me from the side, like he's sizing me up, and his scepticism turns the ground beneath me spongy, infirm.

'It just seems, well, a bit extreme, if it's all for show.' Johnny backtracks, clumsily. 'Just overheard Amanda on the phone to her, probably got the wrong end of the stick,' he says.

I just drink – to disguise my face and calm the agonising cramp of fear.

'Anyway,' he says, 'now you've got yourself into this ridiculous situation, is there anything I can do?'

'I could use some help with Jonah. Company would help.'

'No problem, Tom would love to see Jonah. Call me and we'll make some plans.' He glances at his watch. 'Need to get back, but you will call me, won't you?'

'Yes, I'll call you. Thanks.'

We hug and he leaves. I watch him through the window as he strides purposefully toward the tube and out of sight.

Why don't I hate him? I despise being rescued, it's the kind of dislike that comes with familiarity. I seem to feel most belittled when I have to ask for help; even more so when it's uninvited, like it so often is from my father and from Johnny. It's a knight's complex – when someone saves your life you are forever in their debt, even if there is no obligation or sense that it's desired. But I hate being in debt. I can suffer owing money to the bank, or an impersonal monolith like the Inland Revenue, but emotional debt? The kind I carry around like a rucksack filled with rocks? I received the empty luggage and the first stone as a birthright from my parents, and while they filled it year on year, they never demonstrated the art of unpacking. I need a geologist, an archaeologist as well as a psychologist, and I can't expect my best friend to be all three.

The Bell's Whisky clock tells me it's already one-thirty and I'm well past the point of return. The business phone remains switched off. Emma won't be calling me, I've just seen Johnny and my father hasn't phoned me in ten years – he just turns up like a bailiff with a sledgehammer. And, of course, Jonah won't be ringing me anytime soon. So I wallow like a hippo in the mud of anonymity, shunning the lure of the snug and the glories of a conversation about plastering, wondering about my wife, worrying about my wife, missing my life.

MAUREEN MITCHELL SCHOOL

FOR CHILDREN WITH AUTISTIC SPECTRUM DISORDER

231 HIGH ROAD
GREYBOURNE
WYNCHGATE
LONDON N32 1AQ

HEADTEACHER: DR. C. WARDLE
SITE MANAGER: MR J. HENRY

3rd February 2011

Dear Mr Jewell

Thank you for your phone call regarding a visit to Maureen Mitchell School. I am pleased to confirm an appointment for you to tour the school has been arranged for Thursday 14th February 2011.

I am sure that you will be delighted to discover just what our school has to offer your son, Jonah.

If this date is inconvenient, please contact me on 020 8555 2319 ext 658 to rearrange. If not, I look forward to meeting you then.

Kind regards

Diane Caulfield
Deputy Headteacher

Clown

feel stiff, cold and depressed this morning – Valentine's Day, what a laugh. My dreams kept waking me last night, a recurring scene aboard a jumbo jet. I was sat in the very back row, hemmed in by the largest family in the world. They passed me over their heads to the aisle and I struggled down the length of it towards the front of the plane. But it went on for miles, an aisle stretching beyond the horizon, and when I finally reached a curtain, two burly stewards refused me access. 'But I'm joining my wife,' I kept saying, 'she's in first class.' But they wouldn't let me pass, kept slapping me in the face and from behind the curtain I could hear Emma laughing . . .

'Keep an open mind.'

'Sorry, Dad, what was that?'

'Keep an open mind,' he says.

Jonah is already at school and we sit in the kitchen drinking coffee.

'My mind is completely open.'

'Empty, for sure.'

'No, actually, I am completely open to the idea that it's going to be shit.'

'Emma couldn't come?'

'We've decided it's for the best that I handle things at the moment. She trusts my judgement.'

'She's brave.'

I ignore the sarcasm and drain my coffee. 'Come on, let's go.'

Dad follows me down the hall, where the front door has opened and Maurice waits patiently on the step. Maurice is short and rotund. Toad of Toad Hall in a shiny charcoal suit. The rank entrails of old cigar are clinging to my nose. 'Is he coming along?'

'He likes a day out.'

'What's wrong with Cliftonville? They do coach trips from Golders Green bus station.' My whole life has been film noir, shot through the fog of Maurice's cigars, but their odour has become strangely comforting. He is always here in good and bad.

'I'm not deaf,' Maurice croaks.

'Yeah, but could you just act it for the next couple of hours.'

'Such a charmer, your son.' Even after all these years in England, he still pronounces 's' as 'sh'.

'Maurice will just keep quiet and look inquisitive, won't you?'

'Not a dicky bird, God forbid.'

In four hundred yards you will have reached your destination.

'It's a Satmap,' Dad says over his left shoulder.

'I know what it is, you think I'm a fool? Think I don't know technology? Look.'

An iPhone is waving back and forth between us.

'Look, apps, the whole megilla.'

I'm struggling to find a parking space along this Red Route nightmare and it's not helped by the drumming rain and steamed-up windows. The resulting 200-metre walk to the school's entrance – a box of wire mesh and an intercom cut into a daunting twenty-foot-high metal perimeter fence – has not improved Maurice's mood and he hangs back in the rain with his hand over his mouth as I press the button.

'You coming in or not?'

'Leave him, Ben. Maurice, there's a café across the road, go have a breakfast, we'll meet you there later.'

Maurice ambles back across the glistening road as a muffled voice utters something indiscernible and buzzes us in.

The hallway is narrow, council green and unnaturally quiet. We drop into two plastic, upholstered chairs and await our tour guide.

'What got into him?'

'Sometimes he gets spooked, that's all.'

'Doesn't seem the type.'

My father nods, sagely.

'Mr Jewell?'

We both stand and offer our hand to a thirty-something lady with close-cropped blonde hair, bouncing in her shock-absorbing trainers.

'Jonah's father?' she asks.

'That's me, Ben. This is his grandfather, Georg.'

'I'm Diane Caulfield, the deputy head here at Maureen Mitch-ell. Pleasure to meet you both. I understand Jonah is to join us in September.'

'He's keeping his options open,' I say.

'Yes, of course he is. If you'd like to follow me, I thought we'd start with a year seven class which is where Jonah will be based when he arrives.'

We troop in single file to the far end of the corridor and stand

44

quietly, gazing through a door window at nine children sitting in a semi-circle in front of a teacher. When she gets the nod, Miss Caulfield eases us in. Memories flood back. It's a little shabbier, the children are bigger, but the outlook is pretty much the same. Individual workstations – small desks with side-panels to avoid distractions, little wheeled drawer units, lines of PECS cards on Velcro strips – their simple pictures resembling the reels of a fruit machine – single-glazed windows built for condensation, but no toilet. No en-suite.

'Are all the children in the class dry?'

'No, one of the girls, maybe, but the others are still in pads.'

'So where's the toilet?'

'There is a bank of cubicles down the hall near the front door. You would have passed them on the way to the classroom.'

'What methods do you use for getting them dry?'

She looks at me, confused.

'Well, look, at Roysten Glen each classroom has its own toilet so the kids can be taken every fifteen minutes or so and I still get a steaming plastic bag returned to me with Jonah almost every day. So how are you going to get my son dry when the toilets here are at the other end of the school?'

'It is far more practical to have the toilets situated where they are best for all the children's needs. We went through a long period of consultation before redesigning the school.'

'Oh really, so in an autism-specific school, running them up and down the corridors on the off-chance of a piss is good practice?'

'Mr Jewell, I assure you that those children with autism are perfectly well catered for.'

'Not a blade of grass,' Dad says.

'Sorry?' Dad is staring out the window into the school's quadrangle.

'Not a blade of grass. Not a tree.'

'I don't understand.'

'Where will he play? There is no grass, or plants. Where will he find things to hold in front of his eye like he does, Ms Caulfield? Do you know he needs to twiddle with something to keep himself calm?'

'We have a sensory room and a soft gym. Would you like to see those?'

'He won't like it here.'

'Mr Jewell, we go on plenty of outings to the local park. I'm sure Jonah . . .'

'Don't give me outings. Give me grass and leaves. You think, what? This is good enough? She wasn't a gardener then, your Maureen Mitchell?'

'And we have three guinea pigs.'

'I'll meet you outside, Ben.' And he's gone, striding the twenty yards down the corridor to the exit, blaspheming to himself.

'How do you get out of this damn place?' Dad shouts.

'Press the green button, Mr Jewell,' Ms Caulfield says.

'Huh,' he shouts, 'finally she finds something green.'

She looks at me, quizzically.

'Jonah likes being outside. It's his thing,' I explain.

There is a commotion, a slamming door, pounding feet, shouting, and I find myself on my back watching two sprinting arses head for the entry door. The athlete coming second grabs the winner in a bear hug.

'Fuck off, cunt.'

'Come on, David, back to class.'

'Let me out, you fucker.'

46

A second staff member arrives from an adjoining corridor, as Ms Caulfield helps me back to my feet, and between them they manhandle the giant child back past us, his rubber-soled trainers squeaking on the concrete floor. As they reach me he looks me straight in the eye and pokes a finger in my chest.

'What you looking at, fuck?'

Diane puts a hand on my shoulder. 'That's David,' she says. 'He's in year eleven. He can be a bit of a handful. He has emotional and behavioural difficulties. Sorry about that.'

'He doesn't have any problem with eye contact, does he?'

'No, no, he's one of our special students. From when we were a special school.'

'And now you're what? Ordinary?'

She laughs. 'No, we were a special school before we were designated autism specific.'

'But David, who just "designated" me a fuck, doesn't seem specifically autistic?'

'No, he's special.'

'Yes, you already mentioned that. Is he the most special? Or are there kids more special than David? Specifically?'

'Well, there are still a number of special children in the school who have been here since we were special and before we became autism specific.'

'Define "specific".'

'I'm sorry?'

'Sorry, was I not specific enough? What do you mean when you say Maureen Mitchell is autism specific?'

'It's a school specifically for children with a diagnosis of Autistic Spectrum Disorder.'

'But it's not, is it?'

'Yes it is, Mr Jewell. It was designated as such in August last year. We have a sensory room and a soft play area.'

'They have a soft play area at Jungle Jim's.'

'I don't understand?'

'Clearly.'

She looks at her watch. 'Dr Wardle should be free now. Would you like to meet him?'

'Is he the designated headteacher?'

'Yes, he is.'

'Then I'd love to.'

Dr Wardle has a ponytail. The wall behind his desk is a patchwork of certificates.

'I was head-hunted,' he says. 'Coffee?'

'Thank you.'

He has one of those filter machines with a glass jug on a cabinet next to him. He fills two mugs bearing the legend 'Keep Calm and Hug it Out'.

'It's decaff.'

'Fine. Mr Wardle . . .'

'James.'

'James . . .'

'Did Di show you the sensory room? We're super proud of it. It's pretty psychedelic.'

'Mr Ward . . . James, can I be candid?'

'Of course, Ben, please, continue.' He interlocks his fingers and rests his chin on them.

'I don't want Jonah to come here.'

'But let's explore for a few mos. Indulge me, if you would?'

I'm imagining scissors and fists full of hair. 'Please.'

'Well, Ben, it's about transition, smoothness. Jonah needs

consistency. Let's not make waves for him, let's make it seamless. You see? Roysten Glen,' he draws an imaginary line in the air, 'Maureen Mitchell.'

'I have some questions.'

'Fire away.'

'Speech and language therapy?'

'Once a week from Roysten Glen.'

'Occupational therapy?'

'In the pipeline.'

'Physiotherapy?'

'Ditto.'

'Educational psychologist?'

'You're looking at him.'

'You're a qualified edpsych?' I scan the certificates behind his head.

'Child psychology is my passion, but...'

'So no full-time edpsych?'

'Did I mention I am a reiki master, too?'

'Guinea pigs, I ask you? Not a blade, Maurice, not a single blade.'

'Leave it, Georg,' Maurice says. 'Here, try the black pudding.'

'Nothing like keeping an open mind then, Dad,' I say.

'There's open minds and then there's open minds. JJ's the outdoor type.'

'Georg, Bear Grylls he's not,' Maurice adds.

'Who asked you?' Dad barks.

'I was just saying – maybe his chakras *are* blocked?'

'What do you know of chakras, Maurice? You're a Dutch Jew not a Hindu.'

I finish my bacon sandwich and grab my car keys from the table. 'Come on, Sunshine Boys, let's go.'

The traffic's nose to tail and they don't stop bickering. I try to drown them out with a music station, but they insist on Radio 4. 'The Archers', for fuck's sake, they're both addicted, like their childhoods were spent in some bucolic idyll in the West Country. They have both felt the need for reinvention to some extent, I suppose. I look across and study my father. He has a strong profile, a square jaw, he must have been striking as a young man.

There is a redness on the right side of his neck, it looks swollen and angry. The more I stare, the larger it gets.

'What's wrong with your neck?'

'Uch, it is a shaving rash.'

'Since when did you shave your neck, Dad?'

'Stop fussing, it is nothing.'

'How long's it been there?'

'Since you moved in, I am allergic to you.'

'You need to get the doctor to look at it.'

'It is nothing.' He's indignant.

'Maurice, will you tell him to go to the doctor?'

'Go to the doctor, Georg.'

'All right, if you stop the nagging I'll go.'

'I'll phone,' Maurice says, flashing his iPhone. 'Ben, how do you turn this thing on?'

It's only 3.20 and I need some time to contemplate, and the best place to contemplate is a pub. So I hole up in The Ship for a session of beer and self-pity – my only current hobbies. I used to play five-a-side football every week and go out for a curry every Tuesday with three mates. I used to read books, visit the cinema, go on holiday, sleep, eat out, take more than ten minutes to eat at home, shower and shave every day, have sex and never drink in the mornings.

I cannot blame all this solely on Jonah; any new parent makes sacrifices – most, gladly – swapping perceived freedom for real or imagined parental pride, because that's the expectation. And however hard it is to begin with, there is also the certain knowledge that it will get easier. The full night's sleep will return, the smiles and interaction will arrive, being called 'Dada' is inevitable. The comparison between ages – at first crawling, first steps, first dry night. These are all immutable facts to new parents, as certain as the sun will rise and set each day.

Birthdays are celebrated, toys are bought and played with, teams are supported, educations are planned, careers plotted, holidays with family and friends attended in Spain, Portugal, America – anywhere with a kids' club that provides hours of poolside relaxation and escape. Mothers and fathers smile at their children – as tanned as toast – splashing around in the swimming pool; they smile at each other, hire babysitters while they dine at night in peace, or let their kids roam in packs with a pre-agreed meeting place at a certain time that they stick to obediently.

Many, if not most, of these parents try hard for a second child and repeat the process, forewarned of the pitfalls, which they laugh at when they lose their footing again – oh well.

When they get back they email photos to one another, visit each other's homes, have made new friends – sometimes for life – their kids play together and grow up together, go out with each other, text each other, socialise.

However, every so often, the scribe of procreation decides to write in a new genre – something akin to sci-fi, with a touch of dystopia and plenty of foreshadowing.

And the children in these stories do not make friends, would drown in a swimming pool if left alone, have no sense of danger, no sense of time, can't read or write, let alone text, many never talk, or learn to use the toilet.

And their parents are never invited on holiday, to parties, out for lunch – and on the odd occasion they are, they say no, because while adults just patronise, other children are cruel and your child may unknowingly destroy a treasured possession without intent and will definitely make a mess which Mum or Dad feel duty bound to clear up. But the major reason, in such situations, is that when you exhibit affection, the room's eyes just project pity and disbelief.

By the time I get back, dying for a piss and a little worse for wear, there's a poker game in full flow – Dad's old football cronies from his days in the Maccabi League, where he was Jewish football's least elegant but most effective centre half.

I nod at Maurice, whose chewed-up cigar is lighter in colour than the teeth that grip it.

'You remember Harvey, and this cheat here with the pile of chips is Sammy.'

Sammy raises a liver-spotted hand. 'So this is little Benjamin? No. It must have been . . . ?'

'Two years,' I answer for him.

Harvey looks me up and down. 'Georg, you sure he's yours?'

Maurice and Sammy are roaring, my father sits blank-faced. 'No,' he says. More laughter.

'Nice boy you have in there. Doesn't say much, mind you.'

'He's choosy,' I say, knowing this is good-natured, but feeling like I may end this game with one well-chosen word.

'They're just kidding with you, here.' Maurice pulls out the chair next to him.

'You want to sit in? We're playing seven-card stud,' Dad asks.

'No, Dad, thanks. Where's Jonah?'

'He's inside watching a video, his programme finished at seven.'

Jonah looks like a teenager lying on the sofa with his hands behind his head. I sit next to him, half expecting him to get up and leave, but he's engrossed in *Casablanca*.

The beer and the school meeting have wrecked me, so I take a chance and lay my head on his thigh and he lays his hand on my cheek. I tense every muscle in my body, desperate not to spook him. It was his decision, this physical contact, he wanted to do it, but when he leans down and puts his nose to my nose and his eyes to my eyes, I am in heaven, despite the overpowering odours of Old Spice and chopped herring. Not only does he look like my father, now he smells like him too. It's a stirring smell full of long-suppressed childhood memories and insufferably vague feelings of a trusting love.

'It's okay, Ben? The video? Better than *Schindler's List*? I don't have much of a collection.'

'Get back to the boys, Dad. It's perfect.'

I wake up as Victor and Elsa take off into the fog. My left cheek is bright red and ridged from Jonah's pyjamas, my right bears a sweaty handprint. He is asleep and – in his armchair – so is Dad. I slide out and gently place Jonah's hand where my head has been. Then I flick Dad's ear.

'Can you help me,' I growl.

Jonah is a lump, so it takes both of us to get him up the stairs.

I go backwards, gripping him under the arms and supporting his head on my chest. Dad takes his feet and gently kisses his toes as we struggle – Hillary and Tensing – and by the landing Dad is sweaty and wheezing horribly, and Jonah is awake again by the time we lay him in his bed, before Dad shuffles to his room.

I'm still flushed by the warmth of Jonah's apparent earlier affection and – like the calming effect of the first hit of a whisky – I need to keep chasing that elusive feeling. So few moments feel like true connection with him, I almost grieve when each one ebbs away.

'What is it with you, Jonah? When I was your age I used to pretend to be asleep to avoid listening to my father. I know I don't have the storytelling gift like Papa Georg, but that's okay, isn't it?'

Jonah farts, long and loud, the nappy acting as an amplifier. It makes me belly-laugh and he catches it, like a yawn, and laughs too. I try to lie next to him, but he pushes me away, so I sit across the bed with my back to the wall and he doesn't object. I squeeze his thigh through the duvet.

'Take your Papa Georg.' I feel a pang of guilt. 'He and I can't talk – not like you and I. And we don't hug, whereas I can't keep my hands off you. Yes, I know sometimes it irritates you, but I need to. I can't help it. I wouldn't trade you in – as you are – for anything. I can't imagine you being any other way or wanting you any other way.

'So this business with your mum, all this talk of schools you're going to hear, about going away – you must know that it's because I love you so much. We'll be back with Mum soon, Jonah, I promise, and I know these last two weeks have felt like a year, but I have to tell you this whether it registers or not, I want your days to be full of joy and fun and free of anxiety and pain. Other people may think you're missing out on life. Believe me, Jonah, when I tell you it's not so great. It's hard and confusing and disappointing. I want none of that for you. If you spend the rest of your life in blissful ignorance of all the shit going on around you then I will have succeeded.

'Who else is going to listen to me apart from you? I'm finding it hard to convince myself that my motives are pure, but you won't judge me, will you? You understand that I'd never abandon you. The problem is, if Papa tells me I'm being selfish, I believe him. If Mummy tells me I'm being selfish, I believe her. Maybe I can't find the words with them like I do with you? Just know, Jonah, that whatever anyone says, I'm going to find the belief to fight for you, because you being okay is so important to me, I can't be okay if you're not.' Is he taking any of this in? He's turned on his side away from me, so I rub his back.

'God, your Higher Power, DNA or whatever, has given you certain wonderful gifts, it's just that most other "individuals" aren't programmed to appreciate them. They want you to be like them. Arrogant fuckers. I'm envious of those gifts – your lack of jealousy, self-pity and resentment. Those are emotions, Jonah, that are unattractive and self-harming and if some knob of a doctor came to me and said, I can, among others, allow your son to experience the following emotions, I'd tell him to sling his hook. I know you trust me, because you cling to me in the park when a dog comes near, somehow you know I'll protect you. When you feel threatened, you reach for my hand.

'Well, my gorgeous boy, you need to trust me now too. Because a lot of pit bulls are out to spoil the world I've planned for you and if I have to use Papa's gun to get you there, I will.'

55

I bend down to him and he's already breathing softly through his nose. So I kiss him gently on the forehead. His eyes remain closed. It doesn't matter if he hasn't heard me.

Wynchgate Social Services
The Civic Centre
Brown Street
London N24 3EA

23 February 2011

Dear Mr Jewell
Re: John Jewell D.O.B. 11 May 2000

Adele Latchford, director of children's services, has passed on your recent correspondence and has asked me to provide an evaluation of John's needs. I understand that your circumstances have recently changed and I would like to visit you and John at home at your earliest convenience.

Please ring my office on 020 8555 1000 ext 435 to make an appointment and I look forward to meeting you soon.

Regards
Mary Carey
Senior Social Worker

Witch

After a month, we're settling into a rhythm – my father, Jonah and I – school, food, bath, bed, bollocks and booze. Most nights, when I'm the last awake, I take a spin past the flat – just to check, but the lights remain off. Things are moving slowly and I've caught the inertia like a virus.

I feel like I'm wearing a costume, shuffling around in over-sized shoes, playing the role of an adult. At most if not all of the countless meetings and phone conversations with officialdom, I have taken a back seat to Emma. I have hundreds of email trails about Jonah, cced to me from my wife – but I've read none of them. With the exception of his school, I know none of the significant characters in the unfolding drama of Jonah, but Emma does and that has always been good enough. But with all this going on around me, I wonder what else I've missed and how I'm going to cope.

The shot of brandy I've added to my coffee has frayed the edges of this blanket of dread but, as I spy a human shape through the opaque front-door glass, the blanket engulfs me. I feel I may be less than prepared for this front-of-house role.

*

'Jonah.'

'I'm sorry?'

'His name's Jonah, not John.'

I run my finger beneath his name in the letter.

'I'm sorry, Jonah,' she says. 'You know how it is.' Mary Carey is a picture of robust androgyny, like an East German discus thrower.

'If I knew how it was, you wouldn't be here.'

She settles at the dining table, but I want to move her out of the kitchen before she sees Dad's lethal collection of knives hanging precariously from a rusty magnetic strip.

'Yes, I suppose so.' She takes her pad out and lays a ballpoint on it. 'If you wouldn't mind, I'd just like to observe Jonah for twenty minutes or so and then we can talk. Would that be okay?'

'Be my guest. Maybe it would be better if we moved to the lounge,' I say.

Mary Carey approaches Jonah and he moves away. Then she begins to sign, mouthing along as her bare arms and blinged-up fingers perform t'ai chi for my son. He leaves, through the lounge and out into the garden, and she follows. I feel like giving her my own version of sign language.

It's a coat, hat and scarf day, but Jonah doesn't feel the cold and through the lounge window I watch, amused, as he skips circuits around the garden discarding clothing. Mary Carey stumbles after him picking up items as they fall. Then the cold inspires his bladder and the unfortunate social worker – on her haunches with arms full of school uniform – gets a proper hosing.

He laughs, his head thrown back and uncontrolled. She probably thinks her soaking is the joke, but the truth is it's the least likely explanation. I may think it's hilarious, but with Jonah it's as likely to be the way the wind has caught his hair or the pattern of light created by the bare apple tree. I check my watch. It's 4.30, crapping time, she should count herself lucky.

I grab a nappy and go outside to rescue him. He stands still, twiddling a leaf to the sky as I stretch the sticky straps either side and secure the situation. The soiled social worker hands me Jonah's clothes and heads to the bathroom.

'Can I make you a cup of tea?'

She has taken her vest top off and now sits at the dining table in a leather biker's jacket.

'So he doesn't sign.'

'No, he doesn't.'

'PECS? Makaton?'

'Not really.'

'How does he communicate with you then?'

'He understands simple instructions, otherwise he points, grabs my hand or just grabs whatever he wants for himself.'

Mary Carey is making copious notes when Dad arrives home from his bowls match. The floorboards creak under his loping gait and I can visualise him inspecting Mary Carey's bike and other paraphernalia while he makes a snap judgement about her right to breathe oxygen.

'Good afternoon. Georg Jewell, Jonah's grandfather,' he says, holding out his hand. He sniffs the air like a fox-crazed beagle and I watch the colour rise from his neck to his eyebrows.

'Mary Carey, social worker.'

He takes her hand. 'Can I wash your coat... I mean, take your coat?'

'No, I'm fine, thank you.'

'Where's Jonah? Ah, in the garden, naked again, I see.'

She scribbles more. 'He's a handful, isn't he?'

'He is,' says Dad proudly.

'She wasn't referring to that, Dad. His behaviour . . .'

'Oh, yes, challenging, certainly.'

Her cheeks have reddened. 'So Jonah is currently living here with his father and grandfather. And his mother?'

His mother, my wife. Certainly we won't be back together until after the tribunal is over.

'Not living here. That was the basis of sending the letter.'

'I'm aware of that, Mr Jewell, but is she seeing anything of Jonah?'

'Not since we separated, three weeks ago.'

'Do you know if she has any intention of seeing him?'

'You'd have to ask her that.'

Scribbling.

'So you and your father are his sole carers at present.'

'Yes.'

'And how old is your father?'

'Seventy-eight.'

'And you are thirty-seven. In work?'

'Yes, I run the family business, but of course having Jonah to care for is making that difficult.' Or rather, easier – he's just the latest excuse for not going in.

Mary Carey puts her pen down and grips her chin. 'Could you explain how?'

'Well, Jonah is doubly incontinent, so mornings are a nightmare even though he wears a nappy at night. He needs to be bathed every morning and for that you need his cooperation, which is not always freely given. I should really be at work by seven a.m. but rarely get in before ten, after seeing him on to the school bus. His sleep is sporadic, which means mine is sporadic too.'

She scribbles again.

'So how do you see things improving?'

'Well, while I'd be delighted for some help, it's just a sticking plaster. Jonah needs consistency. From the moment he gets up until the moment he goes to bed he needs consistency and stimulation. There are so many transitions in his life at the moment that he finds it impossible to transfer any of the skills that the school claims he's learnt from there to home. He needs a residential setting.'

I hear these phrases slipping off my tongue with ease and watch for her reaction while they do so. I feel caught in the shame of my use of language, certain Mary Carey will identify the words as the euphemisms they so clearly are – waking day, residential setting, consistency, stimulation. My diaphragm is rejecting them, my heart constricted by them. She knows what they mean – *I can't cope and I want him gone.* As soon as the thought enters my head I mentally bat it away, like fleeting thoughts of slitting my wrists or dining on paracetamol.

'But if we could put together a comprehensive package that would alleviate many of your problems, that should negate the issues that Jonah is experiencing. It is best that he stays with his family.'

'Cheapest, you mean.'

'No, I said best. For him to remain in the community. There are other options.'

'Such as?'

'Well, there's fostering ...'

'Excuse me – did you say *fostering*?'

'Yes, Mr Jewell. When experienced couples – or sometimes

singles – and families, take in a child for a variety of reasons for up to three hundred and sixty-five days a year. Often it leads to adoption.'

'Yes, I kind of knew what fostering meant, Ms Carey. I just cannot for a millisecond understand how a total stranger, albeit one with Health and Safety training, no doubt, could foster Jonah. Do you really think that any couple in the world knows and loves Jonah as I do?'

'No, but if you're truly not coping—'

'Ms Carey, you just chased a naked Jonah around the garden and he pissed on you then laughed. Should we put that on his curriculum vitae and post a crotch shot of him in the local newspaper?'

'But there are people out there—'

'Yes, I'm sure there are. Many well-meaning, kind, patient, saintly people who I admire. But Jonah's not just morose, he's not a pot-smoking shoplifter with a crack-whore mother. It's not just his learning difficulties, or autism, no. Do you know what defines Jonah and makes the idea of adoption both ludicrous and offensive to me?'

'No, Mr Jewell.'

'He's my son.'

Mary Carey sighs, regains her composure. 'Mr Jewell, I object to what you are insinuating about the way Wynchgate Social Services works.'

'You opened this discussion by saying how important it was for Jonah to remain part of the community and yet your next suggestion went past Go and straight to jail. Would it be fair to say that you and your colleagues bend over backwards to keep children with their parents?'

'Yes, that's fair.'

'Despite the recent coverage surrounding Baby Peter?'

'That was a different authority and a tragic set of circumstances.'

'On that we agree. But you do expend an awful lot of energy trying to keep children at home – with the correct supervision.'

'Correct.'

'So why such little effort with Jonah? Why straight to the most drastic solution?'

'No, it's just one of the options. But if you really feel you can't cope...'

There they are, the knowing raised eyebrows – this game of tennis is a sham. She's just fed me a series of dropshots and now she's smashed away the winner. *We know what this is about really, Mr Jewell, don't we? And it's not about Jonah. You want us to make it all better for you, say 'there, there' and make the pain go away? Well, I called your bluff, you lazy, childish waste of space. Stop whining and man up.*

'You do not give your children away. Never! This is the best you have to offer?' Dad's presence has slipped my mind. 'We can cope, now go and get your package together and take your muddy bicycle from my hallway.'

'Mr Jewell, I didn't intend to upset you.'

I'm lost for words, but for once Dad has found them.

'You didn't upset me, missy, you angered me.'

Mary Carey stuffs her sodden vest top into her saddlebag and wheels her bike down the path.

'I'll send my care proposal to you as soon as possible.'

Dad slams the door behind her.

'This is what you have to deal with? These people? Women with spiky purple hair?'

I nod in assent.

'That naked *boychick* in the garden goes nowhere. Now, get me a cherry brandy.'

We both sit and watch Jonah's uninhibited wanderings through the window – he sipping his cherry brandy, me trying to sip my Scotch. The sun begins to set and we're still staring silently. He's not a drinker, my father, I've never seen him drunk – but he's a giggler. I explain to him in bullet points the events as they arose before his arrival.

'All over her? A bladder-full? I knew he was a genius.' Dad chuckles.

'Should I dress him? Don't want the neighbours complaining.'

'What for? Let him enjoy himself, Mrs Colnbach is blind as a bat anyway.'

If he's anything like me, alcohol loosens his tongue and opens his pockets – so I take a chance.

'Dad, I need your help with this.'

'So what's new?'

I avoid the barb, because it's true. 'I'm a bit short. You know how it is?'

Dad sighs. 'Don't think I'm not aware of what's going on at the warehouse.' He suddenly sobers up. 'You are a very good taker, Ben. You want me to keep you while you plot to send my grandson away? No, no, no.'

'It's not sending him away, Dad. It's giving him the best chance, the best opportunity to have the best possible life. It's only a short-term problem.'

He stands up and turns away. 'Nothing is short term with you, Ben.' And to himself he adds: 'He wants me to pay for his booze while he plans to have my JJ locked up.'

'This is not the nineteenth century.'

'No? In Hungary in 1944 they said the same. This is not the nineteenth century, it's the twenty-first and look, look.'

'Dad, it's for Jonah.'

'And not for you?'

That bullet finds its target.

'What? I shouldn't benefit too? Would that be an unacceptable by-product of fighting for Jonah's future? That we should both have a life we're happy to live? Please, I'll never ask you for anything else as long as I live, but please...'

He swings round and stands so close that the smell of cherries is the only barrier between us. I look up to see his eyes – they are amber, they are Jonah's.

'You prove to me that it's for Jonah, you prove to me one hundred per cent that his life will be better away from his family, that he needs what you say and they have what he needs, and I will consider it.'

'I promise you, Dad.'

'Don't make promises, show me evidence. Now go and get him in, it's getting dark. I'm going out tonight.'

I just want Jonah in bed as soon as possible – preferably asleep – so after Dad leaves I call Jonah up and go through the bath routine at double speed, adding a good dose of Medised to his usual drugs to gently knock him out. I kiss him goodnight and stagger down the stairs. I want to flop on the sofa with a large dose of something to numb me while I check my email for the thousandth time today. *Downloading*, my mobile says and up it pops: *I am home, need to see you tomorrow. E.*

I read it over and over, zoning in on 'need' and 'tomorrow' like a whirring Enigma machine. She 'needs' to see me tomorrow. Needs: desires, desperate longing, misses me, can't live without me. Tomorrow: can't wait another day. I daydream about my own bed, satellite TV, the sole burden of Jonah's future removed. Stomach acid bites at my tonsils as the inevitable negatives shoulder their way in like party gatecrashers – the What Ifs Posse from the wrong side of the tracks. I shall retreat into oblivion until I no longer feel their blows.

Four fingers of Scotch help me drift off easily. I doze and wake, dream and doze and wake dehydrated and irritable and Jonah is tugging at my hand.

'Oh, go away, please, Jonah, go back to bed.'

But he won't go, will not budge.

'Look, just fuck off and leave me alone. If you want something, get it yourself.' I jerk my hand away and turn my back to him and doze again. I am vaguely aware of him coming and going, of cupboards opening and closing, of laughing and jumping. Deep down I know I should investigate, but I resent the burden tonight, I'm comfy and he's not driving me mad and I'll deal with him later. The hours pass.

'What is this? I'll kill him!'

I'm jolted awake and remember with horror what I haven't done and what he's probably found. I use the lounge doorframe to prop myself up and try and look awake.

'Benjamin, what is this?'

The hallway is littered with ground-in Oreo cookies, spat-out lumps of bread and what look like thousands of tiny insects, which – on closer inspection – are sesame seeds. At the bottom of the stairs sits a sodden, shit-stained nappy; I watch Jonah tread in it on his way up to his bedroom.

Dad follows him up as I pretend to know where to start. He stops halfway and I sense his glare.

'How dare you allow this to happen, lying drunk on the sofa

while your son could have done God knows what to himself. Useless boy. Now turn down the television and leave us to sleep. I'll clean up in the morning.'

I stand with my head against the wall for what seems like an eternity, but my drunkenness, distilled down to dehydration and edginess, forces me up and, as I pick my way to the kitchen for a glass of water, the full force and devastation of Hurricane Jonah is revealed.

Half-eaten apples on the floor like a deserted game of petanque, dismantled bits of garish feathers glued to the lino with the remains of tortured grapes, a wedge of Parmesan with teeth-marked sculpture, a dozen packets of crisps – their innards ripped violently out, now solidifying like concrete in the sink.

The wall cupboard doors are all gaping. He's been climbing, sweeping tins of fruit, tuna and sardines to the floor like a burglar searching for diamonds. Dare I check the fridge? At first, all looks relatively unscathed – apart from the bag of apples that is now just a bag. There are the telltale teeth marks in an onion – serves him right, that little git – and a banana that looks like it's been through a mangle, but...

'Oh, shit.'

The chicken is gone, he's eaten the chicken. Four raw chicken breasts from the top shelf. Now I panic.

I take the stairs two at a time and burst into his room, but he's not there.

'Dad,' I scream, as I open my father's door. 'Dad...'

Dad is on his back on the right of the giant bed, and a filthy-faced Jonah has his head on Dad's chest. Dad stares me down, his mouth is upturned and his amber eyes burn – get ready.

'Raw chicken, Dad. The raw chicken in the fridge?'

'What are you talking about?'

68

'The chicken, in the fridge...'

From nowhere, a paperback hits me hard across the top of the head. 'Ow!'

'It's in the freezer, klutz. What do you take me for? Go away.'

We meet in a Starbucks in Holborn. She is warm in her cashmere, and I hold her until she pats me on the back.

'I've got twenty minutes.'

'How was Hong Kong?'

'Fine.'

'How are you coping?'

'Fine.'

But as she takes her coat off, I wonder. The shoulders of her tailored jacket fit less snugly and as she fiddles with her wedding ring it rolls too freely.

'I miss you,' I chance.

'How's Jonah?'

'Enjoying Dad's attention, I think.'

She smiles, faintly. 'I bet.'

'Do you want to see him?'

She bites the inside of her upper lip. 'How can you ask that?'

Her anger causes panic. I don't know which words to choose to avoid her ire, to impress her with my stoicism, to placate her.

'It wasn't loaded, Emma. It's been over a month. Tell me when and where and I'll bring him. This weekend?'

'I'm in Geneva this weekend.'

'But you've only just got back.'

She sips from her latte and passes me a sheet of notepaper. 'I've found a barrister. Here are her details.'

I fold it and slip it into my pocket, obediently.

'It's a conference. Don't you have plans for the weekend?' she asks.

'Thought I'd take Jonah to Paris.' It's meant to sound light-hearted, but escapes the leash and barks sarcasm instead.

She leans across the table and stares me down. 'For God's sake, Ben, do you think this is easy for me? I still have to get up every morning, without seeing my husband, without seeing my son, and get on with everything and try and concentrate on my job so that when this bloody business is over at least we'll both have enough money to finally have a life again. Get out of the victim role.'

She sighs deeply as she looks away and murmurs, 'I'm sorry.' On these morsels I shall build my days.

'It's okay,' I whisper and, for a moment, loosen my grip on the bag at my feet, but if it's not possible for me to speak to her when I need to, I'll be wreckage without the reassurance. I place the two identical boxes on the table in front of us.

'What are these, Ben, for God's sake?'

'Pay-as-you-go mobiles. They can't be traced, all we have to do is set a date and time to talk. They're untraceable.'

'You said that already.' She looks weary. 'This is not some covert MI5 mission. Come on, get a grip.'

'I need to be able to talk to you, Emma.'

'Stop wasting your money on toys and take them back to the shop.'

I try to hide the shaking – and my face – as I fake a gulp from my large Americano. I'm behaving like an insecure teenager.

'I had a meeting at the school. They're still going on about Maureen Mitchell, Jenny Porter won't back us. Even if she agrees with us, she's just toeing the party line. I went to see it. It's no good.'

She reaches into her briefcase and passes me a large buff pocket file.

'You'll need these – every document about Jonah from his birth until last week. They're in chronological order and I've made notes, so don't lose them. And anything else that's generated you must keep and you must file – do you understand? There's also a document providing you with temporary custody. You need to sign it and return it. I've already signed.'

'Keep and file, sign and send. I think I can manage that.'

'Now, phone the barrister, I'm told she's the best. You'll need to have detailed reports on Jonah from a speech therapist, educational psychologist, occupational therapist, child psychiatrist, and anybody else that can add to the case. I know this is not your forte . . .'

'But you've already been away for a month.'

'I just can't do it. Not now. I'm already under huge pressure.'

'They on your case at work, then?'

'More than you could know. They have me working all God's hours, meetings every night. I don't have the headspace.'

'But—'

'Ben, you'll just have to cope for once.'

She stands and pulls on her navy coat and picks up her case. I move round the table and reach for her. She kisses me tenderly, but not, it feels, without an invoice.

'You'll have to lay out the money.'

'Why?' I ask. 'Surely we don't have to pretend you're broke as well?' I stare into her eyes as she answers.

'About six months ago I put my available cash into a high-yield bond. It doesn't mature for another year.'

'I don't understand. Why would you do that when we'd decided to go to tribunal?'

Emma picks at her cuticles. 'It was earning nothing where it was, I couldn't let it just sit there.'

'But you knew we were going to need it.'

'I thought the council might buckle,' she says.

'Really? That's not like you. Not your way of planning. What's going on, Emma?' Her eyes wander, I'm conjuring visions of dashing international lawyers and luxury hotel suites. 'What happened in Hong Kong?'

She sits down again and her anger sharpens my sordid vision. 'I worked and I worked and I slept and I missed home. That's all,' she says. 'Do you think I was having fun? I can promise you I wasn't.'

I feel my face set into a Pierrot frown.

'What?' she stabs. I back down, as I always do in the presence of her irritation. We both stare at the table until the air between us cools.

'The money?' I remind her.

'Around thirty thousand pounds.'

'What! You know I haven't got that kind of money.'

'I'll pay you back, don't worry.'

'It's not that, I just don't know where I'll get it from.'

'Ask your father.'

I imagine Dad's twitching fists. 'Emma, come on, that is not going to happen.'

'Why? You keep telling me that he owes you.'

'Yes, but he doesn't agree – there's no fucking contract, after all. It's not written on paper, it's written in years of psychotherapy and washing-up. I am not asking him.'

'For Jonah, you won't ask him?'

'That's low.'

'No, it's just the truth ...'

I'm wounded and my head drops. 'He doesn't want Jonah to go. He says you don't give up your children. Which is a bit rich coming from him, don't you think? Every time I ask him for something, it's like giving up a little piece of my soul.'

'Ben, I can't cope with being your emotional punchbag. We need to win this and we both need to recover, do you see? Everything else is secondary. That is my reality. I cannot be responsible for yours.'

'What is all this psychobabble? You blame Jonah.'

'No, Ben, no. I love and adore Jonah, but I've forgotten how to love myself and I'm not sure you ever did.'

'Love you?'

'No, yourself, you fool.'

We smile at each other and she takes my hand. 'Who will fight for Jonah if we're both wrecked? Where's the sense in it? Now, Georg?'

'I have to tell you he's not keen on Jonah moving away.'

'Then persuade him. He'll come round.'

'Persuade Dad?'

'All right, grovel – I don't care.'

I put the phones back in my bag and we both stare at the table. My Americano has gone cold. It's a strangers' silence, an awkward blind date silence filled with an imbalance of desires – one to leave, the other desperate to prevent departure. It's all businesslike again.

'Now, what are you going to do this afternoon, Ben?'

'Phone the barrister.'

'Don't forget.'

'I won't. I'll call you when I have some news.'

'Okay, but can't you just email me? It'll be better if you email, practically speaking. Can't always get to the phone.' She sees my face drop and puts her hand on my cheek. 'This is the best way, trust me, it will all be worth it.'

She blows me a kiss from the door and is gone, striding back to her legal bolt-hole where she claims to clean up other people's mess and shit just like I do, yet hers is just a euphemism. And I think about money and I think about work, but like an angry reminder of a bill unpaid, which if I ignore it long enough will miraculously disappear, the warehouse is a personal hell I also push from my mind.

She was here and now she's gone again and I'm a worm dangling on a line. I wish I'd recorded the conversation, so I could type it up and pore over the transcript, a proofreader genuinely searching for proof.

12 March 2011

Dear Mr Jewell

Our head of school, Linda Phillips, has now had the opportunity to observe Jonah during a day at Roysten Glen School and I would like to invite both you and Jonah to Highgrove Manor, so that our teaching and therapy teams can assess him and his suitability, while I will give you a tour of the campus and talk you through our role in the tribunal process.

    I have set aside March 19 and if you could arrive by 10 a.m. it would be appreciated.

    I enclose a map.

Kindest regards

Susan Atwater
Director of Education

Excited

'Oh my God, this boy's *tochas* is a shit cannon. Ben, get me a plastic bag, quickly. That's the third today, already.'

'His arse is as unpredictable as he is.'

Dad washes his hands like a surgeon and repeats the process with Jonah. I get him coated and shod while Dad wastes half a tin of air freshener.

'He's no worse than you,' I quip.

'Really? When you get to my age things tend to slow down.'

Jonah is secure in the back, with an apple in one hand and a feather in the other. The sky is clear, the sun low and I blow smoke into its rays before getting in the car. 'What's the post-code? It's on the letter.'

'OX7 3RG. Do you want me to direct you?'

'No, it's fine, I'll use the SatNav.'

'Again with the Satmap.'

'It's great for deliveries.'

'Does Valentine use one?'

'I bought him one.'

'Ha, he has probably given it to one of his kids.'

After refreshing and refreshing, the screen finally becomes

a full-colour map of the surrounding area and calculates both distance and arrival time. Dad's interest is piqued.

'Let me look at this Satmap.'

'SatNav.'

'That is what I said.' He slips his reading glasses from his blue blazer pocket – for Dad, any car outing requires dressing up – and leans close, poking the screen with his finger. 'This is my road. How does it know this is my road?'

The SatNav pipes up: 'Proceed along this road for three hundred yards and take the next left.'

'He's Australian? The one in the box. How does he know our roads?'

'It's a computer-generated voice, Dad – there's a whole selection of languages and accents.'

He seems impressed. 'So how much is a thing like this?'

'Fancy one now? You only go to Maurice's, Waitrose and Florsheim's kosher deli.'

'Just interested.'

We enter the M25 and merge into a traffic jam. I glance back at Jonah – he's finished his apple and is taking the feather to pieces. The plan is to keep him in food and twiddlies for the whole journey and pray his own internal SatNav doesn't object to the computer version. The outcome is never pretty.

'So, where's Mum these days?' I ask.

'You don't know?'

'How should I know?'

'I just assumed you speak to her, occasionally.'

'Not for a couple of years. Had a postcard from the Maldives.'

'Always such a boaster, Myra. No, your Uncle Matthew told me in his monthly duty call that she is currently living in

Norway or Sweden, or some other part of the frozen north. The weather should suit her there, nice and cold.'

I laugh. 'Seriously, though?'

'She always had a thing for herring, maybe that's it,' Dad says.

'Is she with anyone?'

'What is this? Twenty rhetorical questions?'

'No, just wondered.'

The traffic is starting to spread like a drawn-out concertina, which brings bouncing and laughter from the back seat. Dad reaches back and hands him another apple, then puts his hands behind his head and shuts his eyes.

Do I miss my mother? I think about her, not sure that's the same as missing. I was very young when she left and, as my father never tires of telling me, self-obsessed, irresponsible and an embarrassment.

What happened? We've only ever had a single conversation about it and – as ever – he was evasive, fending off my pointed questions like a fly swatter. Did he drive her out? 'I would have happily driven her wherever she wanted to go and dumped her there – but I did not drive her out.' That's what he said. But, apart from this, everything I know is supposition – the result of voyeurism and stealth.

My father is fourteen years my mother's senior. They met, she told me once, through her brother – another Maccabi footballer – and she fell for his no-nonsense manner and his stoicism. There was passion at the beginning, but I remember many nights as a child with her lying next to me, crying into my shoulder. It wasn't long before she was railing against his lack of emotion. Most of their life together was an endless ceasefire.

As I recall, we were poor, then we weren't poor. She wanted, he gave. She wanted more, he gave more. Then she wanted private schooling for me and he put his foot down – it went against everything he believed in, and I never got to choose.

I once confronted him about the unfairness of living according to his ideals, having no choices myself, and his answer:

'Well, let's see. You have two eyes, two ears, a nose – definitely a mouth, and that –' he poked my head hard with his forefinger '– that gives you all the choices you need.

'You've managed to do enough damage yourself. You are the laziest bastard God ever put breath into and you want for nothing. Tell me you were ever hungry or cold and I will cry crocodile tears for you and find you the number for the Samaritans.'

I look across at him and he looks back.

'What?'

'Are you happy, Dad?'

My question is a simple one and yet I sense his answer will be obliquely delivered – in his own image.

'I don't like being happy, it makes me nervous.'

We sit in silence for a while, digesting. He breaks the silence.

'Do you love Jonah?'

I'm disoriented by the cynical tone. 'Of course, how could you even ask such a thing? I love him with everything I have.'

'Then prove it to me.'

'What? Using your counterintuitive method? Is this a riddle, Dad, some kind of trial by fire? What about you, do you love Jonah?'

'Jonah, I love,' he says, with fully downturned grin.

There is silence, while I fight the tears.

'Does the affection gene skip a generation then?'

But he's closed his eyes and his head is lolling and I have a motorway to negotiate. For once, I'm in control.

Bruce the SatNav swings us off the M25 and on to the M40 heading west, but Jonah disagrees. He's been babbling to himself sweetly, but his tone is now gruffer and his bouncing more aggressive. I try to pacify him, but he's gone, shoots forward and clamps his hands around Dad's neck, yanking his head back and forth against the headrest.

'Pull over.'

'I can't, I'm in the outside lane. Hand him a feather, a feather, in the glove compartment.'

Dad is choking and can't reach. When Jonah grips on it's like a hangman's noose. I reach across and flick the catch, just managing to keep my eyes on the road as I locate the bag of feathers and toss them over my shoulder like a hunk of meat into a lion's den. Jonah releases his grip and grabs a feather. It is immediately the focus of my son's left eye. It calms him.

'You okay, Dad?'

'I'll live. Luckily I have four chins.'

'Is his seatbelt still on?'

'Yes, it's still on.'

There's a bottle of water in your door pocket, see if he needs a drink?'

Jonah finishes it in one go, bits of feather stuck to his lips. He smiles again and laughs playing pat-a-cake with Dad's hand. I breathe heavily.

'After four hundred yards, turn left.'

It's a long, sweeping drive leading to high wrought-iron gates. I buzz the intercom and announce our arrival, the gates swings away from us and a Georgian manor house comes into view. As we crawl towards it, open fields, a wood and a stable appear to the right and a collection of lower, modern buildings to the left. The rearview mirror reveals Jonah's face stuck to the window. I park the car outside the manor house.

'Is this what you imagined?' I ask.

'Don't push me.'

'I'm not pushing, Dad, I value your opinion.'

'My opinion is you talk too much, so be quiet and let me make up my own mind.'

A young, casually dressed woman approaches from the manor house.

'Hi, I'm Susan Atwater, director of education, and this must be Jonah?'

Jonah's still fiddling furiously. 'He may be a little tetchy still from . . .'

Susan Atwater offers Jonah her hand and I watch, spellbound, as he takes it.

'If you'd like to come inside we have an itinerary arranged for you.'

Through the double doors of the elegant house is a large panelled lobby with a staircase directly ahead. There are corridors to left and right. From a door off the left corridor a young man appears. He is dressed in a navy sweatshirt and matching jogging pants with the school crest emblazoned on it.

'This is Mike. Mike, this is Jonah's father and grandfather. Mike will show Jonah around while I introduce you to our senior team and show you the facilities.'

Mike pulls a block of laminated cards from his pocket, sorts through them until he finds one bearing a picture of a ball pond and hands it to Jonah. Jonah hands it back and takes Mike's hand and off they trot. Again, compliance.

'We'll see him again in a couple of hours, don't worry, he'll be fine.'

Dad is looking uneasy, his eyes wandering up and down the stairs. 'The dormitory, the ward, it's up the stairs?'

Susan Atwater laughs. 'No, Mr Jewell...'

'Georg.'

'Georg, this is simply the administration block, the children's houses are elsewhere on the site. We will see them presently. First I thought we'd take a walk around the grounds while I explain a few of the basics.'

We step back outside and survey the view.

'Our grounds extend as far as the wire fence you can see straight ahead, about five hundred metres. If you look to the right, you'll see our Countryside Learning Centre where the students learn to interact with our animals – feeding the pigs and chickens, grooming the ponies and, of course, riding them, too.'

'Jonah, on a horse?'

'Yes, horses are highly empathetic animals. We find it a hugely successful therapy.'

'I hope it's a strong horse.'

I find myself unable to take it in. My mind is stuck like an old forty-five. He must come here, I want him here, I want this for him. Whatever it takes, whatever.

Ms Atwater and Dad have strolled off and I quicken my stride to rejoin them.

'And this is our wood. There is a series of paths through it with benches and sensory statues for the students to explore.'

'Jonah will love this,' I hear myself say, like an alcoholic with his own whisky distillery.

'In answer to your earlier question, Georg, we have seven houses that can accommodate up to eight children per house.'

She opens a metal bar gate, secured by a karabiner, and we find ourselves outside a building with a planed roof. She buzzes us in and through a second door lies a huge airy space, two storeys high, with plush sofas, bean bags, a television, kitchen and a wall of glass that opens on to its own garden.

'This is Bell House, where the youngest live. There are currently seven children here. It's empty because they're all in class at the moment.'

The mixture of joy and trepidation is unbearable, like stumbling towards an oasis in a desert only to find it's a mirage.

'The bedrooms are upstairs.'

Dad's stride has begun to spring as we pass through gate after gate, he's like Charlie in the chocolate factory.

'This is our most recent acquisition, the sensory pool. An indoor swimming pool, heated to bath temperature, with both sound and light therapies.'

Change the record; *I* want to move here. Susan Atwater draws our attention to a field, back towards the entrance to the grounds. The grass is cut short and there are what appear to be inflatable obstacles positioned at intervals around a track, like a kids' steeplechase. I can see two figures making their way toward a giant red archway – it's Jonah and he's trotting. The fastest I've seen him move before is between the television and the fridge.

This school, this haven, is fifty acres of Jonahville. Fifty acres, fifty-four children and over two hundred staff on duty day and night. But this level of care comes at a price, so in some way Dad is close to the truth – it does come down to money. We researched these schools, Emma and I, and there wasn't much of a shortlist. Emma visited three and chose Highgrove Manor, now I understand why: it fits our son like a glove. But there are so few spaces and so many children that only a tiny fraction are given what they need. Jonah leaving home makes me shudder, but Jonah not being here makes me shudder more. Him not making it here at all is unthinkable.

In his office, the school's chief executive, Hugh Challoner, runs us through the challenges ahead.

'A forty-four-week placement at Highgrove costs two hundred thousand pounds a year. If Jonah joins us in September and stays until he's nineteen, that's one point six million. We don't accept private funding from parents or any other individuals, however wealthy. Each child here is funded by their local authority.'

'And they pay?' Dad asks.

'Not willingly, no,' I admit.

'You surprise me.'

Mr Challoner smiles.

'That's what I've been trying to explain to you for the last two months, Dad. We have to prove that Maureen Mitchell isn't suitable for Jonah's needs and that Highgrove is. Get it?'

'And the rich can't just pay to get in?'

'No,' Mr Challoner answers.

'So this is a socialist school for children with autism?'

'If you want to look at it that way, I suppose,' the chief executive says.

'So that is the tribunal thing you have been spitting at me day and night?'

'Yes, Dad.'

'Ben, you find a school like this near Muswell Hill and we'll talk.'

*

Dad likes Highgrove Manor, I can tell. He's laid out the dining table for the first time this millennium and, instead of forking out food from containers on the pan-scarred kitchen table, we've been honoured with plates, serving spoons and wine glasses. Jonah refuses to sit with us, preferring to bounce between sofa and table, grabbing handfuls as he goes. Dad seems preoccupied, tutting, sighing, half smiling and teary-eyed as if reminiscing. His melancholy is affecting me, affection for him the result.

'Tell you what,' I say, 'why don't you take it easy while I clear up and sort Jonah out.'

My voice acts as a hypnotist's click of the fingers. He blushes as if he's been caught.

'No, Benjamin, it is a kind thought, but you have been driving all day. Just clear the table while I take JJ up and we can do the washing-up together after.'

'Why don't we both bath Jonah?'

'No, no, we will be fine.'

I hear the slightest rising tone of panic in his voice, but he is right, I am dog-tired, so I suppress my curiosity. 'Okay, but let me do the washing-up too, all right?'

'You know where the tea towels are?'

'Yes.'

'The washing-up liquid?'

'Yes.'

'Okay, but don't get water everywhere. Come, Jonah, let's go up for a bath.'

The washing-up takes me thirty minutes, mopping up the kitchen floor another twenty. The bath is obviously over because, as I trudge up the stairs to kiss Jonah goodnight, I make out my father's voice drifting from Jonah's bedroom. Curiosity overcomes me, so I take the final few stairs on tiptoe and slide down the adjacent wall where I can sit and listen without being seen.

'When I was born in 1934 – that's many, many days ago, my lovely boy – it seemed very good to be a Jew. My father and my mother, Edit, loved me very much and they loved my brother, Jonatan – your great-uncle – too. I worshipped my brother, he was three years older than me, tall and dark with a beaming smile that was always shining on me. But in other ways he was different. Like you, he was a boy of few words. He would often wander off if he wasn't watched carefully and sometimes got so upset that even I couldn't calm him down . . . JJ? Maybe we'll finish tomorrow?'

I can hear Jonah snoring lightly. Any fleeting affection has gone. A brother? I knew he had parents, it's a biological certainty, but an older brother? Jonatan? Why could he not have told me? Jonah gets the story, but not me?

I've got used to the paranoia of my father's 'mistrust' all my life, chewed on it like pep pills, but now I discover it hasn't been paranoia, I feel misplaced. A mother in the Arctic and a father who seems incapable of defrosting. Will I have to eavesdrop like a KGB agent every night to find out where I come from? My own personal 'Book at Bedtime'. I hear the kisses, the soft lullaby and rustling of duvet as Dad tucks him in, and I pad downstairs to the lounge and climb aboard the sofa before he leaves Jonah's room. Dad comes in and stares at me quizzically.

'I thought I heard you upstairs,' he says.

'Jonah all right?' I ask, shrugging.

'He is in bed, he is happy.'

'Good, thanks for doing that. Well, did he like your story?'

Dad raises his hand to dismiss it. 'Pass me my *Daily Mirror*.'

I throw it and it falls apart at his feet, but I get no reaction, he just calmly picks up the sheets and neatly puts them back together before sitting down.

'Am I adopted?' I spit.

'What?'

'Nothing.'

He turns to the centre double-spread that holds the television listings, where he has ringed various programmes with red pen like he's chosen horses at a race meeting. It's the first thing he does in the morning after completing the *Guardian* crossword. He sits in the armchair and flicks on the TV with the remote, silence descends and I cannot be here with this adrenalin coursing through me. I need to find an outlet.

'I'm popping out.'

'Do not do it, Ben.'

'What are you talking about?' God, does he spy on me into the small hours from his bedroom window?

'You'll drive yourself *sedrate*.'

'I'm just off to get some fags.'

'If you say so.'

My car knows the route; I'm just a passenger as it accelerates on to the North Circular, heading east for five minutes and then off, toward Wynchgate. Her car's not there, so I sit in a fog of panic and anger. Ten is late enough on a weeknight; I allow a ten per cent margin for error and Tube delays, but at eleven minutes past, my stomach falls into my arse.

I try to control my breathing, take my own pulse and plot a release of nervous energy through an imagined attack on her hapless passenger. By twenty past I'm talking out loud, shadow boxing, sipping from the flask of whisky warming gently between my thighs. On the half hour, I'm inconsolable, hyperventilating and whimpering.

Then I hear a car, feel its lights silhouette me as it indicates and pulls into her parking spot. When she gets out alone it's like a shot of heroin. Everything calms, euphoria overcomes me and I watch and wait until she wearily opens the front door and begins to climb the stairs. As the light goes on in the lounge window, I turn the key and pull away. I love her like a junkie loves his dealer and yet I want to catch her in a lie.

Mr G Jewell
14 Oakfield Avenue
London N10 4RG

*Department of
Oncology*

12 March 2011

Dear Mr Georg Jewell

An appointment has been made for you to attend Wynchgate
Hospital on the following date: [3 April 2011]
    You will be required to attend the Department of
Oncology in the Heston Building (map enclosed) at 10 a.m.
Please be advised that the procedure – biopsy of thyroid
gland – will be carried out under local anaesthetic, but it is the
hospital's policy that anyone over the age of seventy requiring
this procedure is kept overnight for observation.

Keith Waters-Long
Administrator

Nathan

Worried

x

Jonah's laughing. He's been laughing since 4.30 this morning. He laughed while I cleaned him up and bathed him, laughed as I dried and dressed him and now he can't eat for laughing. I'm not laughing, I'm knackered. It's Saturday morning, it's not yet 8 a.m. and the day feels half done already. Dad is showered and shaved and stands by the kitchen door with a grubby canvas holdall in his left hand.

'I'm going away for the night. Will you be okay?' he says.

Jonah laughs at him and Dad kisses him on the top of his head and ruffles his hair.

There is something shrunken about him, less straight. His eyes have changed from amber to red.

'Where are you going?'

The doorbell rings and then I hear a key turn in the lock.

'What's going on?' I ask Dad, before Maurice saunters in.

'Southend,' Maurice says. 'Kalooki tournament.'

'You hate Kalooki. You hate old Jews. What's going on, Dad?' He can be so inscrutable sometimes, most of the time, in fact, but Maurice is an open book. 'Maurice?'

'Don't look at me.'

'Dad?'

'It's nothing.' There is anger and fear in his voice. 'Doctor Frankenstein wants a bit of my flesh, that's all.'

He hands me a sheet of paper with the royal blue NHS logo in the top right-hand corner.

'A biopsy? You're having a biopsy today? On your neck?'

'No, on my *schlung*. Of course on my neck, fool. Once you start with these doctors they are not happy until they have made you ill. It is nothing, I'll be back tomorrow – and if not, cremate me.'

'For God's sake, why didn't you tell me?'

'Are you a surgeon? No. So what could you do?'

'I'm coming with you. I'm not a child.'

'You'll stay here. It's a nice day, take JJ to the park. Let him destroy some plants. Maurice is coming with me.'

The doorbell rings again.

'That will be the cab, Maurice, get the door.'

'Why did you call a taxi? At least let me drive you there?'

'You can pick me up tomorrow if you have to. I don't want to come home to a mess.'

I sit nursing a coffee after they go. Jonah is spinning around in the garden, pulling a pigeon feather to pieces. His clothes are in a pile by the back door and the remnant of a wedge of Cheddar is on the floor by the open fridge.

I stare at Emma's number on my phone. Already I hear my heart thumping in my ear; with each pressed digit it grows louder. As I stall at the eleventh I feel sick. I press 'call' and it takes an eternity to connect, then rings and rings and rings and rings and goes to voicemail and I hang up.

*

I'm in the back between Jonah and Tom, pretending to share the latter's obsession with football cards.

'Just need to pop into Brent Cross to change something,' Amanda says airily from the passenger seat.

'Can't you do it afterwards?'

'It'll only take twenty minutes, only John Lewis,' she says. 'Johnny'll park outside, won't you, darling.'

'Sure,' Johnny says.

These simple things, little detours, cause me untold stress. Now all bets are off. 'If you have to.'

'We'll be in the park in half an hour. Promise,' Amanda says.

I monitor Jonah's face. So far, so good. His attention is focused on the fur around the collar of his parka. He is plucking and twiddling furiously. As the car comes to a halt in a disabled bay and Johnny releases his seatbelt, Jonah climbs out and grabs my hand like an angel. The only thing predictable about Jonah is his unpredictability.

Johnny grabs a bag from the boot and we troop in after him towards women's wear.

'Uncle Ben, can I take Jonah up to the toy department?' Tom asks.

This is two floors up. Amanda is remonstrating with a sales assistant, Johnny hovering awkwardly behind. 'Come on, I'll take you both,' I say.

I study them standing next to each other on the escalator. Jonah is taller, his hair longer, his fingers squeezing and rubbing the handrail. Tom looks up at him, talking incessantly, desperate for a reaction. They were born three days apart, Jonah the older. Johnny and I had plans for both of them, they were to be best friends or else and Tom has kept his side of the bargain. He never leaves Jonah out, always invites him to his birthday parties, is always excited to see him. Tom wants a friendship with Jonah like Johnny and I have. So do I.

Toys share the second floor with technology, so while I keep one eye on Jonah and Tom, I investigate the latest gadgetry. Jonah joins me, fascinated by the colourful movements of a laptop screensaver. I reach for his hand and hold it gently. My phone rings.

'We're done, where are you?'

'Upstairs, with the boys. I'll bring them down.'

'Okay, see you in a minute.'

I reach for Jonah's hand again, but it's gone. I can see Tom's head above a display of Star Wars figures and wander over, assuming Jonah is with him.

He is not.

'Tom, where's Jonah?'

'He was with you.'

I scan the floor on tiptoes, holding back the sickening panic with imagined sightings of his long, tousled hair. My feet begin to move, carrying me forward, up and down aisles in expectation of relief.

'Uncle Ben, where is he?'

There's panic in Tom's voice. 'I don't know. Tom, go and get your mum and dad for me, please. Now.'

He runs off down the escalator as I collar a besuited floor-walker, but as I try to explain, my words come out like a stroke victim's – confused, disordered.

'My son is missing, he's autistic, doesn't speak, no sense of danger.'

Then Johnny is standing above me. My legs have succumbed first and I sit, cross-legged, on the floor waiting to be saved. I wish Emma was here. My hearing goes sub-aqua, cries of 'Jonah' reach me slowly, I am set apart. Amanda sits next to me and puts both arms round me.

'Sir, please don't worry, we have well-rehearsed systems for this.'

Men with walkie-talkies appear above the water line, I feel hands lift me to standing and lower me into a chair. Tom sits next to me, he's crying. Johnny is describing Jonah; his description is broadcast across the shopping centre.

'We post staff at every exit, he won't be able to leave the centre.'

Johnny puts a reassuring hand on my shoulder. I should be running, sprinting up and down the walkways, shouting his name, screaming at the top of my voice, but I'm frozen because my mind has created scenarios too hideous to live with. He is vulnerable, too vulnerable, so vulnerable. My breath won't escape, it catches in my throat. I am sobbing and will wail, I feel it in my diaphragm; in the reptilian core of me something is building that will shatter glass and level buildings.

My eyes fix on the up escalator. It reveals head after head; body after body. Each stranger's face is ugly to me, contorted, devilish and mocking.

'Ben, don't worry, they'll find him,' Amanda whispers to me.

Tom has burrowed into Johnny's midriff.

The heads of two women appear inch by inch from the escalator and, as their uniformed torsos rise into view, so does a scruffy mane standing between them, one hand held, the other gripping a bright-red cone.

Johnny tells me later they found him in McDonald's. As the relief at Jonah's safe return takes over, I hear nothing.

*

Amanda and I sit on the bench while Tom and Johnny try valiantly to engage Jonah in duck feeding. Her legs stretch way beyond mine and her near-black corkscrew curls cover her eyes and tickle her nose in the breeze. *Different looking*, that's how Emma describes her. Different looking and striking. Tom tears chunks of bread from the loaf in its plastic bag and hands them to Jonah and Jonah eats them himself. I admire Tom's devotion. I know this park is a little boring for him now, the playground's brightly coloured apparatus unchallenging and the swings too low for his feet to clear the ground, but his presence feeds my illusion of Jonah having friends, of maybe one day kicking a football back and forth. There will come a time, I accept, when even Tom will become frustrated with Jonah's insouciance and visits will become a duty, like a visit to a younger cousin or – and the thought makes me shudder – to an aged uncle.

'Have you stopped shaking yet?' Amanda asks.

'Just about. I could murder a drink.'

'He's fine, Ben. Look at him, doesn't even know there was a fuss.'

'I feel like a criminal.'

'Don't be ridiculous, it happens all the time,' she says.

'It's never happened when he's been with me before. Anything could have happened.'

'But it didn't.'

Amanda offers me a cigarette and I take one and light them both.

I feel so raw, that even this gesture of friendship threatens to bring on the waterworks.

'Why wasn't she here with us, Amanda? She should be here.'

'Ben, I know you're angry and confused...'

'So unconfuse me.'

Amanda draws on her cigarette. 'I'm not condoning the way she's behaving, Ben, but she loves Jonah.'

'Then, why?'

'You have to allow her some time,' Amanda says. 'You've both been living in a pressure cooker for so long, one of you was bound to explode. If you ask me, you both have.'

'I haven't,' I say.

'Oh no? I've known you since you were sixteen, remember.'

She pauses as we both pull on our cigarettes.

'Do you know when I first realised you were in trouble, Ben? With the booze,' she continues.

I shake my head.

'You phoned to speak to Johnny and got me, about six months after you joined your dad's business. You were sitting in the car park at Ikea and you dared me to guess what you were doing.'

'And what was I doing?'

'You were working your way through a pack of assorted-flavoured miniature vodkas and you thought it was hilarious.'

At the time, it was. 'I remember now. I went to buy some children's furniture.'

'It was ten in the morning,' Amanda points out.

I pause to light another cigarette, exhale and turn my face from her. 'Bad days,' I say.

'Yes, bad days,' she says, 'And not just for you. Ben, I love you, but you take some looking after. I warned Emma when you first got together, I warned her.'

'Thanks,' I mutter.

'No, really,' Amanda says. 'I told her then if she expected the next Bill Gates, she'd be sorely disappointed. She said you made her laugh and you were kind.'

'Amanda, were we ever right for each other?'

'Life takes over, Ben. Let's be honest, you've not exactly excelled yourself in the responsibility stakes.'

I wince and she strokes my cheek.

'And then, of course, that wonderful lump called Jonah came along and you made Emma suffer for your own misplaced guilt. Give her some space, Ben. Emma's been shouldering the burden for too long. I know it's hard to hear this from me, but step up! Johnny and I will always be here to help you.'

I stare at my feet.

She asks, 'We still okay?'

Johnny arrives, puffing, with the boys following behind.

'So what's with your dad?' Johnny asks.

'It's a biopsy of a lump in his neck.'

'Probably nothing, usually is,' he says.

'Mmm. They might even strike oil.'

'Or sulphuric acid. He's a tough old bastard, your dad.'

'Uncle Ben,' Tom calls, 'Jonah's off to the café.'

I begin to sprint after him, but Johnny stops me.

'Go with him, Tom, there's a good lad.'

'But I haven't got any money on me.'

'It's all right, Jonah's got a tab,' I say. 'Just ask Marie to keep a note and I'll pay her later – and have what you want for yourself.'

'Okay.'

I watch them safely into the little single-storey building and keep staring at the door.

'Seriously though, Ben, your dad's made of Kevlar. It's probably just a glandular thing,' Johnny says.

'Probably, yeah.'

I'd boxed up the feelings of last night, but this talk of my dad has unwrapped them. I watch the reflections of the willows on the surface of the lake, how they change as the sun burns through the light clouds. Focusing on the water is meditation, Jonah does it sometimes too. I sense that Dad is ill, or is it just my natural pessimism? I think it's normal to imagine your reactions to a loved one's death, rehearsing the stoicism, identifying who'll be there to support you.

'And how are you doing?'

I blow out a 'fine' with my first exhale.

'And your mum, does she know?'

'That's all I need. No, I don't even know where she is. Scandinavia or somewhere, apparently.'

'Emma's mum and dad?'

'Murray and Evelyn? I don't know. They only leave Florida if someone dies.'

'And the tribunal?'

'Still need Dad to cough up the money.'

'Ouch.'

'Yep.'

'What about you?'

'You mean apart from the bollocking your wife just gave me?'

'Ben—' Amanda objects, as I pull her head to me and kiss her on the forehead.

The boys are strolling back down the hill from the café, Jonah in front eating an apple, Tom following with gaudy orange ice lolly stuck to his mouth.

'Me? What do I matter? It's not in my hands, is it? Dad decides whether we fight the tribunal, because I haven't got a pot to piss in. Emma seems to have gone AWOL, as you know. I haven't seen or spoken to anyone but you in ages. If we don't fight or fight and lose, the rest of my life is dictated by the bowel movements, sleeping pattern and aggressive mood swings of my son; if we win, my son leaves home at the age of eleven probably never to return, I'll owe my dad for life and I'll be alone and homeless.'

'Could be worse.'

'How do you figure that?'

'You could be a balding middle-aged Jew with a failing business and marriage, and a cock the size of a button mushroom.'

'Where would I be without your pep talks?'

'Uncle Ben, Uncle Ben! Can we go to the playground?'

Jonah's already taken off. Not to the nearest spring-loaded gate, but to the one on the other side of the red circle of railings that encompasses the playground. He always does this, he seems to miss the connection between opening the nearer gate and the apparatus inside. It's like his memory can't handle binary solutions, as if he'll only gain the sensation he's after through one definite action. I can still see him trotting round awkwardly with his hands in the air.

'Come on,' I say to Johnny and Amanda, 'let's go with.'

Tom swings next to Jonah, but they could be in separate playgrounds. I move to sit next to Jonah, but as I do he's up and off to the slide. He climbs to the top and stops, blocking the path of the children behind him. Eventually, he backs up to the steps and tentatively makes his way down again. He never goes down the slide.

'Uncle Ben, I'm really sorry.'

'Sorry for what, Tom?'

He starts to cry, so I kneel in front of him and place my hands on his thighs.

'I should have watched him when we went to the toys, I'm so sorry...'

'Tommy, it wasn't your fault. You mustn't feel guilty.'

'But he's my best friend and I let him down.'

'You're not responsible for Jonah, Tom.'

'But he can't talk, so I have to talk for him. I'm trying to teach him, though, Uncle Ben, so that we can go to the same school next year.'

'Tom, I...'

Amanda is behind me and takes over. 'Tommy, Jonah's going to a wonderful school where they'll teach him all he needs to know, but you'll always be his best friend, okay? So come, give Uncle Ben a hug.'

It feels strange to have a ten-year-old hug me back.

Last night I rehearsed for the worst, but this morning, Dad comes through the automatic doors clutching his bag like a returning package tourist. He has a large dressing on the side of his neck. Jonah bounces and smiles when he sees him. He lets me take his bag and we walk silently to the car and climb in.

'Feeling okay then?'

There is silence as we leave the hospital grounds.

'Well?' I ask.

'Well what?'

'What did the doctor say?'

'Didn't say anything, just stuck a needle in my neck and made me wear a nightie with my *tochas* hanging out,' says Dad.

'What did they find?'

'Have to wait for cytology, histology or something.'

'But were they concerned?' I ask.

'Why should they be concerned? I'm the one they stuck the needle into. I'm starving, you can't eat the food in there, take me somewhere for lunch.'

'Wouldn't you rather go home and rest up?'

'I've been lying down for two days and I'm hollow, I need food. Let's go.'

Of all places, he chooses Goldberg's, on a Sunday, at lunchtime. The tables are packed so tightly together they almost have to hoist the customers into their seats by crane – and the noise is insufferable. This is the place to go to air your resentments and hope that the person you resent is at the next table. It's where the waiters – all ancient and Greek and freelance – are taught to grimace, spill soup, crack bad jokes and pinch the cheeks of fat grandchildren, a little too hard.

But he wants salt beef – nuclear pink and cut like boot leather – oil-oozing latkes, pickled cucumbers, borscht and, most significantly, an argument, a loud argument with plenty of finger pointing. This is a restaurant that keeps an ambulance on constant standby.

'I'm not sure this is the place for Jonah,' I say.

We are queuing. Jonah doesn't understand the concept. 'Dad, he's going to flip if we stand here much longer, can't we go somewhere else?'

Dad looks down at Jonah, who has his hand in a death grip. 'Maybe you're right. You can make me a sandwich at home.'

But all at once, bentwood chairs are hoisted into the air. 'Here we go. Follow those,' says Dad, squeezing between two tables where a gap doesn't exist. 'Just hang on.'

'Hey, control the little *shmerel*!'

I look down at Jonah, who's wedged between Dad and me, munching on a fist full of someone else's salt beef. Then he grimaces, spits out his mouthful, dumps the rest back on its owner's plate and grabs a neighbouring latke.

'What is this? The kid's a pig, a pig.'

Dad turns round and pokes the finger. 'That's my grandson,

shmock.' He waves his hand in the air and catches the eye of a waiter. 'Over here. Another plate of salt beef and latkes for the *Yiddische* Kojak. Happy?'

'Dad, let's go.' News of Jonah's latke larceny has spread like a virus.

'Our table's ready,' Dad says.

'I'm not hungry any more.'

'Did you just come out of hospital? Sit down, you'll eat.'

The table is tiny and round and I grab Jonah's hips to man-oeuvre him into the chair. Through his jogging bottoms I can feel the curve of his arse cheeks. I shouldn't be able to feel his arse cheeks. In the rush to leave the house to pick Dad up from the hospital, I have forgotten to put a nappy on him and I didn't grab his changing bag. The best I can hope for is a piss. I go hot and cold.

'Dad, can you ask the waiter for some serviettes?'

'Here, there are napkins on the table.'

'No, I need serviettes, paper napkins, lots of them, or kitchen roll, toilet paper, anything.' I'd go to the toilet myself, but I can't move. 'Please.'

He looks at me and closes his eyes, contemptuously, then summons the waiter and whispers in his ear. The waiter rushes off.

'How could you?' Dad spits.

'I was worried about you,' I say.

'Useless,' he says. 'A simple bag of things for him you can't remember.'

The waiter returns with a roll of kitchen towel. It is impossible not to draw attention to the process, as I tear single sheets from it and form a multi-layered pad, coax Jonah off his chair and push the hastily constructed pad down the back of his joggers and between his legs.

'How could you humiliate him like that?'

'I'm sorry, I was in a rush.'

'Benjamin...'

That's all he manages. His chin is on his chest. The use of my full name wounds, deeply. It's a childhood admonishment, an expression of the deepest disappointment. Not anger – that is defendable – but a real, winding, draining dismissal that corrodes my soul. It's a hideous realisation that I still care.

And then the smell.

And the darkening stain.

And the two hundred raised noses.

And the heaving.

And the rushing waiters.

And the struggle with Jonah's exploring hands.

And the smearing.

And the frantic wiping.

And the parting of tables like the Red Sea.

And the shame.

The fucking shame.

And the dressing on his neck.

And the panic of what if?

And the silent drive home.

And the only words he utters before retiring to his bedroom with a sigh: 'You pay. You're his father. I gave you the business, Ben, make it pay. If this is truly what you want for your son – work for it. Now bath him, properly.'

I have been in disgrace all week, wandering between the pub, the warehouse and home.

It's Friday and I'm at my catering-equipment-hire empire. I spend the morning daydreaming. For the first time I'm glad that hours of washing-up need to be done. It feels therapeutic, the repetition of cloth on wine glass, watching steam rise from white china plates. Valentine stands opposite me mirroring my movements. He doesn't like to talk – doesn't like me – so it suits us both to keep our own counsel.

The phone rings.

'Jewell Catering Hire.'

'May I speak to Mr Ben Jewell, please?'

'Speaking, how can I help you?'

'This is Valetta Price's secretary. I know it's short notice but Ms Price has a cancellation at four p.m. today...'

'I'll be there.'

Valentine stops glass polishing. 'You leaving?' he asks me after I hang up.

'Yes, need to see my barrister about Jonah.'

He kisses his teeth. 'Deliveries, you know.'

'You can do them, Valentine.'

He puts the glass down and stares at me. 'Aren't you gonna do some? Can't do them all by myself.'

'Look, it's fine, I've already routed them for you...'

'Too many drops, won't be finished by six.'

'Valentine, can't you just do an extra couple of hours, please? I'll pay you extra.'

'What do you think I've been doing all these weeks?' he asks.

'I've been busy.'

'I know, in the pub.'

'Now listen—'

'No you listen, I'm sick of this.'

I put my hand to my forehead. 'Look, just do as many as you can and I'll cancel the rest.'

Valentine goes back to his glasses and drops his gaze. 'Okay,' he says.

HIGHGROVE MANOR SCHOOL

FOR CHILDREN AND YOUNG ADULTS WITH AUTISM

Highgrove Lane, Highgrove, Oxfordshire OX7 3RG

24 March 2011

Dear Mr Jewell

Having assessed Jonah, both in his present school and here at Highgrove Manor, I am delighted to inform you we are confident we can meet Jonah's needs and have therefore reserved a place for him, subject to the successful outcome of his planned educational tribunal.

I wish you luck and look forward to Jonah joining us here in September.

Kindest regards

Susan Atwater
Director of Education

How much?

Lincoln's Inn Field. In a former life, one with aspirations and arrogance, I worked five minutes from here as a marketing assistant. In those days, the hideous recession of the early nineties, the perimeter was choked by multi-coloured one-person tents like bunting and hastily built cardboard shacks in a bizarre pastiche of a rock festival. Right in the heart of London's legal grandeur, the homeless had set up home. It was an affront to the pinstriped barristers who treated the field as their private garden, and when the tennis courts on which they played their lunchtime sets became out of bounds, it was the final straw. One day the tents were there, the next they were gone, the park's gate chained and the rats moved in. The barristers' preference for rodents over people has always amused me.

It's back to its immaculate, manicured splendour now as I stroll through it on the way to the Lloyd Chambers to meet Jonah's prospective barrister, Ms Valetta Price. Barristers don't like to advertise, it seems, for each grand door off the quadrangle is identical and each building's occupants denoted by postcard-sized brass plaques. I walk all four corners and am sweaty before I stumble on the inscription 'Ms Valetta Price' by chance and with relief.

The reception area is surprisingly modern, not at all Rumpole, all shining oak veneer and black leather. I am led down a hallway to an open oak-effect door and ushered through into an equally ascetic office. The desk is pale and huge; Valetta Price small and dark behind it. Her hair is cut in a severe pudding bowl and it's clear from the off that she takes no prisoners.

'You're from Malta, then?'

'I'm sorry?'

'Valetta, the Maltese city?'

'Shall we start again, Mr Jewell? Jonah?'

'Yes, of course.'

Valetta Price is recommended for her tenacity, I keep reminding myself. She is leafing through the folder her assistant asked me to prepare on Jonah when I first contacted her, and it irks me that she hasn't read it before.

'Are you fully aware of what you are letting yourself in for?'

I am beginning to wonder.

'Well, I know it's going to be expensive.'

'This session's for free, but it's the one and only – so it's only fair I provide you with the worst-case scenario.'

'I've experienced a few of those...'

'Indeed. If you are one hundred per cent committed to gaining a place at the residential school then you will do exactly as I say, have Jonah seen by all the experts I name and be ready for a fight.'

'Would you like to see a picture of Jonah?'

'No, thank you. You need to understand this case is not personal to me and you cannot take anything personally, either. Do not expect the local authority to lie down and roll over, they won't. There is nothing in what you have sent me here that suggests that for one second. The burden of evidence lies with us, Mr Jewell, this is not a "guilty, not guilty" scenario, because the local authority – which is?'

'Wynchgate.'

'Oh, how lovely.'

I try my hardest to detect even a jot of sincerity in her tone.

'Wynchgate, as I was saying, only have to prove that Maureen Mitchell is *appropriate* for Jonah.'

'Which it clearly isn't.'

She pulls down a book from the shelf behind her desk. Licks her thumb and opens it toward the front and starts leafing through.

'Appropriate: *Suitable, fitting, apt, proper, right, correct, applicable*. Appropriate, in legal terms is not definitive – it's woolly, general, vague.'

She raises her eyes and tasers me.

'And therefore buggeringly hard to prove. Why do you think they chose that word?'

'So it's a fix.'

'No,' she states and leans back in her upholstered chair, placing her hands behind her head. 'Not a fix, more a term alighted upon by the legal equivalent of an insurance actuary. He or she knows they will win some and lose some, but has to pitch their premiums at the right level to maintain a positive balance sheet by attracting the right number of clients. It's quite clever really.'

'A fucking outrage is what it is.'

'Remove the outrage, Mr Jewell. That's why you're here.'

'No, I'm here to provide the best possible future for my son and so my wife and I can finally share a home again.'

'That's not something I can help you with, I'm afraid.'

'But the fact we're apart will help Jonah's case, won't it?'

'Not in the least, Mr Jewell. This is about Jonah's education only. Your home situation is a social services issue, therefore immaterial. Divorce law is not my speciality, although I could point you in the right direction. Mr Jewell, are you still with me?'

'Immaterial? I'm sorry but you're wrong.'

'Excuse me.'

'My wife has taken advice on this. Being a single father is one of the commonalities of successful appeals. We've been living apart for two months on the basis of—'

'I'm sorry, but I think she's been badly advised. Maybe you should phone her and tell her to come home. Mr Jewell?'

Valetta's look is knowing, the sympathy ersatz.

What kind of an expert has Emma been speaking to? This whole charade, avoidable. How could Emma not know, how could...? I am in agony.

'Will you excuse me for a second, Ms Price? I need to visit the gents.' I don't wait for a reply. I tunnel through the corridor and out into the sobering air. I am sweating and nauseous – staggering between the homicidal embraces of humiliation and rage, I dial her number. Answerphone. I dial her number again, blocking my caller ID. Answerphone. I call her office: she's not in. I call home: answerphone. Her mobile again: answerphone. Message: 'Fucking phone me back, please. Why did you lie to me? All that shit about single parents, commonalities. Shit! And don't try and pretend you didn't know, you're a fucking lawyer. You've made a right dick of me. Why, Emma? This bollocks is over now, do you understand?'

I end the call, yet part of me wants to take the message back, or send another, placatory and grovelling – which only increases the cycle of rage and humiliation. I breathe in deeply as if I'm about to dive underwater, release the air and repeat and repeat, massage my neck. Back inside the building I splash water on my face, pat down my hair and draw from my hip flask. Jonah, I remind myself, this is for Jonah.

Back in Valetta's office, my cup vibrates in my hand. I try to put it down but tea sloshes on to the desk. I'll do anything to get out of here right now. I repeat 'Jonah, Jonah' in my head as a mantra and feign control.

'Thank you for the offer, but I don't need a divorce lawyer, we will be back together soon.'

'Well, good for you,' Valetta says, nonchalantly. 'But let's concentrate on Jonah, shall we? I've already told you, should I be engaged by your solicitors, that will be my job.'

'I don't have a solicitor.' Another blinding piece of ignorance.

'Then you should use these.'

She passes me a glossy A5 folder, with a business card stapled to the top right-hand corner.

'Curran and Partners, Manchester? How am I supposed to travel up there?'

'You won't. Everything will be done via phone and email. Shall I phone them for you now?'

She begins dialling before I open my mouth. Whatever Valetta Price says, I'll say yes to. I feel my will ebbing away as all the anger makes a U-turn and bears down on me. I want to punish myself, sink into a bath of vodka and scrub myself with wire wool. Obliterate myself, feel nothing. Force everyone away from me, care about nothing and have no one care about me.

'Georgia, hi, yes good thanks. Have a potential client, an autism Part 4 placement. I know it's a bit late in the day, but...'

Now I'm sitting forward on my chair clasping my sweaty hands together. Late?

'Yes, I'll pass him over now.'

She thrusts the receiver at me.

'Hello?' I say.

'Hi, Mr Jewell. This is Georgia Stone here at Curran. Valetta is going to get your paperwork copied and emailed to me now. Really, you should have started this process last year, but don't fret, we could still make it by July the thirtieth if we gather everything we need and can get a tribunal date that suits everyone. Mr Jewell?'

Georgia sounds young and disarmingly sympathetic.

'Yes, I'm listening.'

'Okay. Do you have any questions?'

'What happens if we don't get a date before July the thirtieth?'

'Then unfortunately we'll have to aim for a date in September when – thankfully – things are a lot quieter, and Jonah will have to remain out of school until the tribunal has been held and the result delivered.'

I'm doing the computation in my head: that's six weeks of summer holiday, plus probably the whole of September. That's ten or eleven weeks, alone with Jonah and Dad. No. Emma will have to have Jonah for some of the time now.

'We have to get into this session. It's a must.'

'We'll all do our best for you, Mr Jewell. But the quicker we start the more chance we have. Would you like me to advise you of our terms?'

'Yes, I suppose you better had. No, wait, wait a second! What is the overall cost likely to be?'

'They average at around twenty-five thousand pounds. It depends on the local authority, time required by ourselves and Valetta, expert witnesses, etc., but it should be no more than thirty thousand. Mr Jewell?'

No more than thirty grand! Which planet... 'Yes, I'm listening.'

'Our terms?'

'Oh, yes.'

'We require an initial deposit of ten thousand pounds and a monthly standing order of five hundred pounds that will be held in your client account. I could get the ball rolling now if...'

Now this I haven't planned for either. Sickened, I pull out my wallet and check through my credit cards. Could any of them possibly pass muster at credit control – the business credit card definitely won't. I may have to call Johnny, if all else...

'Do you take credit cards?'

'Certainly. Is it a Visa?'

'Three of them are.'

Valetta takes the phone from my sweaty palm, as I wait for the sugary-sweet excuses of dodgy card readers and downed internet for my cards being spat back like a dose of poison.

'So, Mr Jewell, all systems go then.'

I laugh at the shock of it. 'They went through, all eight of them.'

'It appears that way.' She passes me a sheet of paper.

'These are the experts I need to have see Jonah. Some will need to observe him at school and at home, but they will advise you of that. Again, we have had a bit of a false start so need to catch up and, as these names are the best, they're probably booked up by now. I would begin phoning as soon as you get home and tell them I'm acting on your behalf. If they tell you they have no availability, refer them back to me. Any last questions?' she says, glancing at her watch. 'Okay, then I'll see you at the tribunal. Oh, and by the way, the experts will invoice you separately.'

'Of course they will.'

She shakes my hand limply and I'm back in the courtyard without a memory of leaving the building. Somehow I feel I've just been sold a timeshare or joined the Church of Scientology.

Outside, I find a bench and slump down on to it. *Commonalities*, that's what she said. Being a single father would greatly help Jonah's case. I am bored of this sick feeling, this weird haunting ectoplasm that engulfs me the further from Emma I move. Is it possible her colleague was wrong, or misled?

It's only been a couple of months and I'm having trouble summoning the sound of her voice – how can things decay so quickly? How can my senses and memories have such a short half-life? Should I phone her again and give her the 'good news', that Jonah and I can come home? Pretend I do not question her motives? Maybe Jonah and I should just move back into the flat, buy some balloons and cupcakes, a bottle of wine? Surprise her? Yes, won't that surprise her.

Wynchgate Social Services
The Civic Centre
Brown Street
London N24 3EA

30 March 2011

Dear Mr Jewell
Re: Jonah Jewell D.O.B. 11 May 2000 – Care Package

It was a pleasure to meet Jonah recently.

Having reviewed your case I am now in a position to offer you the following care package:

- A care assistant between 7–8.30 a.m. three days per week to help ready Jonah for school.

  As well as the existing:

- Every Sunday – attendance for Jonah at the borough's centre for disabled children 9.30–3.30, including transport. Details to arrive under separate cover.

- After-school club at above site, two nights per week (including travel school to club and home).

- Two nights' babysitting per month.

  Please feel free to contact me with any questions or concerns.

Regards
Mary Carey
Senior Social Worker

Waffle

At least there's no more mention of fostering this time, but 'comprehensive'? They try to dig away at you, inch by inch they take a spade to the foundations of the edifice you build up against them. Bit by bit they undermine your confidence in your own case. None of this was forthcoming before we threatened and started making a fuss about a tribunal. I'm bright enough to understand the concept of limited resources, but fuck, it unnerves me – maybe this is the Gold Standard of Care Packages? And maybe they've got little bits of care to add until the balance just tips against our appeal. They're obviously more practised at this than me. I need to boost my resolve with some serious hatred and anger.

I clear a space on the sofa, attack *his* cherry brandy and swear at the panel on *Question Time*. The rising self-pity is reacting with the brandy, creating a warm glow of indignant rage. I want out of this situation; this is not what I had planned for the onset of middle age. This is bollocks. This is fucking ridiculous.

I pull my mobile from my pocket and scroll back and forth through my contacts, each time pausing at 'Emma'. Why hasn't she called back? How long do I give her before I call her again? I've accused her of lying, I've sworn at her. No wonder.

I tell myself I'll call her at 11 p.m., then at 11.05, 11.10, 11.30. By midnight the cherry brandy is drained, I burp a fruity sweetness and press mute on the remote. Her face flashes up on the screen, smiling. Beautiful and distant and strange, and then the line connects and my finger hovers over the 'End Call' symbol as it rings.

When I worked at Centennial Communications, before Jonah was born, my marketing director was a brute of a man who took pleasure in controlling his staff with verbal abuse. He gave everyone a mobile phone and it was expected to be on twenty-four hours a day. One day I had the bright idea of assigning him a specific ring tone so I would always know it was him and prepare myself before answering. I assigned him the 'Funeral March' and at first it was hilarious, everyone thought so. But after a couple of days it began to haunt me, it began to inspire a direct physical response. Every time I heard that droning 'Da-da-dada, da-da-dada, da-da, dada-da-dada-dada-dada' I felt my bowels begin to fail. And that's how I feel now. Waiting for Emma to answer, half hoping she won't, giving it one more ring before hanging—

'What do you want, Ben?'

Her voice is croaky with sleep.

I pause, think of hanging up. 'Nothing. Did you get my message?'

'Ben? How do you expect me to respond?'

'Look. I can't take it any more, I've had enough, I want our life back. Please, let's stop this. I've hired the best barrister, lawyer, and the experts are in the pipeline. According to her, we don't need to carry on with this.' I hear her sigh.

'Ben, Ben...'

'This is bollocks and you know it. Stop pretending. Did you not think I'd find out? Here I am living with my father. Remember him? Trotsky's ghost? I have Jonah with me day and night. It's too much. And you've just let it happen, pushed us away and taken no responsibility whatsoever. Thank you so much, Emma.'

The silence kicks in and along with it the sickness and dissonant violins.

'Emma. Em?'

She blows her nose; she is a snotty crier.

'Emma?'

'I'm sorry, Ben.'

Again, the drug. 'Don't be sorry, I can carry the burden. Jonah's the important one here...'

'I'm not sorry for that, Ben.'

'You're not? Then what are you sorry for?'

'I'm sorry because you're not coming back.'

'That's fine, I can cope until the tribunal, okay, but—'

'No, you're not listening, you never do. You're not coming back.'

'But there's no need to stay away now...'

'Please, Ben, don't make it any harder than it need be.'

'For who? Me or you?'

'Both of us.'

'And Jonah? He's your son, Emma.'

'It torments me...'

'No, it doesn't, clearly.'

'Ben, please, I'll take all the blame, but...'

I rewind the tape, searching for clues, distraught that I may have missed something crucial, a misused word that could have warned me of this apocalypse.

'And where did all the money go really, Emma?'

'Ben...'

'Tell me.'

I light a cigarette during the silence.

'Emma?'

'I needed the money, Ben.'

'For what? What's more important than Jonah?'

'Ben, not now.'

'Not now? So when, Emma? What the fuck is going on? Emma!'

I can feel her across the line, composing herself, rehearsing. 'Emma,' I say, softly. 'Just tell me what happened.'

'Jonah happened.'

I turn off my phone and bury it down the side of the sofa.

I feel like my pilot light has gone out. The knowledge of my own naivety is crushing me into this piss-stained sofa. People make sacrifices for loved ones, don't they? For each other, for their children? Especially for their children. That should be your primary motivation, but is it mine?

For whom am I performing this selfless charade? For Jonah, of course. But am I? The advocaat tastes too sweet so I cut it with some schnapps. As Emma's truth sinks in, my internal voice screeches: *But I want to run away. Where did she earn the right? Now she's gone, I can't.*

I run to the toilet to throw up. It looks like rhubarb and custard.

Upstairs, I hear their syncopated snoring again. Jonah is lying on his tummy in just a nappy, so I kneel by the side of the bed and gently stroke his back with the palm of my right hand. His skin is still baby soft and warm to the touch. It's golden brown.

If he sees the sun, it tans and never burns – he looks like he's just come back from two weeks in the Caribbean. I rub the back of his neck and push my fingers into his hair then carefully put him in his pyjamas without waking him.

'I love you, Jonah, but sometimes I wish you'd never been born.' I instantly want to take it back, but it can't get past the plug of bile in my throat and then his eyes pop open as if he's heard and understood. He follows me down the stairs in his pyjamas, grabs his shoes and stands by the door. I haven't the strength to argue, just put on his shoes and close the door silently behind us.

My thighs cramp up like a dancing Cossack as I shuffle on my haunches by the BMW parked in *my* spot – if I wasn't dehydrated I'd piss on its personalised number plate. Moonlight flashes off the pliers in my left hand as the shiny black M5 tyre valve comes free and sends me sprawling backwards into a rosebush.

'How did you get out of the car? Get. Back. In. The. Car. Don't laugh at me, you sod, we're not going in.' Of course he wants to go in, it's still home to him. 'Let's go. Jesus, Jonah – stop it.' He is plucking off the rose buds and examining their scent beneath his nostrils.

The third-floor windows begin to blink and then a face – silhouetted against the room's halogens. It's Emma.

The block's security lights have thrown enough illumination on the car park to reveal my current bedding in all its rosy glory. Dragging him away now would be like dousing two shagging dogs with a bucket of ice water – thank God for the pen knife, the Swiss Army and their obsession with attachments. I usher both boy and bush into the car's back seat.

'Ben, is that you?' She is maybe ten feet away, playing Zorro with a stainless-steel fish slice. 'Ben, what are you doing here?' There is no surprise in her voice, just the tiresome version of disappointment that manages to be dismissive and pitying all at once.

'Ben? Do you have Jonah with you?'

'He couldn't sleep.'

'What are you trying to achieve?'

Now that's a question I've been asking myself for twenty years or more. 'Complete humiliation?'

'Take him home. He can't come in now, it'll totally confuse him.'

'Is *he* in there?'

'Ben.'

'Mr PP32.'

'What are you talking about?'

'So he is in there.'

'Ben, I swear to God!' She flops to the wall. 'It's three thirty in the morning, please just take him home.'

'He is home.'

'You know what I mean.'

'He's in my space, Emma, my space.'

'Ben, the car in your parking space belongs to Tricia from next door's brother. She asked if he could use it for a couple of days and I said yes.'

'I'm not talking about the parking.'

'You're not talking any sense. Go back to your dad's, please.'

I hear the car door open and Jonah skips past me and grabs Emma by the hand. She pulls him close and cries into his hair. Everything, at this moment, feels wrong. It wouldn't surprise me to see two moons in the sky, or to see Jonah open his mouth and shout 'fuck off' to both of us.

Instead it starts to rain and he pulls away from Emma and bounces around laughing. Her tears do not stop as she watches our son perform his rain dance and it hurts me like nothing before to see the rain mix with tears on her cheeks as she watches us drive away.

SERVICE
DEPARTMENT

WYNCHGATE

Units 1-4, Wynchgate Industrial Estate, Mutton Lane N27 5YG **Tel: 0208 777 1234**

INVOICE

Inv: PP32-5684898

Mr Ben Jewell
Flat 4, 97 Rutland Road
Wynchgate
London N24 3RS

BMW M5 reg. no: PP32

For the supply and refit of:	Price £	£
2 x Bridgestone 255 Low Profile Tyres	173.73 x 2	347.46
2 x Tyre Valves	18.50 x 2	37.00
Wheel Balancing	55	55.00
Tracking	110	110.00
Labour	90	90.00
	VAT @ 20%	127.89
	TOTAL DUE	**£767.35**

THIS ACCOUNT IS NOW OVERDUE

Paid by Cheque, Jewell's Catering hire

Registered Company: Wynchgate Ltd 23 Garalton St London W1G 5SD
Company Number: RD43344683456

Tasmanian Devil

I've woken up with scratches and bruises before, but usually have no memory of how or where they were inflicted. Not this morning. The rose thorn scratches are stinging and itching. I've only had a few hours' sleep and the smuggled whisky bottle lies empty beside me, but still I take the cap off and stick my tongue in – desperate to catch any remaining drops. I just manage to push the bottle under the sheets as Dad's head fills my vision.

'Where did you take him so late?' he asks.

I pull the pillow over my head. 'Close the curtains, please.'

'You haven't answered my question.'

'Stringfellows.'

'Don't be clever.'

'He wasn't asleep, we went for a drive.'

'At three in the morning? How's he going to learn to sleep if you drag him out in the middle of the night?'

'Dad, will you leave me alone? I'll get up soon.'

'It's midday, you'll get up now. I've got a bowls match in half an hour. Here.'

The tea is sour – the colour of peat – and tea leaves stick

themselves to the roof of my mouth like dead flies. 'I drink coffee, how many times?' I say, but he's already left the room.

I slump across the breakfast bar and light a cigarette. My eyes still refuse to open.

'Going in today?' he asks.

'Later. There's only washing-up to do, Valentine can handle it.'

'So who'll answer the phone?'

I wave my mobile at him. 'Diverted.'

'Well maybe you should turn it on? You want them to go to a competitor? And yes, in case you were wondering, JJ went to school okay.'

I point the phone at him and hold the power button until it sings. 'All right? Don't forget your balls.'

'Bowls.'

'Whatever.'

Back in bed I scroll through the missed calls – all numbers, no names. I turn it off, toss it on to the clothes mountain, have a cursory wank and roll on to my stomach and doze. Wednesday's already half done and I feel no compulsion to get up.

There are books arranged around me on the bed, none opened further than page twenty. A bottle neck peeks out from beneath *War and Peace*. I introduce myself to it, turn on the radio and drift off again.

I am in an airport and the metal detector just keeps going off, even when I'm down to my underwear it keeps going off. Hundreds of travellers queuing behind are laughing and wolf-whistling at me, but it just won't stop ringing...

The doorbell. I haul myself from the bed and almost fall down the stairs.

'Coming, coming,' I shout. Jonah's face is pressed up to the frosted panel, so I kneel down and stare through the glass. 'Afternoon, mate,' I say. When I open the door he passes me without a glance. 'Did he have a good day?'

Minibus Marge, Jonah's regular bus companion and one of Emma's favourite people, looks me up and down. My boxer shorts are creased and rolled and my pecker is peeping out the bottom.

'Sorry,' I mutter, pulling them down.

'Here,' she says, handing me a knotted plastic bag of clothes. Drops of piss and condensation are running down its insides. 'Is his grandfather home?'

'Soon. See you in the morning,' I say to her back and close the door. 'Jonah?' I call, following the trail of clothes down the hall into the kitchen. The cupboards are open, the fridge is breathing arctic air and grapes decorate the floor. 'Bloody hell, Jonah.' On my hands and knees I sweep up the grapes like marbles before being nearly scalped by a family-size jar of Marmite.

'Toast?'

I search the kitchen cupboards, but there's no bread. I check the fridge. Nothing. As I close the fridge door, beneath the hammer and sickle magnet is a note in Dad's classical hand: *Ben, please buy bread.*

Jonah is at me again, banging me on the forearm with the Marmite. He's so desperate he even runs to his PECS book, plucks the correct card and slaps it into my palm.

Bread

127

'I know, but we need to get some, Jonah.'

He's not having it, or not getting it, or both. He objects, his exclamations getting gruffer, and he starts to jump. It's not a happy jump, it's frustration.

'We've *got* no bread, Jonah. Look, we've got *no* bread. How about some crisps?'

This communication system is fine when you have the item he wants. He can request, but can't comprehend the lack of cause and effect.

He bats the crisps out of my hand and they fly across the kitchen. He forces his hand into his mouth and bites down hard until the scar tissue begins to bleed.

'No, please stop, Jonah, please, we've got no fucking bread.'

He releases the jar of Marmite at the top of a jump with some force and it smashes on the floor; brown glass and yeasty brown glue cover the lino by his bare feet. I grab at him and try to pull him away, but he's too heavy. I summon every ounce and just manage to swing him around away from the glass, gashing my own foot in the process.

He's off now. Left hand at my neck, right hand clawing my scalp – uncut nails doing damage. He's a Great White, twisting and pulling. I lose my balance and his weight falls on to me, pins me to the floor. A bloody footprint marks the lino. I feel the unmistakable metallic sweetness of my own blood trickle into my mouth yet I know that if I hit him hard enough – really belt him – I may bring him out of it long enough to extricate myself, but I cannot. I want him to hurt me because I deserve it. I can't even remember to buy a loaf of bread.

I feel his teeth grip on to my nose and I still don't care. I want all his anger, deserve the scars of this. I know the cuts on my face and head are deep and bloody and yet I lie here motionless; like a drowning man facing the inevitable and slipping beneath the surface with relief.

Then he stops dead and starts to cry. Proper tears, fat and salty. A release. His release is also mine and I sit up and pull him to me in an embrace and he doesn't object.

'I'm sorry, Jonah. I'm so sorry.'

I feel his breathing calm against my chest, although it still catches – and his voice has softened to a sweet incomprehensible babble. If he had a speaking voice it would be like a mesmeric peal of church bells.

'I got bread just in...' My father stands and stares. 'I'll get my clippers and do JJ's nails,' he says.

'Make him some toast first, please,' I say. 'There's an unopened jar hidden above the fridge.

And Jonah laughs. His face changes, he laughs, he giggles, he runs back and forth from the kitchen to the lounge – a Marmite toast relay. He settles in front of the TV, twiddles his hair, goes back for more toast, takes an apple from the fridge, eats his dinner with his fingers and just forgets. Forgets that less than an hour before he was at war with me, that he's injured me or that my lack of care made him hurt me. He's forgotten it all, no grudge, no remorse, no resentment. Lucky bastard.

He yawns.

'You want me to run his bath?'

'No, I'll do that, Dad. I'll do that. I'll go and run it now. You stay here and watch TV with Jonah.'

Jonah climbs on to the sofa next to Dad as I mount the stairs, and I hear him start to chatter. More family history, I suppose? More information that I can't be trusted with.

I start down the stairs on tiptoe, then halt. I want to know what he feels unable to share with me, but I want to confront him, not eavesdrop. It may be, I ponder, that this is not about me, but about my father. He can talk to Jonah, because Jonah neither judges nor gossips and, as painful as the information is, Jonah is immune. Whereas I? What could be so bad that he feels I can't be trusted with it? Maybe if I am witness to his catharsis he'll feel powerless. Knowing how that feels, I have some empathy with him. The inquisition will have to wait.

Bath time is my favourite ritual. Firstly, I put a clean sheet on his bed, change the duvet cover and pillow cases and turn the duvet down. Then I make sure the aqueous cream is on his bedside table and close the curtain. Next, I switch on his toy fish tank and check that the brightly coloured plastic tropical fish are revolving freely and, finally, switch on his CD player – always the same CD, Mr Tumble singing children's favourites (number two on the volume dial).

In the bathroom, I use the shower attachment to clean the bath, put the plug in and switch to taps, testing that the water is hot, but not too hot. Then I squeeze hypoallergenic bubbles into the running stream of water for three seconds and watch the bath fill up with a foamy mass. I locate his two bottles of medication that he takes first and last thing – apparently they moderate his mood.

This all takes approximately ten minutes. Finally, I call him up and wait. Sometimes I have to call twice, but usually I hear the 'thump, thump, thump' of his ungainly progress up the stairs and then he bounces into the bathroom, grinning. He is, I think, anticipating an end to the stress and trauma of his own personal groundhog day.

I help him undress, remove his nappy and clean him up with wipes before he climbs in. The nappy and wipes get tied in a plastic bag. The first drug I administer with an oral syringe; the second by spoon. He takes both without fuss.

I kneel by the side of the bath and watch him play, rub the bubbles all over his body before he eats them, and when I wash him we catch each other's eyes and laugh – a father–son connection, hilarious, fleeting and precious.

I let him play for as long as he wants, or until the water is too cold, and then I open his bath towel wide and he climbs from the bath and free-falls into my arms so that I have to brace myself to catch him, and for the thirty seconds that I squeeze him tight and dry him he is a baby again, with his head on my shoulder and his smell all innocent and clean.

When I release him, he runs to his room and bounces on his bed in time with Mr Tumble, and while he does so I dry the bits I couldn't reach before. Then he lies on his tummy – my baby boy with his cellulite bum and spare tyre, fat thighs and soft spotless back, pink from the heat of the bath.

'Turn over, dude,' I say, and he shuffles himself over and raises the small of his back so that I can fit a nappy on him for the night and, as he does so, he is no longer a baby – not quite an adolescent – and he will never, I understand again, as my wounds begin to sting once more, be a man.

I pull his pyjama bottoms on and he sits so I can do likewise with his top, and then he flops to the pillow, face up close to his fish tank as I kiss him, tell him I love him, turn the light off, close the door and leave. Downstairs, I throw myself on to the sofa and bury my head in a cushion.

'Try not to get blood on my furniture.'

Wynchgate and Carlton NHS Trust

**WYNCHGATE
HOSPITAL**

Mr G Jewell
14 Oakfield Avenue
London N10 4RG

*Department of
Oncology*

April 10 2011

Dear Mr George Jewell

We have now received the results of your recent biopsy and would request that you attend an appointment on the following date:

    April 15 2011 at 11:30

where you will be seen by Consultant Oncologist Mr Graham Stonehouse.

    Keith Waters-Long
    Administrator

Empty

Over the past couple of weeks I've been going through the folders marked 'Jonah'. They are beginning to form a tower on my bedside table. Each report is accompanied by emailed comments from Emma. I read her emails along with the reports, searching for clues and looking for excuses to contact her. But they are businesslike and insightful about Jonah and completely free of comments about me, or us. Through my obsession with them both, I have managed to push the terror surrounding Dad's swelling neck out of mind – until today. Jonah is seated with a slice of toast in each hand and Dad is at the sink, rinsing his mug.

'I'm busy,' Dad says.

'Dad...'

'Bowls match, league.'

Oh for God's sake. 'You have an appointment with a consultant in an hour and you're not going to miss it.' And I don't need this. My father acting like a child.

'So what is he going to tell me, their Mr Stonehouse, that I don't already know? What do you think he is going to do?

Measure my inside leg and run me up a nice pair of trousers? It is cancer.'

'What if it is? There are fucking cures these days.'

'Don't use that language in front of Jonah.'

'Why? You think he's going to repeat it? If he turns round and calls me a fucking bastard I'd die a happy man.'

We are both terrified, I realise. At a pivotal point in our lives where the future lies in someone else's hands. I am used to being out of control, but Dad? I look at him fussing around, dropping things, trying to clear his mind of negative thoughts through mindless repetition like he did for years – polishing glasses in the warehouse.

'It is cancer. They do not waste their money on old men like me these days. They have league tables.'

'You don't know that.'

He bangs the letter down on the kitchen table and pokes it with his finger.

'No? Do you see where it says Clap Clinic? Oncology, Ben – cancer. Even an old fool like me knows the difference. Anyway, it runs in the family.'

'What family? All I've had from you is a generic "gassed by the Nazis".'

'Yes, but if they hadn't, they would have died of cancer.'

I look at him closer, my seventy-eight-year-old father with his neck like a prop-forward, and I notice his dilated pupils and the sweat on his brow and I know that he's losing the battle with his demons.

'I'll come with you this time. No arguments.'

But he's not listening. His left hand is stroking Jonah's hair while the other feeds him cornflakes with a spoon.

*

'You have a tumour on your thyroid gland, Mr Jewell.'

Mr Stonehouse is pinstriped and silver-haired and the light-box next to his left shoulder has an x-ray clipped to it. It looks like Dad has swallowed a golf ball.

'And unfortunately it is malignant.'

Dad nods.

'Now, ordinarily, we would operate. Remove the gland and destroy any remaining cancer cells with a dose of radioactive iodine. Then it would simply be a case of taking thyroxine on a daily basis. Please sit down.'

Mr Stonehouse waves us to two chairs opposite his desk.

So that would be the simple solution, but we don't do simple in our family. Dad has an anaplastic tumour, Mr Stonehouse tells us. It is extremely rare and very aggressive. They can't operate, can't guarantee to remove every single cell which would send it racing round the rest of Dad's body – if it hasn't already done so.

'So what can you do?' I ask.

'Well, the first step is an MRI scan to check whether the cancer has spread to any other organs.'

'And if it has?'

Mr Stonehouse turns to my father. 'Mr Jewell, I need to be candid with you. Your cancer is incurable. The average life expectancy from diagnosis to death is three to fifteen months, depending when we catch it.'

And my first thought is of Jonah's case and the money, not of my father's pain, and it drenches me in guilt. Is this normal? Does the impending death of a loved one turn your mind to practicalities? And then I think of the old Luger and its two bullets, how I must hide them because he's capable, pig-headed, fatalistic and fearless.

And then I finally notice him crying, and the sickness and

bagel in his mouth, he stares at me poker faced, shining lumps of butter in his wild bed hair.

It's not unbearably painful. Is that good or bad news? Surely it should be agony? Has my toe been killed off totally?

'Jonah!' He's off back toward the kitchen.

I shuffle down the remaining stairs on my bum, then pull myself up on the banister and begin hobbling after him, my toe still flipping me the bird at every step.

'Fuck you, toe.'

There's a new pack of wipes under the kitchen sink and I manage to grab both Jonah and the wipes without putting pressure on my ailing toe, until he steps back and puts his full weight on my disfigurement. The scream is of shock, there is still no pain, and as he casually saunters off towards the lounge, half a wet-wipe still lodged in his bum crack, I look down and see that my lump of a son has restored my toe to its regular position. I perch on a kitchen chair and reach down to touch it – it moves easily in all directions like a video game joystick. Then the pain begins.

'Aaron said you have to go to A&E for an x-ray in case there's any blood-vessel damage,' Johnny says.

'Do I really? He always was a bit of a tart.'

'Aaron's the doctor, Ben.'

'I can't take Jonah to A&E. Can you imagine? Could you have him, Johnny?'

'We've got the captains playing in at the golf club.'

'Jonah likes golf.'

Johnny laughs down the line. 'Just go there with him and explain about his autism. It's a hospital, for goodness' sake, they'll understand the situation.'

Jonah's sprawled on his back on the sofa, crumbling his bagel on to his bare chest. He smells a bit. I try to sit by his feet and he kicks me in the small of the back. I pour myself a medicinal whisky and slump on to one of the dining chairs.

This is a scene. Curtains closed at midday, behind which sit a naked father and son staring into space. I am devoid of options as my father, Johnny and Amanda are the only people Jonah trusts that can cope with his rock 'n' roll lifestyle and will actually have him in their house. Why couldn't it have happened on a school day?

School. His teacher, Maria! Where did I put her bloody number? I know it's not in my wallet, but I search there nevertheless. It's not there.

I think back to when she gave it to me in the school car park. What did I do with it? I got into the car, began arguing with Dad. The door pocket! It's in the door pocket!

'I'll be back in a minute, Jonah.'

There's no answer, so I leave a garbled message on her voicemail and begin the half-hour process of dressing, stroking my toe and licking my wounds.

Jonah won't leave the automatic door alone, jumping up and down in wonder and excitement as people wander past him into North Middlesex A&E. Each passing emergency represents another twenty minutes' wait for us and I'm getting edgy as my toe begins to throb.

'Jonah, in you come,' I say, slapping my thigh. 'Come on, Jonah!'

I manage to pull his torso through the door, but not his legs. I put my arms around his chest, clasp my hands behind his back, lift him off the floor and swing him into the heaving waiting room. A fuzzy giant LCD monitor on the wall tells me the average wait is currently four hours – this is not even remotely possible. I pull Jonah with me to the reception window.

The nurse addresses me with her head down.

'Name?'

'Ben Jewell.'

'Ben Jool,' she repeats as she types. 'Problem?'

'Badly broken toe,' I say.

'Possible broken toe. GP?'

I give her details twice then pull Jonah in front of the window.

'Look, I've had to bring my profoundly autistic son with me, he just won't be able to cope with being here very long. Is there anything you can do?'

This time she looks up, her thick glasses reflecting the strip lighting back into my eyes. 'Take a seat and a nurse will assess you as soon as possible.'

No points for that, then. Perversely and irritatingly, Jonah has calmed down. He's fiddling with some thread-like thing he's found on the floor. I daren't imagine what it is.

This A&E is a United Nations of the unwell – babies, burkhas, hoodies, sandals, saris, smatterings of European languages I recognise, cluckings of African ones I don't. I wonder what they make of Jonah and his personal, evolving language for one. Why does everyone in A&E have a cough, even if they're here with a gashed head or a broken ankle? Are we that insecure that we always feel the need to embellish? I look at Jonah, quietly fiddling. Jonah doesn't embellish, Jonah just does.

The piercing sound of unoiled trolley wheels announces the arrival of a miserable-looking sixty-something black man and his even more miserable selection of chocolate and crisps. Jonah sniffs the air like a meerkat. I've got no cash with me and the packet of pitta bread in my bag will be hurled if I offer it now. No, I'm going to have to say no.

He's at the trolley before I have a chance to move, a family-size bag of bacon-flavour crisps gripped in both hands. I try to take it off him and the growling starts. He releases one hand from the packet and makes a grab for my neck, then he presses the swollen packet with all his force and bacon crisps erupt from it with a *bang!* This only makes him angrier and he turns back to the trolley and sweeps the remaining bags on to the floor and jumps on them and, as much as it hurts, I cheer him on in my head, 'Go on, my son!'

In an instant, A&E is all activity and a triage nurse is miraculously available. An arm has gone around Jonah's shoulder and is clutching him in an embrace. Maria's red bob appears above his right shoulder.

'Sorry it took me so long,' she says.

'No, no, I'm just so grateful that you're here.'

Why do redheads blush so readily? I wonder.

'Leave him with me, we'll be fine, won't we, Jonah?' she says, as one of his tears rolls down her cheek.

They're both waiting for me when I re-emerge from the x-ray room, little toe strapped to the next in line, clutching a box of high-octane painkillers. Jonah has his hand palm down on a pad of paper, fingers spread, while Maria traces round it with a ballpoint. Occasionally the pen touches the soft skin connecting his fingers and he giggles. Maria laughs back at him. They both spot me. Maria looks up with a smile.

'All done then?' she says.

'Apparently I'll live,' I reply.

'Thank heavens for that! How would we cope without him?' she asks Jonah.

Now I'm blushing. At least, I feel hot. Her eyes have not left Jonah. *How old are you? Twenty-seven, twenty-eight?* I follow them out to the car park where we stand in a triangle by the car.

'So what else have you boys got planned for the day, then?'

'A supermarket, then back to the hospital to pick up my dad.'

'Yes, I heard, I'm so sorry. Let me come and help. You're injured, remember?'

'But I've taken up enough of your Saturday already.'

'I was only going to slob around. No, I'd like to help, if you don't mind?'

'Of course I don't mind, and Jonah would love it, obviously. Where did you park? Do you want to follow us to Tesco?'

'I came by bus,' she says. 'It's why I took so long.'

She came by bus? I think: Jonah, you're a lucky boy.

'Well, hop in!' I say, opening the passenger door. 'And don't worry about the mess on the floor, just stamp on it.'

I feel self-conscious strolling the aisles of Tesco with Maria at my side. Jonah fills the trolley with apples, crisps and Smarties, eating as he goes – it's the only way to get him round. Emma and I developed a system whereby a 'double' is kept of whatever he eats, which is then scanned at the checkout and handed back.

Maria laughs at Jonah as he examines each shelf like a seasoned bargain hunter.

'He's such a sweet boy,' she says. Her voice is soft. BBCish, Dad would call it.

'I feel really guilty,' I say. 'Keeping you from your weekend, from your friends.'

'Please don't, really. I'm so sorry for the way things have

143

worked out for you. I find it so disheartening that we can't just be honest.'

'I'm sorry,' I interject. 'Jonah! No butter, leave the butter alone.'

He drops it and skips towards the bakery. Instantly, Maria follows him and, sensing her behind him, Jonah laughs loud and high and speeds up. I hear them both laughing and skipping as they turn down the canned vegetable aisle and Maria trying to slow him down as they reach world foods. They're skipping hand in hand when they arrive back next to me.

'That seemed like fun?' I say.

'It was, wasn't it, Jonah?' she says. 'I don't know why anyone would deny that Jonah needs the waking-day curriculum you're fighting for. How could you say no to him? I mean, look at this face,' she says, gently taking Jonah's face between her hands. 'Who could resist this face?'

'It's one only a father could love,' I quip.

'How does that work, when you've got the same face?' she says.

We sit nursing watery coffees in the supermarket café, while Jonah turns a chocolate gingerbread man to dust.

'I speak to Emma every Thursday,' Maria says.

I didn't know. 'What do you talk about?' I ask.

'Jonah, of course!' She laughs. 'What else?'

How shit am I? The fantasy that has been swiftly coalescing in my head reforms into visions of unfaithfulness and recrimination. I feel my toe throbbing again and throw back a painkiller with my coffee. Women tie me in knots. Always have. Am I surprised by Emma's weekly updates from Maria? Not when I think about it, it's just I feel shitty because it has never occurred to me to do the same. I feel ashamed and jealous that Emma does these caring, responsible things for Jonah and it has rarely crossed my mind to do so. This knowledge chips away at my sculpted monolith of Emma's culpability and leaves me coated by the dust of shame – shame at the kernel of an idea, a fantasy of a relationship with Maria. Talk of Emma has popped the dream bubble and the reality is all pain and a sense of foolishness, that a desire for more than I have could ever be realised or deserved, that I'll ever be over Emma. Silly middle-aged sod.

'Ben, I'd be really happy to spend more time with you and Jonah, if it would help?'

This hasn't ended the confusion. Of course it would help, but here's the strange paradox of my thinking: if she finds me attractive then it would be unfair to lead her on right now; but she can't truly find me attractive, so she is offering out of pity and I can't live with that either. I am arrogant and insecure, simultaneously. *How to Turn One's Life into a Lose-Lose Situation* by Ben Jewell.

'I understand,' she says in the face of my silence, her words muffled by Jonah's crazy thick hair.

'No, no,' I say, 'it would be great, but with Dad and everything, it's difficult to make plans.'

She removes her face from the back of Jonah's neck.

'Could we play it by ear?' I ask.

She holds my gaze and I notice that she has dimples. 'Absolutely,' she says. 'Plus, I'm travelling all summer when school finishes, so.' She shrugs.

'Where are you going?'

'Latin America,' she says.

'Amazing,' I say.

'By myself,' she adds.

'Brave.'

She grins. 'It's an organised eco-tour – guides and everything.'

'Very sensible,' I say. 'You must send us a postcard.'

'Deal,' she says, holding out her hand to shake on it.

After dropping Maria home, Jonah and I head back to the hospital, where we find Dad sitting up in bed drinking a cup of tea. Jonah slumps in the armchair and stares at the heart monitor next to Dad's bed.

'Even has a battle plan, this cancer of mine, like Hitler. First he took Czechoslovakia, then Poland. Mine? Invades my neck and has designs on my lungs.'

'It's in your lungs?'

'Three little lumps like Myra's *matzo* balls, only less toxic, he says.'

'Do you want me to contact Mum?'

'After I am gone, I could not bear to think of her miserable face at the funeral. Have you called Maurice?'

'Don't have his number.'

'Here,' he says, thrusting out his hand, 'pass me your phone.'

'You need to do the 020 . . .'

'I know, I know.'

It takes him three tries to enter the correct number, but it's answered immediately.

'Maurice. Georg. You need to practise the Kaddish. Yes, that bad. Wellington Ward. No cigars.'

He hands me back the phone without ending the call, so I catch the tinny whimpering of his diminutive friend.

'He will be here in an hour.'

Do I have to wait here with him until Maurice arrives? The whole hour? I can't spend sixty minutes talking to him, cancer or no cancer.

'Shall I go and pick Maurice up?'

He answers without looking up from his paper. 'No, he needs the time to calm down.'

'Tumours in the lungs, then?'

'Yes.'

'But nowhere else, thank God.'

'What? The lungs are not enough? You don't need to breathe?'

'I just meant...'

He pats my hand. 'I know what you meant.'

I unlock my phone and flick through the latest news stories. My attention is drawn to the picture of a mouse with a human ear growing from its back. Surely if they can do that they can knock him up a new thyroid and a couple of lungs. Medical science. Whatever the incurable condition is, the scientists always claim to be *just on the verge*, rather than saying: *yeah, we can fix that, no problem*. I study Dad with his red pen and his *Daily Mirror*. He is regrouping, preparing for a battle, I can feel it. I feel proud of him, this man of mystery with his camouflage fatigues on, getting ready for his own personal Stalingrad.

Jonah is up from the chair and is twiddling a feather in front of his eye by the window.

'So what are they going to do?'

Dad sighs and folds his paper neatly, placing it next to him on the bed.

'Apparently, they are having a conference this morning to decide. Probably radiation with chemotherapy for dessert. But if I do not like the menu I may not eat at this restaurant.'

'What are you saying?'

'I'm an old man, Benjamin.'

'You have to try.'

147

'For who? Me? You think I want you and JJ watching me shrivel like a prune? I will not have it.'

This is not the kind of bravery I want from him. No! Not surrender, it doesn't suit him and it doesn't suit me. The pride has turned to the vertigo of abandonment. Selfish old bastard.

'Oh, you're just so noble, aren't you?'

'There is nothing noble about death.'

'You've got to fight it, Dad.'

'What, death? Cannot be done.'

'The cancer. Do the radio and chemo, please.'

'Ben, I'm seventy-eight.'

'Jonah...'

'That is unfair.'

'Maurice.'

'Will agree.'

So I'll work on Maurice. No, Maurice is his lapdog. Jonah, Jonah is the only way of changing his mind. I put my face in my hands and press the trio against the mattress. Then I sit up and clasp his hand.

I say, 'Tell you what. We'll make a deal. You start the treatment and if you can't take it, stop, and I'll say nothing else.'

'The outcome will be the same.'

'But it could give you another year or so.'

'To see what? My grandson sent away and my son leave too, as soon as the cock crows the day after?'

As if he understands, Jonah skips over to Dad and sits on the bed next to him. Now I see it. Now I know. Cunning old bastard. He is looking away from me, but I can still catch the corners of his mouth turned down in a smile. How do I feel good about either of the sides of this bargain he's foisting on

148

me? You can't bluff my father, you can't bluff a man with a Luger, two bullets and a belly full of cancer.

'Tell you what,' I say.

'I'm listening.'

'Look at me then.'

He turns to face me, knowing, the sly old sod.

'Jonah will stay at home, with both of us, while you are alive.'

'So you'll cancel this tribunal . . .'

'Postpone it. It's the best you're going to get.'

There's no way I'm going to postpone, so what am I doing? Hoping that he dies sooner rather than later, before I have to admit I'm lying?

'I do not believe you.'

I don't blame him.

'You'll just have to trust me. Bit hard to swallow?'

'Everything is hard to swallow,' he says.

'Everything will proceed until all the reports are in, then I'll halt it, but only if you have the treatment.'

'Suddenly my son is a haggler.'

'You're the stall holder, Dad. It's either take your medicine and have another possible year with Jonah at home, or be the martyr and say goodbye to him in three months.'

'And you will stick to these odds? Honour a winning ticket?'

'Absolutely.'

'But you are betting against your own team?'

'You're both my team.'

But in the end, I have to make a choice and make a promise I have no intention of keeping.

'It's a win-win situation, Dad.'

'Don't treat me like a *shmock*. When do they start to fry me?'

When Mr Stonehouse arrives from the conference he says

that they'll start radiation tomorrow. 'Would you like me to explain the procedure to both of you?'

Dad points at me. 'He has an O-level in Chemistry, tell it to him.'

Then he turns away and sticks the hospital radio's earphones in his ears.

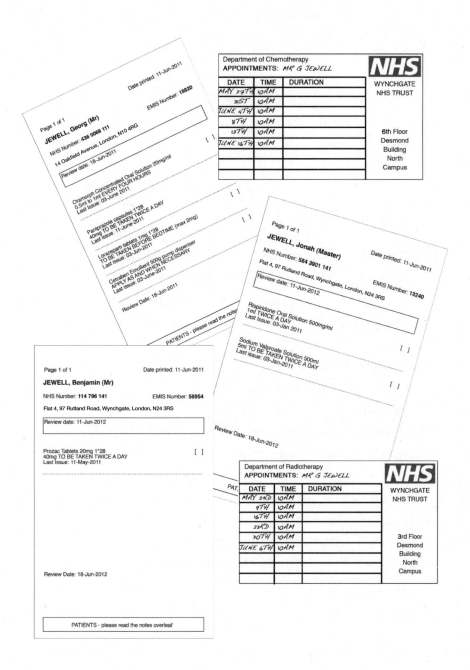

Department of Chemotherapy
APPOINTMENTS: MR G JEWELL

NHS

DATE	TIME	DURATION
MAY 27TH	10AM	
31ST	10AM	
JUNE 4TH	10AM	
8TH	10AM	
12TH	10AM	
JUNE 16TH	10AM	

WYNCHGATE
NHS TRUST

6th Floor
Desmond
Building
North
Campus

Page 1 of 1
Date printed: 11-Jun-2011

EMIS Number: **18820**

JEWELL, Georg (Mr)
NHS Number: **436 0069 111**
14 Oakfield Avenue, London, N10 4RG

Review date: 18-Jun-2011

Oramorph Concentrated Oral Solution 20mg/ml
0.5ml to 1ml EVERY FOUR HOURS
Last Issue: 03-June 2011   [ ]

Pantprazole capsules 1*28
40mg TO BE TAKEN TWICE A DAY
Last Issue: 11-June-2011   [ ]

Lorazepam tablets 1mg 1*28
TO BE TAKEN BEFORE BEDTIME (max 2mg)
Last Issue: 03-Jun-2011   [ ]

Cetraben Emollient 500g pump dispenser
APPLY AS AND WHEN NECESSARY
Last Issue: 03-June-2011

Review Date: 18-Jun-2011

PATIENTS - please read the notes

Page 1 of 1

JEWELL, Jonah (Master)
NHS Number: **584 3901 141**
Flat 4, 97 Rutland Road, Wynchgate, London, N24 3RS

Date printed: 11-Jun-2011

EMIS Number: **13240**

Review date: 11-Jun-2012

Rispiridone Oral Solution 500mg/ml
1ml TWICE A DAY
Last Issue: 03-Jan 2011   [ ]

Sodium Valproate Solution 500ml
5ml TO BE TAKEN TWICE A DAY
Last Issue: 03-Jan-2011   [ ]

Review Date: 18-Jun-2012

Page 1 of 1
Date printed: 11-Jun-2011

JEWELL, Benjamin (Mr)

NHS Number: **114 796 141**
EMIS Number: **56954**

Flat 4, 97 Rutland Road, Wynchgate, London, N24 3RS

Review date: 11-Jun-2012

Prozac Tablets 20mg 1*28
40mg TO BE TAKEN TWICE A DAY
Last Issue: 11-May-2011   [ ]

....

Review Date: 18-Jun-2012

PATIENTS - please read the notes overleaf

PAT.

Department of Radiotherapy
APPOINTMENTS: MR G JEWELL

NHS

DATE	TIME	DURATION
MAY 2ND	10AM	
9TH	10AM	
16TH	10AM	
23RD	10AM	
30TH	10AM	
JUNE 6TH	10AM	

WYNCHGATE
NHS TRUST

3rd Floor
Desmond
Building
North
Campus

Sad

He is not a good patient. Stoicism may be bonded to his haemoglobin but the house has become his own private clinic, complete with personal nurse – Maurice; personal porter and lackey – me; and entertainment – Jonah. With all the radiotherapy, I'm run off my feet. God knows how I'll cope when the chemo starts next week.

'Do not forget the prescription requests.'

'I have them.'

'No, you do not, they are still on the kitchen table – why should Jonah and I suffer more because you have a head like a sieve?'

I grab the three slips of paper. 'Have you got a spare twenty quid?'

'What for? Jonah and I don't pay for our medicine and yours is only about seven pounds. What do you need twenty pounds for?'

'Sundries.'

'I am lying here like a burnt offering and he wants cigarettes. What a sensitive boy I have raised. Behind the carriage clock, there is some cash.'

the car the three hundred yards round to the warehouse. The ancient white Luton is still parked outside.

'For fuck's sake, Valentine.'

He should be well on his way with pick-ups by now, but there's no sign of action whatsoever. I jump out, light a cigarette and walk to the metal shutter door. Not only is it pulled down, but the padlock's there too. As I bend down to check if it's locked, I spy an envelope poking out from underneath. It's brown and addressed to me and marked 'Inland Revenue'. My stomach churns the Liffey Water as I pull it out. It's already been opened, which is strange, but there is a letter inside it that I unfold like a set of exam results.

I QUIT
VALENTINE
P.S. FUCK YOU!

Which for Valentine is verbosity gone mad.

As I drag the shutter up, the smell hits me like the Delhi-to-Mumbai express. Sunday's Indian wedding for four hundred. Four hundred of everything: plates, side plates, knives, forks, spoons, glasses – all unwashed and piled high and hopelessly muddled, a shanty town of glass, metal and ceramic with an exponentially growing population of flies.

I check the cash box in the office and count through the notes. It's all there bar Valentine's weekly wage. He's paid himself and taken nothing else. Twenty-two years of dirty slog has finally proved too much for him. Well, really, ten years of me. I pocket the wad of cash with no thought of pleading with him to come back, just a mental note to drop in some money for him, and stand staring at the shit. I'm not going to do it. I know I'm not. So it won't get done. Even with the industrial washers it

155

will take me all week to run the stuff through, then count and wrap and stack ready to go out again.

I'm done. Dad's business – gone. My income – gone.

The phone rings.

'I need a water boiler, dolly, for a shiva, this afternoon. And could you bring twenty tea plates for the marble cake?'

'Where to?'

'Streatham.'

'No.'

'No?'

'No.'

'*Nu?*'

'Bye.' I slam the receiver down, pull the phone from the wall and toss it into the pile of washing-up.

I have a pocket full of cash, a mild Guinness buzz and a few hours to kill. Jonah is at school, Maurice is with Dad and I can't think of a single solitary thing to do that will give me any pleasure whatsoever.

I may as well have driven to Streatham, but all I know there is the Jewish cemetery where I attended the funeral of some distant cousin.

I sit and spin myself around in the office chair for five minutes until I'm giddy, then pull at a bulldog clip hanging from the wall, holding a thick wad of invoices addressed to customers stamped UNPAID in red.

I go through the debtors' invoices with a feeling of rising anger, directed both at them and at me – this is Jonah's money and I've been too lazy to call in the debts.

The warehouse is a shithole, because I've allowed it to become so. Valentine has left because I treated him with contempt and these people never bothered paying me because I couldn't be bothered to chase them, while other regular clients melted away because I got orders wrong, never checked properly and on some level wanted to destroy the house that Dad built as my only means of escape from my personal prison camp.

I work my way through the invoices carefully – some of them date back three years – and divide them into private clients with home addresses and caterers that may still, or no longer, exist.

I arrange them into date order and pin them on the map of London, pasted on the office wall.

Finally, I grab a calculator and tot up the money owed to me.

There are seventy-two outstanding invoices. It takes me ten minutes to finish and then there is a sudden surge of adrenalin and shame.

TOTAL OUTSTANDING: £18,724.84

Trick or Treat

I could ask God for a favour, but my call would probably go straight to voicemail. The warehouse is quiet and cold and I warm myself with whisky as I run the numbers through my head and prevaricate as I always do when something awkward needs to be done. How can I ask these people for money after – in some cases – three years? If they say no or deny the debt, I'm likely just to say sorry. They may even laugh at me, at which point I normally become abusive and threaten violence. *You'll never be a captain of industry*, Mum used to tell me, in a self-fulfilling prophecy, *but you'll always be the captain of my heart*, which is clearly bollocks. I could hire debt collectors, but that would require letters, phone calls and proper procedures. I don't have time for that.

I visit the warehouse's filthy toilet, where there's a mirror. My hair is unwashed and matted, my eyes glassy from the Guinness and my face adorned by six days of stubble – not a proper beard by any means but a dirty-looking straggle that enhances the effect. My fleece is rank with weeks-old sweat and my combat trousers are streaked with archaeological curry stains all the way down to my heavy black boots. And I see, as I examine my upper torso from various angles like a bodybuilder, that all the years of schlepping tables and chairs in and out of venues and up and down stairs has beefed me up, considerably.

It's the perfect look.

I start to shadow box, but have a coughing fit.

I phone Johnny.

'We're going into the debt collection business,' I announce.

'You are joking?'

'No, Johnny, I'm deadly serious.'

'Can't you find someone else?'

'I don't know anyone else, so short of phoning Equity...'

I explain the full extent of my negligence and he laughs at me.

'And it's your money?'

'All of it, every penny.'

He is truly the only person I can count on, Johnny, apart from Jonah. It's the kind of friendship that endures despite intermittent periods of a lack of contact – always instigated by me, always for no reason other than my own retreat into isolation.

'I don't do violence, Ben, you know that.'

'Just stand behind me looking mean, it'll be a doddle. I only need you for the refusers anyway.'

'That's comforting.'

'Oh, and your hair.'

'What about my hair?'

'Get it cropped, clippers, number one at least.'

'You want me to shave my head, too? I'll end up staying at yours tonight if...'

'Please, Johnny. If not for me, for Jonah.'

'God, the things I do for you. Where do you want to meet?'

'Pick me up tomorrow morning at eight-thirty,' I say.

'You think I'm letting you use my car for this nonsense?'
'It's gangster, screams drug dealer.'
'One scratch...'

Jonah has already left for school when I drag my carcass down the stairs, so I clear up the breakfast things and fumigate his room. As I collect up the Tesco bags containing Jonah's soiled nappies and ruined underwear, Johnny pulls up in his pristine car, the sun bulleting off his newly skinned head. I sit next to him reading the addresses and laughing at his baldness while he programmes his SatNav.

'She's going to kill me.'

He looks at the plastic bag on my lap.

'Please tell me the old man's Luger isn't in that bag?'

'Thought about it.'

'You're insane.'

I open the carrier, to reveal a bottle of whisky.

'I hope that's to celebrate with afterwards?'

'Dirty, angry and smelling of booze – wouldn't you pay up?'

'I don't know, but I'd have you arrested.'

'Don't worry, I'll ask politely first and save the menaces for later.'

Johnny looks unconvinced as he starts the engine.

This seems crazily like the start of a holiday, the drive to Gatwick for a flight to the Alps, or a weekend in Dublin. The freedom and drinking, for drinking's sake, rather than the current reality of drinking insanely for sanity's sake. A memory creeps into this strange revelry – arriving at the airport on the way to France fully aware that I had no money and asking Johnny to lend me some. Johnny obliging without question. Never paying him back. I just keep taking, I realise. From

Johnny, from Emma. Even from my dad. I need to start clearing my debts.

To me, asking Jewish widows for payments relating to the catering after their husbands' funerals seems the height of callousness. But I just keep reminding myself that they've played on that sense of grief to avoid paying me in the first place – so fuck 'em. Johnny, on the other hand, lies cowering on the back seat whenever we reach an address he recognises – which is a lot.

'Come on, it's fun,' I shout, jumping out of the car and running up to a doorstep. Johnny's presence rids me of my awkwardness, always has.

'Fuck off, that's my mother-in-law's house. Don't ring the doorbell, I'll pay her debt, just get away from there.'

His protestations are too late. The chime rings out in the hallway and the door opens. It's the cleaner, Mrs Caplin's playing golf. 'No,' I say, 'no message.'

'Bastard,' Johnny says, climbing back into the driver's seat. I lay the Caplin invoice on his thigh and give it a pat.

'You're a very generous son-in-law.'

We make thirty-one house calls before lunch – such is the convenience of a ghetto – and it is proving surprisingly easy. Most people, it transpires, are relieved to pay, many others explain they thought I'd gone out of business because the phone just kept ringing and ringing. Even Johnny appears to be getting into the spirit of the exercise, happily bouncing along to Dr Dre as we pull into a Sudbury pub for lunch.

Johnny counts and writes down neat columns of numbers as we eat.

'Well?'

'So far, £6,411.50. Not bad for a morning's work.'

'See, what did I tell you?'

Johnny's club sandwich nods. What I haven't told him is they were in my 'easy' pile and I don't know what to expect from the afternoon, but I keep reminding myself that this is for Jonah and throw down a touch of the old Dutch courage. I phone the hospital to find out how Dad's latest radiation blast went. When I finally get through to the nurses' station, I can hear him shouting at Maurice in the background.

Back on the road, I feel the roll of notes and the thick fold of cheques in my pocket. I don't think I've ever carried this much money before. How much have I wasted over the years? I recall the rush when a customer asked to pay in cash, the delight of feeling that power in my pocket, the guarantees it provided of decent drink – a celebratory bottle of malt rather than blended whisky. Drunk in exactly the same fashion, of course, from the bottle and in the van. The shops and houses become familiar.

'I'll probably need you here,' I say as he pulls up outside a three-storey Victorian in Kilburn.

'Oh God.'

'I'm sure it'll be fine, just stand behind me looking gormless and don't say anything.'

The bell doesn't work. So I begin thumping on the door. The curtain twitches next to me in the ground-floor window.

'Afternoon, Kieran.' Now I'm banging on the window. 'Kieran, I know you're in there, open up, please.'

The door opens and a wiry six-foot-two-inch Irishman stands in his boxer shorts and a grubby t-shirt. He looks groggy and my knocking has obviously woken him up. I get into role.

'What, not going to offer us a coffee?' I say, pushing past him into bedsit land.

'Come to the kitchen, then.'

I step over boxes of computer components lining the hall-way, with Johnny behind, and into a kitchen that could do with a drop of Dettox, to say the least. Kieran puts the kettle on and I hand him the invoice. His eyes widen in shockwaves like pebbles hitting a pool.

'Jesus, Mr Jewell, I don't have this kind of money.'

'Well, you should have thought of that before you hired twenty of my trestle tables for your computer fairs and fucked off without paying me the money or telling me where you left them. It took my colleague six weeks to recover them all,' I say, thumbing over my shoulder at Johnny.

Kieran stares at him. 'Yeah, I'm sorry about that, it was a bit of a mix-up.'

He hands me a coffee in a chipped mug, but Johnny declines.

'I wish I could help you, Mr Jewell, but I'm potless at the minute.'

'Well, Kieran, so am I and mainly because of people like you.'

'I just don't have anything right now. The fairs have gone to shite, do I look like I'm loaded?'

No, he doesn't.

'Off somewhere, Kieran?' It's Johnny.

'T'visit family, yeah – how'd you know?'

'American family, by any chance?'

'Jesus, Mr Jewell, is your mate psychic?'

Johnny steps in front of me with a passport in his hand. It is stuffed with dollar bills.

'Oh, come on, that's me spending money,' Kieran pleads.

'What's the pound–dollar exchange rate today, boss?'

I take out my phone and Google the question. 'Well it seems that each and every dollar today buys you sixty-six pence.'

'Well that means at the current rate of exchange, Kieran here needs to hand over...'

Kieran snatches the fold of dollar bills from Johnny.

'Two thousand six hundred and twenty-five dollars.'

'Ah, come on, I don't have anything like that. Let me make you a gesture of good will.'

He licks his finger and hands Johnny $500.

Johnny moves closer to him; they are a similar height, but Johnny likes his food.

'Look, five hundred more but that's all I can manage.' He hands another $500 over.

Johnny puts a hand on each of Kieran's shoulders and growls: 'That's a grand, now you just keep peeling them off.'

Kieran complies with jittery fingers, until it's all there. But guilt invades me. It's his holiday money, look where he lives, he's quite a nice bloke really, maybe we could give him half of it back, it's partly my fault for not chasing him up. I throw a pained expression at Johnny.

'No!' he says, manoeuvring me to the front door. 'Oh, and Kieran, have a nice holiday,' Johnny calls as we step on to the street.

'You are one scary fucking tax accountant,' I whisper as we walk to the car.

'It's a dog-eat-dog world out there, don't let the suits fool you.'

'Respect.'

'Right,' he says, rubbing his hands together, 'who's next, boss?'

We grin at each other once we're back in the car. Proactivity it seems is not a fantasy dreamt up in an LA marketing brainstorm. I can feel my mood lifting. Not just because Jonah's war chest is beginning to fill, but also because I am out with my best friend, for a whole day, and we are laughing and joking and behaving ridiculously. But that is what's called for – crazy behaviour, for a crazy situation. I almost wish I had brought the Luger.

The rest of the afternoon isn't perfect; we hit some walls of denial and the vicious thug act doesn't go down too well with a couple of receptionists, but by the end, we have just over £11,000 in cash and cheques. It's 6 p.m. and we're both exhausted.

'Right, let's head home, I need to face the missus.'

'Just one more stop.'

'No, Ben, my acting days are over, I'm knackered.'

'It's on the way and you can stay in the car.'

I direct him to pull over behind an old VW Golf on a small 1950s terrace. 'Won't be a second.'

I press the bell at the familiar red door. I hear feet coming down the stairs. The door opens and a teenager kisses his teeth when he sees it's me.

'Dad, it's for you,' he shouts, and immediately runs back up the stairs. I wait on the doorstep; I've never been inside.

Valentine appears from the lounge in a grey sweatshirt and jogging pants. His frame fills the front doorway.

'What you want?'

'I'm sorry, I'm a dickhead,' I say, handing him £1,000. Not a fortune, but a month's money. He takes it and pockets it without comment.

'What will you do?' I ask.

'Going back to Barbados.'

'Good for you.' And I mean it.

'How's that boy of yours?' he asks with a smile.

'Good.' And I smile back.

He closes the door without further ceremony and all that enters my head is 'God, I must have been a nightmare for him.'

Back in the car, Johnny is admiring his new haircut in the rearview mirror.

'Thank you,' I say. 'I really mean it. I just couldn't have done it by myself.'

Johnny reaches into his glove compartment and takes out a cheque book.

'You don't have to pay me for your mother-in-law's tea urn, Johnny, let's call it wages.'

But he grabs a pen from the car's door pocket and begins to write anyway.

'No, seriously.'

He finishes with a scratchy signature and hands it to me. All that's filled in is my name and his signature.

'I don't understand.'

'Whatever you're short. When it's all over, with the lawyers and everything, just fill in the numbers.'

'I can't . . .'

'It's agreed. Both of us discussed it last night.'

'Amanda, too?'

'Both of us.'

'I'll pay you back.'

'Pay us back by winning and smiling. I can't stand looking at your miserable face any more.'

Something about today has lifted me. I have achieved something. It's not perfect, but with the money raised and Johnny's help I feel a part of the solution, rather than the problem. I can manage this situation until Emma pays me back. I feel I'm finally helping Jonah and I don't need Dad's money.

I arrive home elated, but it shrinks away as I see the front door – there is a blue balloon tied to the brass knocker with string.

Oh, no, May 11. More balloons are bouncing around the hallway and gruff, poker-school voices are battling for supremacy. They are in the lounge.

'Head like a sieve,' Dad says.

A marble cake adorned with eleven garish candles sits proudly on the coffee table, one half of it mangled.

'He couldn't wait.'

He's sitting on the sofa, crumb-spattered, twiddling a length of shiny gold ribbon with a green crepe crown atop his head. I go to kiss him but he turns away.

'How did you know?'

'He's my grandson, why wouldn't I know?'

'Really?'

'Also, Emma's here.'

'Here?'

'No, Maurice's. Of course here.'

'You let her in?'

'Why not? A mother shouldn't see her son on his birthday? Besides, you have enough anger for both of us. She's in the kitchen.'

She has her back to me, dropping tea bags into mugs. 'So, you thought you'd just turn up?'

'It's Jonah's birthday, Ben. Please, let's not do this now.'

'So when? When you decide to take my phone calls? When are you going to tell me the truth?'

She turns to face me. 'Ben, please. Please just let me spend a little time with Jonah on his birthday. I miss him.'

'No one's stopping you from seeing him, Emma. You're the one who—'

'Leave her alone!'

'Stay out of this, Dad.'

'No. You will leave her alone, Ben.'

'Georg, maybe I—'

'No, no, you should see JJ.'

I stumble out into the hallway and lean against the wall, breathing hard. From the kitchen I hear soft tears and low talk, but the words are unclear. Minutes later, she's passed me and is in the lounge, then she runs to the front door and is gone. I try to compose myself and wander back into the lounge.

Dad's poker buddies, Harvey and Sammy, are trying to attract Jonah's attention, holding badly wrapped bundles under his nose, but he's glued to the television screen. I have nothing to give him.

'Open them for him, Sammy, he won't do it himself,' Harvey says.

Sammy rips the paper off the parcel. Inside is a blue velvet bag the size of a folded newspaper, with gold-embroidered Hebrew characters. He unzips it and takes out a blue and white silk *tallas* – a prayer shawl – and a blue suede *kipah* with the Tottenham Hotspur crest on it.

'Is this some kind of joke?' I ask.

'A Jewish boy shouldn't have a *tallas*?' says Sammy. 'What should I buy him, an apple?'

'He doesn't need any of this, he doesn't know any of this. He'll never be bar mitzvah or married, he'll never go to a synagogue. Whose stupid idea was this anyway?'

'Mine,' says Dad.

I look to him. 'Yours? The atheist.'

'Yes, mine.'

We both turn to Jonah, whose face is engulfed in silk. On each end of the *tallas* are a multitude of threaded silk fringes. Jonah's fingers are all over them.

'For the twiddling, not because he is going to be a rabbi.'

I look to Sammy's hurt face. 'I'm sorry,' I say.

'So what have you bought him?' Dad's eyes are blazing.

'I left it in the boot, just go and get it.'

I sit in the car with the air-conditioning up full blast, but my blood is still on the boil. Rage and shame are difficult to chill. She wasn't as I imagined she'd be. She was less than I remembered, her confidence withered. No rejoinder, no argument, no stoicism and now I feel like a piece of shit.

The only place to buy a toy now is the 24-hour Tesco. I drive like a lunatic down the North Circular, believing somehow that my forty-five-minute absence will not be noticed. I swing on to the slip road with a screech and immediately my dashboard is awash with disco lights – red and blue, red and blue.

I pull over, concocting: *it's my son's birthday, he's autistic, my wife's left me, I'm really a good person.* A torch beam blinds me, then moves around the inside of the car like a descending UFO. The window is rapped, hard. I press the down button.

'Can I help you, officer?'

'Do you normally exit a dual carriageway on two wheels?'

'No, officer, I'm a very careful driver.'

'Could you please step out of the car, sir.'

Standing with my back against the bodywork, I run through the day's drinking. Impending incarceration is attacking my knees and I stumble. The policeman looks at me ruefully and turns to his colleague, who heads to the rear of my car.

'Have you been drinking tonight, sir?'

'No, officer.' Which is true, because I haven't had a chance yet.

'I'm going to have you breathe into a breathalyser.' He removes a plastic-sealed tube from his pocket, just as his colleague opens the near-side rear door. The sound of a xylophone pierces the traffic noise.

'Gavin, I think you ought to see this.'

PC Gavin guides me by the elbow round the back of the car and stands me facing the open door.

'What's this?'

'Empty bottles, officer.'

'Don't be clever, sir. What are they doing falling out of your car?'

'I was taking them to the bottle bank behind the store.' Which is feasible.

'Really? Never heard of plastic bags?'

'Bad for the environment.'

'So are drunk drivers. Breathe into this tube, sir, but don't take a deep breath, just breathe until you think you're going to faint.'

I feel like fainting already, but I comply. Standing up in the dock is something I've managed to avoid, but given my recent luck... He takes the tube from the black box and puts it back in plastic and then we both stare at the three coloured diodes. Never have I willed a traffic light to go green with such force. The three lights flash like a fruit machine: green, amber, red, green, amber, red. It hesitates on red and finally settles on amber. I don't know what this means.

'You're lucky. You see that light? It means you're currently a fraction under the limit. I want you to put the bottles in the boot, get back in your car and drive carefully home before it goes red.'

'But I need to go shopping.'

'Tomorrow, sir. We'll see you off, goodnight.'

They follow me for the first five hundred yards and when they peel away, I pull into the first pub.

Jonah is in bed snoring with his *tallas* still gripped in his hand. I kiss him on the forehead and, when I gently remove the prayer shawl from him, Emma's perfume catches in my throat like ammonia. It makes my eyes water. I escaped from one prison tonight, I think, but could it be any worse than the one I'm already in?

All the joy I thought I'd feel at the demise of the business hasn't arrived. This wasn't the way I dreamt it would be, the perfect scenario, the phone call out of the blue from a giant marketing agency telling me – while I sob with relief – that they've seen some old copy of mine and just had to employ me. The walk away with pride, the resurrection.

No, it can't end like this. I'll just have to keep it ticking over – with or without Valentine. There are staff agencies, I can get a driver, washer-uppers, I'll phone them tomorrow, I decide, as I also pledge to park up in a side street tomorrow and drink myself stupid.

Lomax and Partners
Solicitors at Law
132 Furnival Street
London EC4 2JR

30 May 2011

Dear Mr Jewell

Re: Petition for dissolution of marriage on behalf of Mrs
Emma Jewell

I am writing on behalf of my client Emma Jewell, to petition
you for a divorce.

I understand from Emma that you have been officially
separated for approaching four months and that you have,
between you, decided that you be assigned temporary custody
of Jonah as Mrs Jewell currently works full time and, between
yourself, your father and social services, Jonah is currently
well cared for. We reserve the right to review this when
circumstances allow for joint custody. This, of course, makes
everything a lot simpler as it negates the need to go to family
court to resolve such a dispute.

I also understand from Emma that the former family
home in Wynchgate is in her name alone, which again
removes a great deal of negotiation and confrontation.

Emma has asked me to assure you that she wishes no
enmity to arise from the proceeding and would implore you
to sign the enclosed documents so that we can get the ball

rolling. You will notice that she has specified the marriage breakdown due to 'irreconcilable differences' and hopes you will not contest this.

I am conscious that you are currently investigating the possibility of an Educational Tribunal for your son, Jonah, and Mrs Jewell wishes to reiterate that she will contribute half the cost, when she has funds available.

Mrs Jewell will, of course, be covering this firm's costs. But if you choose to contest, I would advise you to find a solicitor to represent you.

Yours sincerely
Phillipa Lomax LLB
Partner, Lomax and Partners

Cow

screw up the letter and shoot it basketball-style into the black
bin liner hanging from the cupboard door. What is there to
contest? What is there to split? By rights, I suppose, she could
pay me maintenance and child support now that the business
has gone tits-up and I have no income, but I won't ask for it.
Don't want to upset her, it's not over yet.

Dad's too weak from all the treatment to bath Jonah – or to
bollock about opening my post – and so social services have
been sending care workers round to help with Jonah in the
evenings. On the whole they're pretty good and I can't complain,
but at the same time, they represent the harbingers of doom
to me. He isn't going to get stronger, Dad, when I thought he
would go on for ever.

I find Dad asleep in his armchair with his hands resting on
a half-finished *Guardian* crossword. The blanket has slipped so
I pull it back over him and make my way wearily up the stairs.

A young woman – it's never the same one twice – has Jonah
in the bath, but I see that the water level's too low and the
water's too cold. She smiles at me as I enter. Jonah ignores me.

'It's okay, I'll take it from here.'

'Are you sure, I'm booked for another hour?'

'No, it's fine, you get yourself off.'

'Well, if you're sure?'

'Go,' I say, with a smile.

I wait for the sound of the front door closing then turn on the taps and squeeze in the bubbles.

'Come on, dude, let's do this properly.'

He places his left big toe under the tap and giggles as the falling water tickles him. I swoosh my hand around the bath to raise the bubbles and start the ritual again.

I lie back on the bathroom floor and rest my head in my hands, while he splashes and babbles.

'Is this strange for you, Jonah? One minute you're in your own bed and Mum and Dad are with you, then next Mum's not there and you're in a strange house with just Dad and Papa?

'Well, it's strange for me. We're not that dissimilar, you and I. I know we look nothing alike, but that's not what I'm talking about. Neither of us likes change, do we? And I know it upsets you and I'm sorry. I'm upset too. Yes, really. We just show it in different ways. You get angry and frustrated and I'm just fucking horrible to everyone and get pissed. Whatever you do, even when you're old enough, stay off the booze. It doesn't change anything and just makes you more miserable. You stick to water. And for God's sake avoid cigarettes. I know you'll do what you want, just like I did, but look at me, I'm no great example, am I? Don't answer that.

'There are so many people that love you, Jonah. Mum loves you, even if she has a strange way of showing it, and Papa loves you more than he loves me...'

'No I do not!'

I pull myself into a sitting position.

'Didn't hear you come up.'

'What makes you think I love Jonah more than I love you?'

'It just seems obvious by the way you...'

'Never make that assumption again. Do you hear me, Ben?'

'Yes, Dad.'

'You are both of my flesh.'

'I know.'

He pats my shoulder. 'I'll be in my bedroom.' I watch him as he leaves, the floorboard creaking on the off-beat, in time with his failing balance. His movements, once marching band, have slipped into the unpredictable, edgy disharmony of jazz. The whistling from his chest leaves him breathless and me unable to breathe.

Jonah is in bed. Dad's in bed. I am lying on the sofa with a tumbler of Scotch resting on my chest. I haven't the energy to watch TV or read, so the radio is on, but just for company, just a warming soundtrack. I've succumbed to Radio 4 and it's 'Book at Bedtime'. I have no idea what the story is about and it doesn't matter, because the female narrator has an Irish accent, Southern and soft. I love the sound – all stories should be read in this lilting tone. I sip at the Scotch. It's warming my insides while my Irish companion relaxes my overloaded synapses. I don't want to go to bed in case my mood alters. If I could stay just like this, with all the needles pointing at neutral, I would. For ever, I promise. Then the padding footsteps. Jonah. Before the cancer, I'd have ignored it, but Dad needs his sleep desperately now, so I reluctantly rise to investigate.

I take the steps barefoot and slowly. If I maintain calm both in demeanour and sound then there's a chance I can coax him back to his own room without waking Dad. I check Jonah's room first; the duvet is lying on the floor and multi-coloured fish are swimming the walls and ceiling.

Dad's door is open, so I creep in.

'I'm awake, don't worry.' His voice has dropped an octave through the therapy and cancer and is hoarse.

'I'll take him back, Dad,' I whisper. 'Come on, Jonah.'

'It's okay, let him stay. I like his warmth, I like to listen to him breathe. He likes my stories, don't you, JJ?'

My dad winks at him, conspiratorially. I can't argue, I know the feeling and I don't feel jealous about it any more. It's not personal, nothing about Jonah's behaviour is personal. He has bias and preferences but they're not based on enmity. I think of my 'Book at Bedtime' narrator, how her voice soothes me but may grate on somebody else's ears. We are all individuals. It may just be that Dad's cadence, the tone of his voice, the syntax of his sentences and that strange, almost imperceptible wisp of Hungarian soothes him like my Irish lady soothes me. And then again he may just prefer his smell. Either way, it's all right by me. For now, let Dad tell Jonah his life story if it makes him feel easier with himself. I will ask him about it all, sooner rather than later.

Cheque book

My solicitor, Georgia Stone, has applied to the Tribunal Service for a date and, through a cancellation, has secured July 28 – two months from now. I mention this casually to Dad and reiterate my promise of halting the tribunal. 'Really,' he says.

'Are you calling me a liar, Dad?'

'That is what you are, even if you don't know it.'

I feel caught in a trap. 'Dad, that's just—'

'True? It doesn't matter, Ben. You promised something you could not possibly keep to. We both knew that at the time. What should a dead man do?'

'I wanted you to have the treatment, Dad.'

'But you want what you want for your son as well. Ben, we are both fathers and fathers have always, since the dawn of time, been squashed between their own fathers' dreams for them and their dreams for their own children. It is folly to believe that you can carry both in outstretched arms like the scale of justice. Maybe I forgot that myself, but you haven't. That is as it should be, so we'll say no more about it.'

I feel like hugging him, but grip his forearm instead.

*

The twenty-eighth is already after Jonah leaves Roysten Glen and only three days before the Tribunal Service begins its month-long summer recess. I begin tapping out Valetta's list of 'crucial' experts like a stenographer. She is right, of course, the experts are booked up months in advance and I start to despair. I try pleading by email, then phone again, then email again, then phone Valetta.

'They're all booked up, it's hopeless.'

'Leave it to me.'

The following day the phone calls start to arrive, cancellations have suddenly multiplied like a flu epidemic and Jonah's assessments and visits can miraculously be fitted in – just.

I phone Valetta to thank her.

'Thank me when we win,' she says.

A subsequent invoice reveals that the plea and thank-you phone calls cost me fifty pounds each.

I have opened a separate bank account for the tribunal costs and the money Johnny and I collected is safely deposited; the solicitor's monthly £500 standing order set up. I promise myself to fill in the cheque book stubs and keep an up-to-date record of the financial situation. I also resolve to keep chasing the remaining outstanding debts owed to Jewell's Catering Hire.

I even buy a diary.

June 2011

RG: Roysten Glen

Sunday	Monday	Tuesday	Wednesday	Thursday	Friday	Saturday
1	2 Radiotherapy 10am	3	4 Anne Birch RG Home 4pm £1275	5	6 Claudia Lack RG Home 4.30 £845	7
8	9 Radio 10am	10	11	12 Prescriptions!	13	14
15	16 Radio 10am	17	18 Jennifer Smart RG Home 2.30pm £920	19	20 Valetta Price Progress 12pm	21
22	23 Radio 10am	24	25 Ben GP 2.10pm	26	27 Chemo 10am	28
29	30 Radio 10am	31 Chemo 10am	1	2	3	4
5	6	7	8	9	10	11

July 2011

Sunday	Monday	Tuesday	Wednesday	Thursday	Friday	Saturday
29	30	31	1	2	3	4 Chemo 10am
5	6 Radio 10am	7	8 Chemo 10am	9 Prescriptions!	10	11
12 Chemo 10am	13	14	15	16 Chemo 10am	17	18
19	20 Chemo 10am	21	22	23	24 Chemo 10am	25
26	27	28 TRIBUNAL	29	30	1	2
3	4	5	6	7	8	9

Dad is weakening, the chemo has taken over as his sole chance of extended survival and his hair is littering the house, being twiddled by Jonah and ignored by my father.

He refuses to sit in on the experts' visits to Jonah; refuses to read their reports when they arrive. He may be dissolving, but when I offer him Anne Birch's educational psychology report on Jonah, he bats it away angrily.

'No one,' he tells me, 'can see anything in my grandson that I cannot see.' He goes back to his crossword.

As the weeks wear on, the reports pile up, as does my work-load, the cost and my stress level. I am forcing myself to be forensic in the study of the reports and forthright when making notes when I disagree, or feel that the wording could be stronger.

There is iteration, after iteration, after iteration. Filing them is a nightmare. Every piece of correspondence is sorted by date and sender. Each paid invoice bears the payment date, and a running total, each cheque stub covered in information.

After Jonah has gone to bed, we sit together in the lounge while I do this. Most evenings, Maurice joins us, ferrying tea and coffee to us and unpacking containers of pre-prepared deli food that, for Dad, he cuts and mashes so he has a chance of swallowing it. Radio 4 is the soundtrack to this operation. The television on only when Jonah gets home from school.

I, of course, have to read the reports on my son and there are no punches pulled, adjectives are plucked from the more emotive pool of synonyms. These three expert women are Jonah's generals; Valetta his field marshal. They are the top brass of our tribunal army and their services do not come cheap.

I find myself writing cheques in my sleep: £850, £975, £650, £1,050, £975, £1,150, and stare at my laptop when I'm awake, watching the balance in the account dwindle.

This is a full-time job. If I hadn't killed the business and driven Valentine back to Barbados, I could never have run it in parallel with this tribunal preparation. It's the hardest job I've ever had, by far, but the one I'm doing the best at – because it has meaning and purpose. The future of Jonah Jewell, the future of Ben Jewell – currently employed as professional son-lover and father-carer.

Then the local authority drops its atom bomb.

Bull

They've added a third school into the mix – a residential school, The Sunrise Academy. It's autism accredited and – significantly for the LA and its case – vastly cheaper than Highgrove Manor. Valetta says this is a serious challenge.

I'm apoplectic. 'So, let me get this straight, if they can convince on Maureen Mitchell, Jonah will go there, but if not he ends up in this, this, what? Counterfeit good? Emma visited the place a year ago and said it gave her the creeps. I've looked at its website, it's surrounded by dual carriageways. I can't see Jonah there.'

'You'll need to visit it, Ben,' Valetta says, 'and so will our edpysch, Anne. Of course, this makes things harder, but not insurmountable.'

Valetta is calm. I am not. What if I do like it when I get there? What if I think it will be difficult to argue against it?

'With two weeks to go?'

'It's a strategy.'

'To save money.'

'Of course, but the LA is also tacitly admitting that they feel they will lose with Maureen Mitchell, so now we concentrate on

The Sunrise Academy. When you see it, you may even change your mind.'

'Bollocks, Valetta.'

'They will try to deal, Ben. It may be in all our interests.'

In whose? I think, as I imagine the fifty green acres of High-grove turning into the over-extended semi of Sunrise.

How proud Emma and I were on Jonah's first day at nursery. I remember taking photos of him in his uniform – navy blue sweatpants and bright orange polo shirt, matching orange Converse high-tops, a mop of light-brown hair and a nappy. We both took him that first morning, watched him stroll in nonchalantly while the other children cried and clung to their parents. Johnny and Amanda lived close by at the time and we were heartened because Tom would be with him, on that first day and – we hoped – throughout his school years.

I recall watching through the window as Tom took Jonah's hand, so protective, seeming so much older. I smile to myself at the memory. Tom's speech had an amazing fluency, while Jonah was wordless, but Tom believed that he could translate Jonah's guttural lexicon – which only he understood – and would concentrate, with his ear close to Jonah's mouth, before regaling us with extraordinarily detailed accounts from our poet, astronaut, secret-agent son.

It turned out to be the only year they spent together. Jonah repeated nursery before transferring to Roysten Glen, while Tom graduated to reception class and upwards. Jonah had lost his translator and protector and time stood still for us.

And now here I am, sitting next to Tom's father in his BMW, struggling around the North Circular Road to see another school that believe they can help Jonah more than anywhere else and for less money. It seems as if Jonah's been put out for tender like the East Coast mainline.

The lights finally change and we crawl across Kew Bridge.

'South London, passports at the ready,' Johnny announces.

'Thanks for doing this, Johnny, I really couldn't face it by myself.'

'While we're down here, any punters we can call on who owe you money?'

'No, I think we'll leave the debt collecting for today. God, I hate South London. It's all causeways and British Rail and concrete.'

'Never been to Greenwich, or Dulwich Village?'

'Don't contradict me, I'm venting.'

'Fair enough.'

We sit in silence while the SatNav commentates. Eighteen miles to go, forty-eight minutes.

'Where are we heading to first? The school or the accommodation?'

The school and accommodation are six miles apart – which is a boost to my fault-finding agenda, given Jonah's difficulty with transitions in his daily routine. Hence the beauty of Highgrove Manor – it's a rural campus where his movements will be minimal.

'The school first. And look, even if you like something, don't say so, please,' I say.

'Okay, whatever you want.'

Johnny makes a final left turn and pulls into a car park adjacent to the metal gate of The Sunrise Academy. Surprisingly, I hate it on sight. It's a single-storey mashup of cubes and covered walkways. We're buzzed in through the gate and again into the school with little question and, once inside, no one seems overly eager to meet us. Finally a slender blonde in a sports tracksuit and trainers arrives.

'Can I help you?'

'Ben Jewell, we booked a tour of the school?'

'Oh. Tribunal. I'm Julia Makarova, chief psychologist. Follow me, I'll show you around.'

Johnny and I troop off behind her. I'm a veteran of this by now and know our educational psychologist will do the proper grilling, so I'm half bored, feeling mildly belligerent, and I know what to spot.

A loud bell rings.

'What's that for?'

'This is the change of lesson bell.'

The walkway we were strolling down alone just moments before is now heaving with students – autistic students – desperately trying to avoid each other and find their way to the next class. Some have carers with them, others not. It's like central Rome on a Friday afternoon. Johnny is taking it all in like a meerkat. I have to shout above the noise.

'Why don't the kids stay in the same class all day?'

'This is secondary school curriculum, this is what we model.'

'And they have different teachers for each subject?'

'Yes, of course.'

I feel my confidence growing every minute as each checkbox of negatives is ticked. I look at Johnny who, with his knowledge of Jonah, also appears to share in my scepticism. I ask leading questions, like a paperback detective, eliciting the answers I want to back up my case.

'How do they deal with the transitions?'

'They stay in their classroom and wait for children to join them.'

I don't bother clarifying my question.

'You want to see a classroom?'

'Yes, please.' We walk through a door which no children are queuing outside. Tables.

'Tables?'

'Yes, as you can see.'

'Individual workstations?'

'No, as you can see.'

'Is there somewhere we can talk?' I have seen enough. Even objectively, this place is unsuitable. It assumes a level of awareness and understanding that Jonah just does not have.

'Come to my office, I have ten minutes.'

'I only need one.'

The din evaporates as she closes the door behind Johnny and me.

'How much does it cost?'

She sits at her desk, mousing and tapping, then without looking up states: 'Eighty-six thousand four hundred pounds per academic year.'

'Fucking hell.'

'Johnny!'

'Sorry.'

'Thanks, I think we have everything. Could you show us the way out.'

Back in the car he's still aghast.

'Eighty-six grand? You're expecting the council to pay eighty-six grand a year to send Jonah to school? No fucking way.'

'No, I'm asking the council to lay out nearly two hundred grand a year to send Jonah to school.'

'That's more than double.'

'I know – and that's the problem.'

'I never realised...'

'No, no one ever does,' I tell him. But how much is Jonah worth? Thirty thousand, eighty-six thousand, two hundred thousand. These are just numbers, but to those who will decide his fate, so is Jonah.

I'm hoping that the accommodation will be equally unsuitable, but the massively extended Victorian house halfway down a leafy suburban road appears quiet and comfortable. But it has taken us twenty-five minutes during the middle of the day to get from the school to here along some major roads, so during rush hour? Forty? Fifty? An hour? I make a note in the back of my diary.

A lady greets us with a smile, older, maybe fifty-five, and she can't wait to extol the virtues of her house, but the stairs are narrow and steep, with half-landings and turns everywhere – a Jonah nightmare – and when she reveals that they only take weekly boarders, I've seen enough.

It takes us ninety minutes of hell to get home.

After kissing Jonah goodnight, I head for the lounge. Dad is asleep in his chair. Maurice is on the sofa, watching Dad sleep in the chair. The radio is down low, but 'The Archers' is still faintly audible. I take a beer from the fridge, I feel dirty, my throat dusty and my head now horribly conflicted.

After what I saw and heard today, given the choice, I know I'd prefer Jonah to join Maureen Mitchell rather than Sunrise, but I don't know if I'll be given the choice. All the groundwork is now laid. Some of the reports have still to come in and will need to be read, reread and redrafted before the tribunal – only two weeks away. Somehow we have got this far. Soon, it will be time to climb aboard the troop carriers and head for the beaches.

THE SUNRISE ACADEMY
Autism Accredited School

Mr B Jewell
Flat 4, 97 Rutland Road
London N24 3RS

25 July 2011

Dear Mr Jewell

Based on the current evidence, Jonah will be offered a residential placement starting from September 2011, on a standard package reviewed during the first six-months assessment.

Yours truly,

In your dreams, bitch.

Julia Makarova
Lead Psychologist
120 Hopewell Lane
Hopewell
London SE32 9DX

Uranus

So here I sit at the dining table the night before battle. In front of me lie eighteen inches of A4 paper, binders, wallets, folders, emails – £24,000 worth of words that could mean nothing by this time tomorrow night. An unauthorised biography of Jonah, of God only knows how many words, certainly more than the Bible. All this for one not so little boy who couldn't give a shit what anyone else thinks.

All that money, the price of a terraced house in Sunderland, has bought me just one episode of *LA Law*. Whatever the outcome, I can't claim any costs back; however thin the council's argument – and its pile is anorexic by comparison – not a bean will come back my way. But at this moment, just like Jonah, I couldn't give a fuck.

I've already fantasised about occupying the council offices should the worst happen. The truth is that I can't afford the second appeal I'd be entitled to, so this is Jonah's golden shot, the last arrow left, bullseye or bust.

This is a racket, a gravy train, a lot of people are making a lot of money off the back of my son – I recognised this months ago – but again, I am entering willingly. I am, I suppose, an independent expert on fucking up marriages and businesses – but I don't see anyone employing me at a thousand pounds a day to advise them.

I think what I find most difficult – as I begin scanning the reports on Jonah for the last time – is that the local authorities don't recognise this, or worse still, they do and have some geeky maths turd in a back office somewhere telling them it's still better value than treating a vulnerable child correctly – all vulnerable children correctly. That's what I hate the most about this process, the selfishness it forces on me. At this point, I'm not thinking of Jonah's classmates at Roysten Glen, many, if not all of them, as bad as Jonah. It's hard to admit that I don't give a shit about them. Some of them have existed in space and time with Jonah for six years. But they've ignored him, as he they, apart from the odd physical attack. I don't know them, couldn't tell you their names, or the names of their parents, and they'll all be off to Maureen Mitchell for another seven years' babysitting until it becomes adult services' problem.

Whatever others may think, Jonah's tribunal and his possible victory is only for those with the capacity for all-out war, for those with the acceptance and knowledge of their children's true condition, and those who have the requisite cynicism to identify officialdom's true strategy: divide and conquer. What could be an easier enemy to defeat, a community to corral and pacify, than those who lack the basic skills to interact with each other? Autistic children have no field radios, not even the antennae.

I sit at the dining table with a whisky next to me and keep scanning. These pages are my son's behaviour writ large, acceptable exaggeration in the face of enemy disinformation. And tomorrow I will hear this argued over. I will sit there, hands clasping the sides of the chair, no doubt listening to a justification of incompetence, the description of my living, breathing, loving son in terms of 'scales' and 'cognitive age' and 'levels of continence'. I will also have to listen to the truth and bury deep the yearning to jump up and punch the opposing barrister in the face.

I feel the anticipation rising, I imagine my last meal with Jonah, my life alone, and out comes the exhaustion and fear. I have spent the best part of a year hammering away at the walls that keep my son at home, close to me, while in my heart I'd rather have been building watchtowers and laying barbed-wire. What the fuck is that all about? I see no prospect on the horizon other than solitude. I feel such bitterness. If I believed in a god, I'd be railing at him daily.

My mother has hardly entered my thoughts at all, but occasionally – as now – one of her bloody platitudes arrives like a neon sign: Growth Through Pain. 'Thank you, Myra, and fuck off', I say to myself.

She walked out and left me, left us, and yet all I wanted was the opportunity to be the kind of parent I never had. And the only way to be that now is by letting my son go. Of all the fucking ironies. It seems so Victorian, so unenlightened and punishing, so personal. There are moments when I feel so unneeded that a quick morphine high followed by a swift death seems logical and appropriate. Growth through pain? Yeah, right.

Whack! Dad slaps a notebook on to the table next to me as he lowers himself tentatively into a chair.

Why are you crying?

The cancer has finally pilfered his vocal cords and he's taken to pad and pen. Conversation is laborious and irritating – even more irritating than normal.

'Have you read these? It's hard to see Jonah in black and white like this.'

Why read them then? it makes no sense to me. Who are you crying for? What do you think these words are? They are nothing. Listen carefully to me, just for once, sit quietly without that pitiful look on your face and listen.

He puts his hand up to stop me and carries on scribbling. It takes a minute.

Words are just shapes, one squiggle after another. And you think people are so clever to use them this way and that way; stitch them together and shoot them like bullets and watch them wound or caress, hurt or disgust?

The hand again. This is torture.

Then more scribbling and it's thrust at me once more.

Let me tell you, I have heard enough words to last me this lifetime – words in Hungarian, in German, in French, in Dutch, in English, in Yiddish. So I have enough. Did I understand all of them? No. And I'll tell you why: because I'm deaf to anything I don't want to hear and most of what I've heard in my seventy-eight years is other idiots like me using words to tell other idiots what they want by using words that mean the opposite of what they truly mean. Are you following me?

I shake my head and he snatches back the pad. He writes more slowly, he is getting tired.

Still no? Because you're an idiot too. How many words do the Eskimo or Inuit or whatever they're called this week have for snow? Thirty-two or so. Idiots! Move somewhere warmer and have done. The Japanese and Chinese waste their time drawing pictures – ach, no! Not pictures, pictograms, because one word isn't enough. Maurice speaks five languages and he's the biggest

*fool I know. Spent his whole life making shmutter dresses for fat
women who think they're 'voluptuous', or 'zaftig'.*

This time he bats my hand away in frustration and continues
to scribble.

*That Rosetta Stone – they should have smashed it up, saved us all
the trouble of understanding what any of those ancient shmocks
didn't mean. Your Ancient Greeks, Egyptians and Sumerians, they are
laughing at us. And don't get me started on the Bible.*

*You and your words, Ben. What are you today? Devastated?
Bereft? Heartbroken? Broken? Melancholy? Distraught? Does
it matter? Why on earth do we need all these words – especially
you – when you can be described by just two of them: self-pity.
There, I even gave you a hyphen for free.*

*It's not words. It's not words. It's actions. But you don't see
with your eyes, like every other fool you see with your ears. You
heard love from Emma, you heard devotion from Emma, you heard
yourself tell yourself that you love Emma, but what did you see?
What did you do?*

'You know nothing about my marriage.'

He scribbles.

You think so? Why? Because I never interfered?

'Because you didn't care.'

He scribbles.

Because it wouldn't have mattered.

'You never liked her.'

He scribbles.

Not true.

'Then what? You pitied her for marrying me?'

He scribbles.

*No, I like Emma. But you, I have watched you for thirty-seven
years and you have never finished or taken responsibility for*

anything. *Even as a child you would never wipe your tochas
properly. If you crapped in your nappy you would deny it was you.
Never a jigsaw, a game, a model, your homework. You are not a
finisher.*

'I'm sorry I am such a disappointment.'

*Here he is again with the self-pity. You are not a disappointment,
you are a positive reminder.*

'Of what?'

Of the utter pointlessness of expectations.

'So you had no expectations for me?'

*Not one. So how could I be disappointed? But it doesn't mean I
don't love you.*

'Then I'm confused. Why are you so opposed to the possibility
of Jonah going away?'

Dad pauses and looks at me, his eyes bloodshot, his pen
hovering.

*Look at that pile of paperwork in front of you again. Tell me,
what does it represent to you?*

'Jonah, you know that,' I say immediately.

Nothing else?

'Oh fuck off with your quizzes, please, Dad. So what else does
it represent then? Half a rainforest?'

*It represents YOU, Benjamin, and your love for your son. All that
paper? Your determination, your single-mindedness. This whole
thing was never about convincing me, it was about convincing
yourself that you can decide on something and see it through to
the end whatever happens.*

*I was wrong to say that you never finish anything, you have
finished this and I'm proud of you. Now you must tell the Gansa
Macha lawyers to win so I can go with visions of my JJ skipping
around that beautiful school, laughing.*

I can't identify *all* the feelings, but these tears are of relief and regret. Relief that I have finally seen him as a father and regret that it should come so late and at such a price. He is still scribbling furiously and it's difficult to read through the water, so I wipe my eyes with my sleeve. There is the pad and a separate leaf lying next to my elbow.

Here is all the pad says. But the other cream-coloured note is made out to Mr B Jewell. It is a cheque for £40,000. Elation? Yes, but still the shame that I couldn't have written the cheque myself. I have his agreement, it's worth more than money, it justifies everything I've done. Now he is with me, I can be right.

'Thank you,' I say, leaving the table to sit near to him on the sofa. We both stare at the silent TV screen and I lean across and squeeze his hand and, in this new era of Glasnost, I chance another question.

'Dad, why tell Jonah your life story, my history, when you've always refused to share even a speck of it with me?'

He stands, shuffles to the sideboard and returns with two brandies, his with plenty of water. Then he sits and grabs the pad.

You didn't need to know. I have protected you from my agonies as best I could.

'But you gave me no choice?'

He ponders, takes a sip and scribbles

Be patient.

It is a full stop.

'Come on, it's one o'clock, we should go to bed. How are you feeling?'

Scribble.

Tired, sore.

Then a virtually inaudible croak creeps up from deep inside him. I can see the effort on his face as he speaks.

'Nu? Jonah, did we wake you? Come and sit with us,' says Dad.

Jonah's waiting hopefully at the door. So we sit, three generations of Jewell men around a fat, dark, ugly oak table – a séance of silence. Dad and I simultaneously reach for one of Jonah's hands, but we don't complete the circle with our own, as if it would release something too powerful – like love. I can't resist pushing him, just once more tonight.

'He's the last Jewell, you know, Dad, that's the end of the line. No more. It's sad.'

He reverts to his pad, his voice now nothing but fetid air, and with his free hand writes:

Peh! I changed it from Friedman in 1945, but you know that anyway, from all your eavesdropping, so what's the difference?

'I guess I should thank you for that morsel at least.' I have so many questions, but I'm tired, nervous and panicky. I'll save them for after the tribunal, I think. I need an hour alone now to prepare myself and what I need to say tomorrow, to calm down before I try to sleep.

Jonah frees his hands and picks up the crystal paperweight, summoning the colours like a wizard, while I try to summon the courage to study my father's grotesque neck, ignoring its pus-yellow colour like a coward.

'I'll change him,' I yawn, 'but let's get you to bed first.' His energy appears to have eloped with his voice.

Need something to help me sleep. In drawer of sideboard.

'Lorazepam?' I ask, searching through the boxes of drugs.

Yes, two.

'It says one on the prescription label.'

Give me two! Are you the one dying of cancer?

So I give him two – each cut in half so they can pass through the capillary of his throat – and a glass of water. Still, it takes him fifteen minutes to force them down. Without his pen and notepad, without me, he is totally helpless. Without my help he wouldn't eat, be able to make it to the bathroom or sleep comfortably. I take the notepad to bed with me and re-read his scribbling, then turn to a clean sheet and begin, once again, to write my submission for tomorrow's tribunal. I've had weeks to do this. I've started, scrubbed out and started again on numerous occasions. Emma will speak and I must find the words to make them understand, to tell them what Jonah would want to say. What would he say?

I hear the thump at 3.17 a.m.

'Not now, Dad, please, not now. I have the tribunal in the morning, please…'

He's on the floor, his legs awkwardly wound around each other like a stretchy children's toy. Saliva is dribbling from his mouth and he's mumbling incoherently.

'Do you need the toilet? Is that it? Were you trying to get to the bathroom?'

The cancer has constricted his throat to a needle eye, making it impossible for him to eat without the regular thimbles of Oramorph that relax him enough to take anything down. This and the chemo have wasted him. Wires of silver hair have begun to poke through the back of his head. He weighs nothing. I rearrange his body and put him in the foetal position, then gradually into a sitting position. His pyjama bottoms glide to the floor and his nakedness appals me and, as I lift him into a standing position and hoist him into my arms like a baby, he urinates on me. Burning hot and smelling of rubber.

I carry him to the bathroom and gently place him on the toilet. His head rolls to the left and I kneel at the right of him holding him steady.

'Was it the Lorazepam? Did I give you too much?'

He has trouble sleeping because he can't breathe. Lying in my bed for the past few nights has been like attempting to sleep in a carpenter's workshop.

He doesn't have the strength to strain, but the cocktail of chemicals and cancer cells that has gradually replaced the blood in his veins is doing its job. His backside is running like a tap.

Jonah is at the door. I smell him before I see him.

'Go back to bed, Jonah.' But he doesn't move. I should be glad, glad that the discomfort of his soiled nappy woke him up, that he realised – on some level – he needed changing.

'Jonah, go back to bed, please go back to bed, I'll be in soon, I promise. Jonah, please.'

My pleading has led to tears. Dad is half-smiling, but there is no malice there, just the flushed, skewed mouth of an imbecile.

'I am not wiping your arse, Dad. Not yours too, please not yours too.'

But I reach for a fresh toilet roll and thrust the entire thing between his legs with my head turned away and roughly push and pull it a dozen times before throwing it into the bath. I grab his arms and wrap them around my neck and lift him to his feet by his waist.

His bed sheet is wet, but there are no clean ones left so I place a large towel over the wet patch, lay him down on his back and cover him with the duvet. I look at my son.

'Your turn, Jonah.'

The night takes pigeon steps while I sit on the floor in the hall. I turn to Radio 4 for company and judge time's passing by the hourly chimes of Big Ben.

Dad is between sleep and death but not captured by either, yet. It's now 5 a.m. and I've tried Emma, but she's a voicemail junkie these days, so I sit vigil by the side of his bed with my hand on his corrugated chest, timing my own breathing with his in a futile effort to finally bond us in some way, any way. Jonah has mercifully stayed in his room and I hear him giggling in his bed. The dawn hours are finally here.

My father is going to die.

No last-minute flight to a New York clinic.

No miraculous, unexplained remission.

Just a horrid, undignified end.

He'll be philosophical despite the pain.

And I hate myself because I'm in pain.

And even more so because I resent him for it.

For making me need him and then fucking off when he's supposed to watch over me.

I phone social services at 6 a.m. 'My father's going, it could only be hours. I need someone here to wait with Jonah for the school bus while I go with my father to the hospice.'

'Someone will be there as soon as possible, Mr Jewell.'

She arrives at 6.30, just as they carry the unconscious remnants of my father into the ambulance and I climb in after. Through the ambulance's blacked-out rear windows, I see Jonah skip back into the house as we set off for Hampstead Hospice.

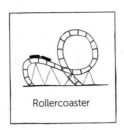

Rollercoaster

He is settled – I have time to wait that long – in a bed with a morphine drip in his twig of a left arm and a nurse gently bathing him as he lies unmoving. I tell him I'll see him later, although I can't be sure. Maurice arrives as I leave and we embrace awkwardly.

'I wish you mazel,' he says, his eyes teary.

My phone rings on the walk down to Hampstead tube, a number I vaguely recognise but can't quite place.

'Hello, Ben?'

'Maria? Where are you?'

'At Heathrow. I just wanted to wish you luck. I'm so sorry I can't be there to celebrate with you and Jonah.'

'I wish I had your confidence,' I say. 'Anyway, you're going on an adventure, put all this out of your mind.'

'Not possible, I'm afraid,' she says. 'Remember our deal?'

'The postcard, of course.'

'Well, I'm changing the terms,' she says.

'Not sure that's legal.'

'I reserved the right, check the small print,' she says.

'Okay, what's the deal?'

'You must email and keep me up to date.'

'I promise,' I say.

'Good. By the way, how's your dad?'

'Hanging in there,' I say. 'Please be careful, Maria.'

'Around snakes or Latin men?' she giggles.

'Both, please.'

'I have to go, they're calling my flight,' she says through more giggles. 'And remember, write to me!'

'I will,' I say, as the line goes dead.

How many cigarettes can I smoke before entering this nondescript building? The butts decorating the rain-mottled pavement at my feet suggest enough to join my father in the next bed with unnecessary haste.

I haven't worn a suit for months and I'm dishevelled, stained, creased, unshaven.

The waiting area is like a catalogue for budget office furniture. I appear to be the first of our 'crack squad' to arrive and settle in a royal-blue tub chair. This is not what I imagined – no wood panelling in sight, no powdered wigs. Functional and quiet, businesslike. The mood belies the purpose, I think, and the anxiety I feel. I wish I had swiped a couple of Dad's Lorazepam. Instead, I go back outside.

She approaches me like a pickpocket.

'Today is about Jonah, not about you and me. Okay?' Emma's lips are set in a determined pout. I light another cigarette as she heads into the building. I knew she would be here, but I feel marginalised by her presence. Resentful of her riding in like Sir Galahad to save the day. I remove the photo from my inside pocket and stare at Jonah's faraway eyes. This is for him, all else follows.

Valetta is the next to arrive, wheeling a hand-luggage-sized suitcase, and within ten minutes there are six of us crammed into a cupboard of a meeting room. The airless space and the body heat is making me sweat and – after the night's exertions – I'm conscious that a few more pound coins could come my way if I stand by Holborn station during evening rush hour.

'The first good news is the judge,' Valetta says from the head of the table. 'She's generally sympathetic. I've come across her before and she takes a dim view of a lack of preparation.'

'There's more good news?' I ask.

'The local authority's brief, De Vries. He's South African – easily riled. Your basic arse.' She leans forward in her chair and stares me down. If this were a rugby match she'd be an All Black performing the haka.

'Listen, Ben, Emma, you are going to hear some things today from the opposing side that will upset you, things that you believe to be false and things that you know for certain are false. Whatever happens, and I mean *whatever*, do not react – don't grimace, gesticulate, get up from your chair, and do not interject or interrupt. That is my job. Do you understand?'

I nod.

'We have a good case. I don't like to lose.'

'But we'll have a chance to say something, won't we?' I ask.

'Yes, the judge will invite you and Emma to talk about Jonah at the end of the proceedings.'

I glance at Emma, she is looking down. A hundred thoughts of what she'll say are vying for my attention. I instinctively reach for the typewritten sheets in my inside pocket, words that I have sweated over late at night for weeks. I hate what I've written, how can I claim to know so much? What right do I have to deliver them? If only he could—

There is a knock at the door.

'Okay, that's two minutes. Does everyone have the paperwork in order? Good, then let's go.' She suddenly stops. 'Oh, Ben, how is your father?'

I can't find anything to say as I step into a mystery future.

IN THE FIRST TIER TRIBUNAL
SPECIAL EDUCATIONAL NEEDS & DISABILITY

Between

(1) **BENJAMIN JEWELL**
(2) **EMMA JEWELL**
Appellants

and

WYNCHGATE COUNCIL
Respondent

Attendance

Ms Valetta Price, barrister, represented Mrs Jewell and Mr Jewell – who attended the hearing. Their witnesses are Ms Anne Birch, independent Educational Psychologist, Ms Claudia Lack, independent Speech and Language Therapist, Ms Jennifer Smart, independent Occupational Therapist and Mr Hugh Challoner, Chief Executive and Principal of Highgrove Manor School, observing.

Mr Francis De Vries, barrister, represented the LA. Its witnesses are Dr Anita Kaur, LA Educational Psychologist, Mr Donald Davies, Deputy Manager Social Services, and Ms Claire McDonald, NHS Highly Specialist Speech and Language Therapist.

I sit behind the main players with my head against the wall, trying to stay awake, the fatigue partly from last night's trauma and partly in anticipation of the traumas to come – both in this utilitarian room and the one that holds my father a few miles away, awaiting his own judgement.

> JUDGE: *Good morning, everyone. As you are all aware, we are here not just to hear evidence of two opposing sides, but to decide the future of a young man called Jonah Jewell.*
>
> *It should also be noted that Mr Georg Jewell, Jonah's grandfather, is currently in Hampstead Hospice where he is in the late stages of cancer. My sympathy, Mr Jewell.*

All these months of work and I just can't stay awake. My chin keeps falling to my chest. I can blame the tiredness on last night, but something else is dragging my mind away from these proceedings.

Those hidden vodka miniatures and the need for more take me back almost twelve years, pre-Jonah, to a memory of lacerating humiliation.

A hand gripped me hard beneath the armpit and pulled me violently from my swivel chair before my heart or eyes or brain had accepted I was awake. Dissonant violins struck up. The floor was cotton wool. I desperately needed to defecate. I was vaguely aware of people standing open-mouthed – some shocked, some wearing the smiling mask of schadenfreude.

> DE VRIES, opposing barrister: *It is the LA's view that it is in Jonah's interests to transfer with his peers to Maureen Mitchell*

and for his care package, which is already substantial, to continue.

The LA is opposing the parents' appeal in relation to Part 4 because it considers the parents' choice of school represents unreasonable public expenditure.

It is the LA's view that Maureen Mitchell School can meet Jonah's needs and the LA does not feel that it should fund a significantly more expensive placement elsewhere.

Unreasonable public expenditure? So it's really all about money then, nothing to do with what's best for Jonah. At least, finally, someone's got the balls to admit what this is really all about.

A second hand hooked my other armpit. I would have run but my legs felt stripped of bone and cartilage and I was dragged, toes scraping the carpet, through parallel lines of suited people in a parody of a wedding party – no confetti or claps, just gasps and sighs.

Then I was in a lift, the doors closed. My escorts remained silent. The sound of my heart caught in my ears, my mind was a washing machine. Ideas, tossed and turned, twisted back on themselves, crazy, insignificant details – I'd left my laptop open, my jacket was over my chair. The lift dropped to the basement, my stomach stayed on the third floor. I felt fingers dig into the soft flesh of my upper arm. My ear began aching again – I had had an ear infection for weeks that wouldn't shift – I felt it weeping, mingling with the sweat running from my head. I could smell myself. Acrid. Rotten. Different to the sweet sweat of exertion – it was the smell of fear.

The lift ride went on forever. Chris de Burgh piped from the tinny speakers. My mind hummed the funeral march.

The lift juddered to a halt and the doors screeched open. We were in the basement, below ground. I thought I was in Hell.

'What are you going to do to me? What have I done?' My voice sounded monotone, lifeless, haunted like the voices of those downed RAF pilots captured by the Iraqis and made to confess on TV like Thunderbird puppets.

There was silence as I was led through a metal door and out into the blazing sunlight. I squinted, my eyes blinded, but when the macabre dance finally stopped and the flashes began to fade, I made out the grubby form of my company Mondeo and the guillotine dropped. Alec stood next to my open driver's door clutching a roll of black bin bags.

The grip was released as I was thrust forward and dropped to my knees in front of him.

Alec stared down at me and handed me the bin bags.

'Clean it out, you fucking piss artist.'

The others left as Alec stood over me, his foppish blond hair glistening in the sunshine.

'Count them in,' he demanded.

I started counting in my head.

'No. Out loud.'

I pulled my hands through the piles of bottles festering in the foot wells, scraped the door pockets for miniatures and empty fag packets.

'Thirty-two, thirty-three... sixty-seven.'

DR KAUR, borough psychologist: *Staff reported that Jonah's self-help skills have improved. He is now able to dress and undress himself for activities in school, such as swimming.*

Jonah is able to indicate that he needs the toilet by standing

*near the toilet entrance and is developing his ability to exchange
a toilet photograph to make this request.*

Which child has she been observing? Sure, he can strip off, but
he can't even put his boxer shorts on by himself, and as for the
toilet bollocks . . .

The inside of the car was clear.

*'Now the boot.' Alec handed me another bin bag and peered
over my shoulder as I leant into the boot. It was full to bursting
with half- and full-sized bottles.*

'Keep counting. I want to know the exact tally.'

*My tears fell heavily, mixing with the discharge from my ear
and the vinegary remnants that leaked on to my shirt and trousers as I continued this humiliating ritual.*

*'One hundred and twenty, one hundred and twenty-one, one
hundred and twenty-two, one hundred and twenty-three, one
hundred and twenty-four, one hundred and twenty-five, one
hundred and twenty-six.'*

*I pulled myself up using the bumper for purchase. Six black
bin bags sat neatly against the side of my car. Alec tied knots in
the top.*

'That's the lot,' I wheezed, puffing from the exertion.

*'Now carry them up to the skip. You'll need to make more than
one trip, I reckon.'*

*It took me three trips to get the six bags the hundred yards
to the office's rubbish skip. The journey took me past banks of
windows. In each, voyeuristic colleagues jostled for space, like
rubberneckers catching a glimpse of a dead body at a motorway
pile-up.*

BIRCH, EdPsych: *Jonah was not able to point to objects in response to complex questions, e.g., 'Which one do we drink?'*

Or anything else preceded by which, why, where or when or how. These kind of statements are so obvious, so simple and so devastating. Surely the judge will understand that the LA is talking bullshit?

I smelled my hands, they reeked of stale wine and beer. My face was smeared with dirty tears, my shirt and trousers stained, and all I could think about was Emma's pitying face and the month's impending mortgage arrears.

'O'Brien wants you on the tenth floor soon. You can't leave the building or attempt to go near your car,' Alec instructed me.

I was held in the emergency stairwell for twenty minutes as Alec stood silently guarding me. Did he think I was going to run? I smoked frantically.

Alec was just the chaperone, the leg-shagger. O'Brien would do the damage, all six foot five inches of him. But the fear of this brute was nothing to the fear of Emma. I needed to dream up a deception to excuse myself from losing a £30,000-a-year job and everything that went with it.

The twenty minutes felt like an hour. The stairwell was a grey concrete funnel. I looked over the banister, instantly imposing vertigo on my already spinning head. Was I looking to leap? I counted the number of metal balustrades, imagining how many times my head would crack into each before I finally ended it all with a crunch . . .

PRICE: *It is interesting, when looking at Mr Hatton's report in 2003 I see he described Jonah's self-help skills as being very much different between home and school and stated: 'This seems to vary from home to school, depending on how much he can get away with being lazy. Perhaps for similar reasons, Jonah is not yet toilet trained.' Eight years later it seems clear that this is not a result of laziness.*

Laziness? How stupid does that sound now? That bastard condemned him – and us – in 2003 with his nonsense. He was supposed to be the borough's leading child psychologist. Maybe if he'd have listened, and yet, at that moment, I so wanted him to be right, Jonah was just lazy, like me . . .

These words are Chinese water torture – drip, drip, dripping on my head. I begin listing stops on the Piccadilly Line, Cockfosters, Oakwood, Southgate, Arnos Grove; I scrabble for memories of a Mauritian beach – Emma next to me, pert and shining with sweat. But this is not a local-anaesthetic situation, this calls for a general. I want to wake up when it's over and scream for water and strong painkillers.

'GET IN HERE NOW,' O'Brien bellowed.

I hated being shouted at, anything but that. Punch me, knife me, just don't shout.

But O'Brien was in his element. He had the floor to himself. A horseshoe of desks where he'd browbeat underlings, reduce them to tears. A vast empty space where he paced while on the phone and when angry.

And he was angry then. I prepared to tell him anything, every-thing. I wanted his sympathy. I needed to live past those next few minutes. I needed, I needed, I needed a drink.

And then it came.

'I GET CALLED BACK FOR THIS, BEN. I'VE A HUNDRED

MILLION THINGS TO DO AND I GET CALLED BACK BY ALEC TO DEAL WITH A FUCKING DRUNKARD.'

'I'm sorry,' I muttered, staring at the floor.

I couldn't help myself any more and my legs gave way. I didn't mean to kneel at his feet.

'GET UP. YOU'RE PATHETIC,' he snorted.

But I couldn't move, I was frozen and I was pathetic, it was true. And then I begged: 'O'Brien, please, please don't fire me. I've just been going through a bad time, things are tough at home, my medication's gone haywire, I'll go back to the doctor, I promise. It won't happen again, just please don't fire me! I need this job.'

He paused. The silence was almost worse than the bawling. People claimed that they aged under pressure, went grey, grew lines on their face. But the opposite was true of me. I regressed, shrank, cowered. I was twenty-six at 8.30 that morning. By then I was no more than eleven.

'Ben, I like you. Everyone likes you here. I'll give you one more chance.' His tone was quieter, almost conciliatory. 'I want you to stand in front of me now and admit to me that you're an alcoholic. I want you to say "My name is Ben and I'm an alcoholic." Say it now, go on, "My name is Ben and I'm an alcoholic." '

'My name is Ben and I'm an alcoholic,' I lied. Maybe that was the end? Maybe that was it? Tell him what he wanted to hear, tell him it would never happen again and I'd escape.

'Look, these are my terms. I want you to go to Alcoholics Anonymous and I want proof that you're going.'

'But how am I supposed to prove it to you when the thing's supposed to be anonymous?' It was my final gambit. I couldn't go to Alcoholics Anonymous even if I had wanted to because I'd have had to explain it to Emma.

'There's sponsors or something. Get him to sign a letter, take a photo – I don't care.'

As if by magic, Alec appeared beside O'Brien, clutching in his hand a bottle of wine, Cloudy Bay – my Cloudy Bay! Alec whispered in O'Brien's ear and they laughed...

BIRCH: *Dr De Rossi, Consultant Child and Adolescent Psychiatrist, noted in a letter dated 22 October 2009: his behaviour was increasingly difficult to manage, including significant self-harming, biting his hands, causing them to bleed, bruising on his legs, stripping himself naked and frequent mood changes, from laughing for no reason to head banging or biting himself. He also tried to strangle his parents.*

God, that was the beginning of the end. Those horrible months when every day we'd wait for the tales from school of Jonah's metamorphosis into a wild animal. It was heartbreaking watching him bruise and batter himself. All I could do was drink to numb myself. It just got worse and worse – the rage of not being able to help, the horrible decision we had to face. It was time we looked for a residential school.

... And then I had a vision of the two of them, O'Brien and Alec, sharing my thirty-pound bottle of Cloudy Bay, draining it while they laughed at my predicament, and suddenly my fear and humiliation – so complete and genuine moments before – was displaced in an instant by righteous indignation and anger.

And the revelations of that past hour – all the admissions, pledges, shows of regret and apology, and any hint of damned gratitude – passed and it became as clear as day what was going on there, what the charade, the injustice and travesty's purpose was. O'Brien wanted to subjugate me further, he wanted me as his gimp, to do his bidding, to draw out and display whenever he felt it necessary to boost his own flagging ego. And even worse: that monstrous man, that bully, that hypocrite, wanted to save me! Me! He wanted to save me and use me as an example. Tell people how he, O'Brien, master businessman and paragon of compassion, had taken that poor broken, alcohol-sodden soul and saved him. Saved his life, his job and his family. Well fuck that and fuck him, I thought. He was one of the reasons I needed to drink in the first place. I was incandescent. If anyone was going to save me it was fucking well going to be me!

And so after banging in my resignation, I repeated this mantra all the way home on the bus. I was going to save myself, no other arrogant bastard was going to take the credit, I'd show them all who was in charge and I'd do it my way. I'd stop drinking my way – just not then.

In the time it took me to walk from the bus stop to the off licence I was King of the Fucking Universe again and bought half a bottle of cheap vodka as a big fuck you to both of them. The bottle was already waiting in a bag as I walked through the door.

I necked half of it during the remaining hundred-metre walk and hid the rest in my laptop bag, then – suitably armoured – I put my key in the door, fixed the smile on my face and stepped confidently into my other life – jobless, hopeless, but reassuringly pissed . . .

It is our contention that the LA in this case fundamentally ignored the deteriorating situation within the Jewell family until it became clear that they intended to appeal to this tribunal.

And then the agonies carried on for us and we stopped communicating, everything between Emma and me laden with stress and anxiety.

. . . I moved to the bedroom doorway and watched her apply makeup in her dressing table mirror.

'You going out?'

'Yes, you'll be pleased to hear,' she said, without turning round. 'I'm seeing Amanda, so you'll have to make something for yourself. Please don't make a mess and don't drink too much. I want you up early – or have you forgotten that as well?'

'No, I haven't forgotten,' I lied. How could I forget the mechanics of procreation?

I peered through a crack in the net curtains to make sure she'd gone. I watched the heavily financed four-wheel-drive's headlights disappear down the road and waited for the indicator to stop flashing before I retrieved the remainder of the bottle and plummeted on to the sofa, finally alone. The silence was soothing. But then I remembered the horrors of the day and I thought about the following one. It hadn't occurred to me to own up, or even to lie about redundancy, or other legitimate reasons for not going to work. It seemed I'd drunk away my capacity to tell the truth, as if all the barriers against deceit, depravity and normal human behaviour were fizzing and dissolving away, leaving no defence against a debilitating, slow death-by-shame.

There was just enough left in the bottle to stain my lips. Before I knew it, I was outside, sprinting. Arms pumped like pistons, feet hammered the pavement, faster and faster, until the neon of Regal Wines rose out of the gloom like Las Vegas from the surrounding desert.

I burst through the door and joined the queue. A verbal battle was ensuing – chardonnay versus sauvignon blanc. Just fucking get on with it! I remembered my confiscated bottle of Cloudy Bay and the anxiety returned, little needles piercing my scalp. The wine conversation was finally over and the Indian man whose name I did not know, but who knew me better than anyone alive, stared at my feet. I looked down. Just socks. I looked back at him and shrugged. He didn't smile at me, just shook his head and passed me another bottle of vodka. I held the money in my hand, but he indicated I should drop it on the counter, which I did. He took an envelope from beside the cash register and swept it up.

DE VRIES: *Value for money, Miss Price . . .*

PRICE: *But we're not comparing brands of washing-up liquid. How can the LA, Mr De Vries, not blush when suggesting other-wise. It has tacitly admitted as much by introducing The Sunrise Academy at such a late stage in the proceedings, despite having had two years now to engage with the family on the matter. My clients find it cynical in the extreme.*

And I can't forget how things were before Jonah. I just wasn't ready to be a father, I was too ill, too fucked up, I was spending every night till two, three in the morning trying to dissolve the anxiety in alcohol. How could I be a father in this state? The alcohol fuelling the fear and vice versa.

I settled down to watch a DVD – beached on a sofa I was still paying for – bottle of vodka perched on my chest, favourite film playing over and over again because I passed out periodically and kept missing crucial bits. I was unnerved by the prospect of leaving the house the next morning with absolutely no idea of where to go for eight hours, or how to lie my way into another job soon enough for the whole sorry mess to have remained a secret. But first, the trauma of the alarm call needed to be negotiated and I feared there would be no escape from that.

It was 2 a.m. and I was drinking a can of 7-Up in the kitchen. My eyeballs had turned to beach pebbles after crawling into bed at midnight. It was almost worth the dehydration just to have felt the relief as my eyes plumped up, moist and taut like shrivelled tomatoes dropped in ice water.

Our bed was king-sized. Emma slept on the left, on her left side, her back to me. I mirrored her to the right. I always waited until she was asleep before I came to bed.

It was 4 a.m. and I lay with my arms behind my head listening to Emma's snoring. It was funny, sometimes the alcohol sedated me almost into coma territory, but that night I couldn't even buy a yawn. The curtains in our bedroom were inherited from the previous owners and they didn't quite fit, so a shaft of streetlight divided our bed in half almost perfectly down the centre. It was like a James Bond-style laser and I fantasised about gently placing Emma's arm across its beam, the burning smell of flesh as it cut a perfect incision. Then my imaginings wandered to me. Maybe I could have used it to perform a vasectomy? Cutting off Emma at the pass, so to speak.

I couldn't wait to get out of bed and out of the house again, but as the clock ticked ominously toward six and Capital Radio began to caress my ears, I detected a staccato quality to her breathing. She roused, edged her backside towards me in the bed and I felt myself shrink back further toward my side, as the duvet rustled and she removed her underwear and dropped it to the floor. I wanted to scream. I was screaming in my head. It was the scream of despair from The Deerhunter, when Robert De Niro tried in vain to plug the bullet hole in Christopher Walken's temple. It was the result of his promised last shot in a game of Russian Roulette. I hoped my chamber was empty.

Then I removed my boxer shorts and searched my memory for an image, an encounter – however fleeting – anything that would have provided me with the means to fulfil that service. I moved my hand down to my groin and took hold of myself. I squeezed and pulled in desperation, but there was no reaction. I removed my mind from the room and searched back five years, ten years and the first stirrings, the smallest sensations began to work their way from my brain to my groin and I finally began to swell.

I was with Michelle. We were seventeen, lying on my bed in my parents' house. We were friends, but there had always been an attraction and then somehow, without warning, she was on top of me and my hands were under her green dress, we were dry humping, my hands had found her breasts. I had admired them for so long, masturbated at the thought of them nightly and suddenly they were in my hands and they were much softer than I had imagined and her nipples were small – two five-pence pieces – and pointed.

And I pushed my torso towards Emma's backside, pulling my legs and chest back from her so that the only contact was between my daydreaming penis and her dryness. I spat on my hand and wiped it on the end of my cock and pushed and pushed until I was inside and then it was Michelle, on all fours, the curve of her buttocks in my hands, and I was driving and thrusting, my heart pumping until I came and started crying and the illusion shattered and Michelle disappeared and I pulled away, clawing for the side of the bed and escape. I felt sick as I watched Emma prop herself up on her elbows with her legs above her head, businesslike and oblivious – she seemed relentless in her pursuit *of a fertilised egg, while I prayed that the alcohol had damaged my sperm beyond repair.*

I was in the bathroom, naked in front of the full-length mirror. God, I was a sight to behold. My eyes were bloodshot, whether through drinking or crying, I didn't know.

BIRCH: *Small time-out rooms are used both at Roysten Glen and Maureen Mitchell and provide an outlet for Jonah when his levels of anxiety increase. These facilities are not readily available at The Sunrise Academy and, it seems, the strategy is perceived by Dr Makarova as a punishment.*

Punishment? Yes, maybe this is my punishment for not wanting to be a father. Jonah's autism, my failed marriage.

My urine was the colour of cola and stung and I had pain where I thought my kidneys were. A sickly-sweet odour rose from the toilet. I had heard of ketones. I wondered if I had diabetes.

The shower was mercifully hot and I leant my forehead against the tiled wall as the water cascaded over my head and down my back. There was a banging on the door.

'Ben, open the door, I need to use the toilet.'

'I'll be five minutes,' I shouted, above the noise of the shower.

'Come on, I'm bursting.'

Irritated, I jumped from the shower and pulled back the lock. I returned to the shower as she seated herself at the toilet.

'I thought you were supposed to be in the bicycle position?' I said, in a tone edged in mockery.

According to Lisa, Emma's permanently pregnant friend, lying on your back and doing bicycles for twenty minutes increased the chances of fertilisation by fifty per cent. I wondered whether the introduction of alcohol and anti-depressants had a bearing on that marvellous piece of scientific data. I suspected it did, not that I shared on the subject.

In the kitchen, a Russian coffee steamed my eyes open while I worked out my timings – when to leave, when to get back, lunchtime phone call. I checked my watch – it was seven. I thought I could leave. I drained the rest of my coffee.

'I'm going. Have to get the bus, remember?'

'Can't they give you another company car? How long is it going to take?'

'I don't know, couple of weeks?' I said, buying some time.

Emma looked up from her mug of tea and I saw her bottom lip begin to quiver.

How do people cope with living together? How do they negotiate the minefield? I realise I have no memories at all of living in tranquillity, even as a child.

My parents' house – that unchanged fleapit. Sat in the lounge, on the floor, watching the test card. My school uniform was still damp from the walk home in the fading daylight, my belly grumbled from the spaghetti coated in butter and black pepper. I was what? Nine? He was home, I heard the front door slam and the muttered curses and the growled 'Myra!'

She was in the bath, with the Scotch and American I had mixed her. I could hear the radio and her tuneless accompaniment. And then the shouting started, the cat and the lion. I was inured to that muzak. *It was usual, expected, banal. But then the pitch changed and the cat began to scream and cry and it beckoned me up the stairs to the bathroom and the sight of my father with* balled-up fists and my mother screaming and splashing as water crashed over the sides and soaked the lino.

'Go to bed!' he screamed and I was caught between my own fear and my mother's.

'Bed, Benjamin.'

Her whisky was on her bedside table, oily and sweet, so I drained it as I'd seen her do a thousand times. My throat burnt, but my fear dissolved in the heat and my bed was suddenly a haven of peace, the clattering and banging went on around me but I was transported.

He left with another attack on the front door and the calm extended like drifting incense. Then she was in my room, towel-clad and whimpering. She sat on the edge of my bed with her hand clamped around my wrist.

'You understand me, Benny, don't you? We are like two peas in a pod, you and I.'

'Yes, Mum,' I replied, with a mixture of pride and revulsion.

'Good. Then go downstairs and mix Mummy one of her special drinks.'

I did this, but before I poured out the rehearsed two fingers, I slugged from the bottle myself.

I never knew for certain what the arguments were about, but could they have been about anything other than me? Later that night, lying drunk in the darkness, I vowed to be better, to do whatever it took to make her happy.

BIRCH: *Using the early-years assessment from BASII, Jonah was able to demonstrate some skills.*
Verbal ability (nine months)
Block building (developmental age of two and a half years)
Nine-piece puzzle (two and a half to three years)

Copying task he merely scribbled randomly (eighteen months to two years)

By any measure, my son is still a toddler and they argue that more of the same will help him? He needs something different! More support, more recognition, more encouragement, less stress. Look what it's done for him so far ...

When I was eleven, I raced home from school with my report, the first from my new secondary school. It was a column of As – not a single blemish, perfect. 'Benjamin is a credit to himself and the school,' the headmaster had written at the bottom. I burst through the door: 'Mum, Mum?' It was my dad sitting with the Daily Mirror *on his lap.*

'Where's Mum?' I asked.

'She has gone, Benjamin. Now it is just us.'

'Gone where?'

'Ask her, she will call you at seven.'

I sat by the telephone for three hours. Then I ran to the garden and set my report alight with a match.

Emma phoned me at eleven and I scooted from the bar in Euston station.

'Ben, I'm pregnant. We're going to have a baby!'

I didn't feel joy, just relief and fear. Relief that the sex could then finally revert to the pastime of abandon it once was; fear at the prospect of going home and admitting my job loss and tube-riding fortnight. My feigned surprise and delight gave me cramp. What choice did I have? So I phoned him. 'Dad, I need to talk, can I come to the warehouse?' He said yes and I drove straight there.

The steam and the noise from the industrial washer set my teeth on edge. My father stood opposite Valentine as they polished glasses in perfect sync. Neither looked up.

'What's so important?'

'I need to talk to you.'

'That much you said, so?'

'Can we go to the pub?'

Valentine kissed his teeth and Dad checked his watch.

'Half an hour...'

One pint downed and one in front of me.

'I want to come and work with you.' He left me to fester in the silence, while he cracked his knuckles.

'You want to work for me all of a sudden? Why now, after all these years? What have you done?'

'You keep saying that it's getting too much for you.'

'You honour me with your concern...'

'Dad. Emma's pregnant, you're going to be a grandfather.'

'Have you told your mother?'

'No, I'm telling you. I need the stability, Dad, I need to provide properly.'

'Emma provides, stay at home and look after my grandchild. That is what this is about – all of a sudden you're too proud. What's wrong with the job you have?'

'It's not pride, it's responsibility. I'm just not earning enough yet.'

'And whose fault is that? You too would have a stable profession like Emma if you had only applied yourself.'

'Okay, fine, forget it.' But I knew I had to swallow that, it was the price of his patronage, the hard lessons he predicted. I stood still, with my head down.

'Why should I rescue you?'

I could have given him a million reasons. 'Because I need you?'

'Because you need my money, as ever. I need to get back, come over tonight at seven and we'll discuss it.'

'So that's a yes?'

'Come over, do not forget, and congratulate Emma for me.'

The phone wouldn't stop ringing and it was only eight-thirty in the morning. I sat there, fending people off, when my mobile rang and flashed 'Valentine'.

'Van's broken down.'

'What do you mean, broken down?'

'Dead, nothing.'

'Where are you?'

'Southbank.'

I felt the lack of sleep and anxiety rush to my tear ducts. I let the phone drop to the desk.

'Pull yourself together, Benjamin.'

'But Dad . . .'

'How will this help?'

'All these Christmas orders . . .'

'Stop crying, please. Always I have to wipe your nose.'

LACK, Speech Therapist: *Jonah began using words at a year and eleven months, but these were sporadic, and then lost his speech when he was around two and a half years. Jonah never progressed to using sentences.*

Why? It just keeps haunting me, why, once he'd started, did he just stop? Could we have done any more?

Tom and Jonah sat side by side in the bath, bubbles so thick and high that only their heads were visible. 'Peter Pan, Peter Pan,' Tom shouted, raising his hands to Johnny.

We lifted both boys out of the bath, their chubby, two-year-old bodies glistened with water. The towel wrapped around Jonah radiated warmth, his head smelled of baby shampoo. Emma and Amanda reached the top of the stairs carrying coffee.

'Peter Pan, Peter Pan,' Tom cried again, and Johnny unwrapped him, gripped him around the waist and started flying him round the landing, crying high and loud: 'Peeeder, Peeeder, Peeeder...' Tom laughed and, by my feet, Jonah laughed too and stretched his arms out toward Johnny.

Amanda took Tom in her arms. 'Johnny, look, Jonah wants a go, do it with Jonah.' Johnny was about to pick Jonah up when Emma stepped in.

'No. Make him say it before you do it, Johnny. Make him say Peeeder.'

'Come on, Emma, that's cruel, look at him,' I said. Jonah was more desperate than ever. Emma crouched on the floor with him. 'We've got to push him, Ben. It's the only way.'

And she began to call to him: 'Come on, Jonah, if you want to do it, say Peeeder, come on, Peeeder, Peeeder, Peeeder.'

I hated it. Jonah bounced up and down on his backside and Emma wouldn't let it go. I was about to intervene when a shrill cry filled the air.

'Peeeder, Peeeder, Peeeder.' It was Jonah, and the words were not just identifiable, they were pitch perfect, tone perfect like a recording of Emma's version. We all looked at each other, stunned. Johnny picked him up and flew him round, crying Peeeder himself. Jonah had said a few words before – bubble, door – but that was months earlier and we had begun to question whether he'd really said them at all. But this felt different, like a spiritual moment, an awakening. The evening was a joyous one, full of laughter, hope and relief. The breakthrough had come and we went to bed happy.

It was the last word he ever spoke.

BIRCH: *Jonah has a diagnosis of ASD, but, in my view, this does not convey the severity of his condition and it should be noted that he is at the most severe end of the Spectrum and, as such, falls within the small range of children displaying complex ASD.*

And then it just got worse and worse and worse. No words, no eye contact, no bodily control, no physical affection . . .

I watched him play inside the plastic Wendy house, opening and shutting the windows, through the door, round the back and in again, back to the windows. Emma chewed her nails, crossed and uncrossed her legs. The door opened and we were called in. I called Jonah, but he ignored me. I put my head through the Wendy house window and tickled his tummy. Finally, he took my hand and allowed himself to be led into the office. He started flapping his hands as if he'd been engulfed by a cloud of midges.

The consultant was small behind his desk, near to retirement, his accent sing-song Indian.

'So, you must be Jonah?'

Jonah ignored him.

'And how old are you, Jonah?'

'He's two and a half,' Emma said.

'No language at all?'

'He had some, maybe forty words or so.'

More like six, I thought.

'But he just stopped using them.'

'How long has it been since he spoke?'

We looked at each other, Emma answered. 'A year, maybe.'

The consultant made some notes. Jonah was fighting to get off my lap.

'I have the report from his school. I have also observed Jonah on two occasions.'

We didn't know this.

'Mr and Mrs Jewell, all the indicators suggest strongly that Jonah is autistic.'

'But he had words, he had words.'

'This is common among autistic children, Mrs Jewell.'

I watched her eyes redden, but I felt calm, somehow, like I'd already known.

'But why? Why?'

The consultant scanned some more paperwork and looked up at me.

'You have an alcohol problem?'

'Had,' I said.

'But you were drinking heavily around the time of conception?'

'Yes, I suppose so.'

'You are aware that this could have caused Jonah's autism?'

Could have. God knows I'd trawled the internet until the Google logo was burnt on to my corneas and couldn't find any evidence that it was my fault. But despite that, after hearing someone say my worst fear out loud, I walked from the office overcome by shameful tears.

Minutes later, Emma and Jonah followed me out. I watched

her as she picked Jonah up and marched to the lift. She couldn't bring herself to look at me.

PRICE: *Mrs Jewell was out with Jonah on Sunday 5 June last year and experienced the worst, most aggressive public outburst she had seen from Jonah since Christmas the previous year. Lasting approximately twenty minutes, Jonah attacked her and two strangers (who tried to help) as well as self-harming. The key point here, according to Mrs Jewell, is the suddenness of this meltdown – 'although he had clearly not been in the best of moods for a few days prior' – as well as the severity of the aggression. It shook her terribly and left her in no doubt that she could no longer manage these outbursts on her own in public owing to Jonah's size and strength.*

What's going to happen when he's older? When he's too big for even me to handle. Will he kill someone? Maim them? What happens when I'm dead? Where will he go ... ?

'Don't come back until five,' Emma had said.

I'd been driving for forty minutes and I had an hour left. We'd been to the park, we'd been to McDonald's, we'd been back to the park, back to McDonald's. I had a Costcutter bag on the passenger seat. Contents: ten apples, six bags of Quavers, a loaf of white bread, eight tubes of Smarties, a large bag of Minstrels, a bottle of water, forty Camel Blue and half a bottle of vodka for luck.

My left leg was cramping from the incessant clutch use, so I pulled over – careful to ensure I was not overlooked by a house. Then I spun the bottle lid and drank. In the back, six-year-old Jonah pulled apart the feather duster I had bought. I had given up feeding him individual Smarties and he had emptied the tube beside him on the seat; he banged on the sprung cloth like a bongoist and the bright tablets jumped up and down in time.

How long would I get? Two minutes, ten? Thirty, sixty? Each movement, each exclamation made me flinch. I tossed food back at him like a zookeeper feeding a lion. I dropped the window and felt my face spotted by rain. I lit a cigarette and furtively took another swig while the digital clock flashed the seconds and the radio banged on about Manchester United.

My God. It. Was. Hard. How could I explain it to anyone? The feeling of utter failure, the battle that raged in my head between love and desolation. I could abuse him like that because he couldn't tell anyone. I could sit in my car inhabiting a different universe, not engaging with him and dreaming of solitude and the end of fear, because he was locked away elsewhere and knew no better. We would arrive back home at the appointed hour and I'd make up some drivel about how great a time we had, list the places and activities encountered, how good he had been, and he couldn't contradict me.

What did that make me? A bad father or a prison-camp guard? A fantasist or a simple liar?

He started to laugh and bounce on his seat – this might have given me another ten minutes, or his mood could have changed in three. It was the constant uncertainty, the unpredictability. It was the way I felt when I walked past a pit bull terrier on the street or in the park, primed for an expected attack.

But Jonah wasn't an animal. This was a vodka conversation, self-pity and self-loathing all wrapped up in one easily breakable package.

Thirty minutes left. I would start up when there were ten.

My phone rang: 'Could you make it six?' she said.

'No problem,' I said – although it was, I knew it was, but the words were out before I had a chance to think. It was always like that, I was unable to say no, then I was cursing Emma, and myself, for being so weak.

An hour and thirty minutes was left. Too long to drive, too long to sit. I flicked through the contacts on my phone; was there anyone I felt comfortable just dropping in on? My father? Johnny? I'd try Johnny. My finger hovered over the call button, then my heart thumped as I pressed it and it rang. I was just about to hang up when he answered.

'Sorry, mate, you should have called earlier, we're off to the cinema. Why don't you meet us there?'

Then I cursed Johnny too. Didn't he realise? Jonah wouldn't sit in the cinema. I was as lonely as I'd ever been, with just a silent boy and a bottle of vodka for company.

'We are not wanted, sweet boy,' I told him. I couldn't face Dad because he'd guess why I was there. He'd shame me more than I'd shame myself. He'd smell the vodka.

And then I felt his fingernails in my neck and I cried in pain. Jonah's eyes were glowing, he took another swipe. I grabbed his wrist and squeezed harder than I needed.

'Will you just fuck off and leave me alone!'

Tears erupted from his eyes and mine caught on like a yawn. Where could we go from there?

PRICE: *If it pleases the tribunal, Mrs Emma Jewell would like to address the tribunal.*

Oh.

Emma stands and opens the leather-bound folder in front of her. I have never seen her in action before. In all these years I have never once visited her at her offices, met her colleagues, joined her at functions. This Emma is a stranger to me. She is tall and elegant and poised. I do not recognise the line of her lips or her eyes as they cast around for an audience. They alight on me briefly and in that instant I believe I know how it must feel to be prosecuted by her. She holds it within her power to flay me, she always has, but now I feel that she will expose me. I cannot show my face. I bury it in my hands and await the knife as she coughs and closes her folder. I anticipate the words she delivers now will pierce my carefully constructed stoicism. There it is again, *words*. If nothing else, I have come to this moment of clarity: I fear words more than anything. I can find whatever meaning in them I wish, twist them for my own purposes, beat myself up with them, use them as an excuse to drink, to rage against the world, to withdraw from the world. If only others would use the words I want to hear, I'd be happy – but there's as much chance of me successfully willing Jonah to speak as there is of Emma or my father speaking the words I feel I need. Even if, by some miracle, Dad expresses remorse for my shitty childhood, or Emma begs me to take her back, I would find alternative motives for their words. But, just by looking me straight in the eyes, or inviting some physical contact, in a moment Jonah informs me of his true feeling without words and I believe him. Words become meaningless if you don't tell your truth and they become weapons if you try to tell someone else theirs. Through his silence, Jonah allows me to listen to him – there is no wall of words to clamber over, no self-defence of the reality of him. I need to follow his example; silence will allow me to evade the internal clamour for regret and retribution. As Emma clears her throat, I try to clear my head.

'Some of you may think harshly of me for leaving the care of my son to his father and grandfather, or for leaving my husband.

'I won't make any excuses, because I can't make you walk in my shoes any more than I can make you walk in Jonah's, all I can do is relate my story in so far as it relates to Jonah and Jonah's in so far as it relates to me.

'You have seen his picture, I know. He is beautiful. Everyone commented on it when he was born – and yes, I know that every new mother thinks her baby is the most beautiful baby ever born and that everyone tells her so, but with Jonah, with Jonah it was true. He looks like neither of us, Ben or me, he looks like himself; apart from his grandfather's amber eyes he is as individual as it is possible to be.

'When Jonah was born, one of my closest friends had a three-year-old boy who just would not talk. He was difficult, odd, his behaviour irritating and I'm ashamed to admit that I pitied her. Somehow – or at least that's what I believed at the time – she pulled him out of it, bullied him, demanded that he speak and he did. Slowly at first and then in great flowing sentences. I was in awe of her, sang her praises at every opportunity. He has Asperger's, is now sixteen, goes to a mainstream, selective school and is a virtuoso on the piano.

'It never occurred to me that I would follow her down the same path, but it happened. Jonah's early milestones were severely delayed, but I didn't panic – we put it down to him being top heavy, Ben and I, and laughed about it and made up rhymes about him: "He's fat, he's round, he must weigh fifty pounds, Jonah Jewell, Jonah Jewell."

'But it wasn't that at all.

'He wasn't talking and he wasn't walking, he wasn't playing with other children and I convinced myself he was shy.

'Then, when he was about two and a half, he forced out a word. Ben and I had reported words to each other before then,

233

but we were both lying to ourselves. But this was a word. My son's first word, the sound that lit up our world, was "bubble". In the bath, with us both present, Ben blew bubbles in the air for him to pop and as we both pressed the word on him, he repeated it. "Bubble," he said. "Bubble, bubble, bubble." And then everything was okay. "Bubble" was followed by "door" which was followed by a handful of other words and we were off and running.

'But it stopped as suddenly as it had started. Jonah would use a word, just once, and never use it again, however much I prompted him, pushed him, cajoled and withheld his favourite food. Then "bubble" disappeared and he was silent.

'This doesn't happen. Once you know a word, you know a word and then two and three. Once you know one, others follow, you build sentences, you speak, it's natural. I became desperate and Ben didn't. I don't know why he could accept it and I couldn't. But I resented him for it and started looking for causes. From which side of the family did this nightmare emanate? Was it the Jewells or the Carlins that carried this devastating gene?

'When Jonah started Northlea Nursery it was painfully obvious how different he was, but still I hoped. And the cruellest thing sometimes is hope.

'There he was described as "lazy" and "within the broad range of average intelligence". All hope – and when we had the big meeting, the statement meeting to decide just what was wrong with my beautiful son, the borough's educational psychologist was adamant that he didn't have autism, that he was just suffering from Global Delay. How cruel is that kind of hope. *Delay* – I hung on to that word like a life preserver. *Delay* – the very word meant that he would catch up, that at some stage he would reach his destination like everyone else, there were just leaves on the line. The real Jonah would arrive, I just had to be patient. Ben didn't agree. He wanted Autistic Spectrum Disorder on Jonah's statement, he argued endlessly at that meeting for the inclusion of the diagnosis that we had already obtained, but in my head as he argued I was screaming "No, no, I want him to be delayed. Shut up, you quitter."

'Ben finally won. I hated him for it, as if the inclusion of ASD on his statement confined Jonah to life's waiting room for ever. Ben had torn up his ticket.

'My son was now officially autistic and transferred to Roysten Glen, a special school. The phrase made me feel sick. I'd seen those minibuses with children staring blankly out of the windows and I'd look away, embarrassed. Disability made me uncomfortable. I cried the first morning one of those buses arrived to pick Jonah up.

'And yet still, in my mind, I thought, *he's delayed, he'll be at Roysten Glen for a year, they'll sort him out and he'll back at Northlea again*. But the minibus kept arriving day after day after day and, of course, he never went back.

'Then the charlatans started to arrive with their programmes and promises and hefty invoices, like some gang of venal, money-grabbing evangelists. False hope is an industry like any other. That was five years ago. I have watched my son grow from a beautiful silent baby, smelling of poo and baby shampoo, to a beautiful silent boy on the verge of adolescence, smelling of poo and baby shampoo.

'Towards the end of last year, the cogs finally slipped into place. Jonah is autistic, he will never speak. Being attacked, scratched and punched, having your home constantly smell of air freshener, acts as quite a truth serum. And after ten years of denial, resentment and quiet anger, I decided to fight for him and was told time and time again until I could take it no longer that really, he didn't matter. Essentially what we are being told is that there is an epidemic ravaging our children, but let's pretend that no treatment is available rather than spend the money on administering it.

'Do any of you know how it feels to know your child will never call you Mummy?

'I was never able to share any of this with Ben. Maybe that's the biggest irony of Jonah's condition. Not only has it robbed Jonah of the ability to talk and interact like a human is supposed to, but it has robbed those around him of the ability to admit their pain to each other.

'I love my son. Some may doubt it, but I do. I always want to be in his life.

'But I want others to take over the shame that I have felt for ten years and, mostly and simply, I want to watch my ten-year-old child wee on the toilet. Thank you for your time.'

I feel worthless. It's shameful that I never asked the right questions and never accepted her pain could be anything like my own. I had heard the shouting, seen the crying, but it repelled me. I heard, but I didn't listen; her words were just background noise, the shriek of seagulls over a waste dump, an incessant car alarm. Nothing else I say here now is going to add to Emma's powerful portrait of her life – our lives – with Jonah, and it may appear as a pitiful exercise in one-upmanship.

'Mr Jewell, would you like to add anything?' the judge asks.

I rise, self-consciously. I feel foolish and fraudulent. I must do him justice. This wonderful, exhausting, terrifying, vulnerable, beautiful son of mine. I clear my throat.

'Jonah does not have a voice, he cannot tell anyone what life truly feels like for him. So I must be his voice.' I pull the leaves of paper from my inside pocket.

'Apparently, my name is Jonah Jewell. I know this because they repeat the sounds when they're looking at me and I'm off somewhere investigating. Light fascinates me a lot, especially when it splits into colours and when it reflects off a leaf close to my eye.

'I don't really know what time is, but when there is no light for me to investigate, I like to play with the water and bubbles and float in the warmth until he, Dad, tells me it's time to get out. I don't always get out when he asks, but he sits and waits for me and when I step into a towel, he cuddles me and dries me and squeezes me tight. He does this, I think, because he knows that I like it and I think he likes it too, and if he doesn't do it, I feel anxious as if it is light again outside and everything is in the wrong order.

'When I'm dry, he lets me run into my bedroom and jump on my bed and he puts my music on. I know it's mine because it's always the same and it means everything's all right. Then he puts on my revolving fish-tank light and I lie down on my bed and watch the colours go round, which keeps me calm, and he takes the towel and dries my back. Sometimes – when I'm in the mood – he rubs my back and legs and bottom with his hand and sometimes it tickles and I laugh and then he laughs and I really like that. When I've had enough he gets a nappy and I lie on my back and push my bottom in the air so that he can slide it underneath me. Then he gets some cold white cream and smears it all around my willy and balls and the tops of my legs and around my bum which sometimes makes me laugh too. He does this, I know, because I wee and poo during the night and if he doesn't use the cream I get very sore, but I don't tell anyone. Then he puts my pyjamas on and I pull the duvet up to my chin and stare at my fish tank as he kisses me four times and turns the light off and I can finally disappear to wherever I want. This is my best time.

'When I see the light again I wake up and meet him in the room with the water and the bubbles. My nappy is heavy and I want it off and it's the first thing he does while filling up the water and bubbles again. Sometimes I wee and poo so much during the night that it leaks on to the bed which upsets him; and sometimes I push my hands into my nappy because it feels warm and squidgy and draw pictures on the walls with it and then he sometimes shouts at me. He cleans my bottom with lots and lots of wet tissues and puts me in the bath in the light. Then he dries me and dresses me quickly so I can go downstairs for Marmite toast and if there isn't any Marmite I throw the plate across the kitchen because I have Marmite toast for breakfast. I jump up and down and pull at his hand because I have Marmite toast for breakfast and then I grab at his face and hair because I have Marmite toast for breakfast and I won't let go so he opens the back door and forces me outside into the garden where I skip round and round screaming because I have Marmite toast for breakfast. Then the door opens and I run in and there is Marmite toast on the table so I sit and eat it because it's what I have for breakfast and he sits on the floor with his head in his hands.

'When I've finished my Marmite toast I pull grapes out of the fridge and eat them and roll them on the floor with my toes and squash them because I like the feeling of cold and stickiness and it's part of my breakfast, I think, because he sits on the floor with his head in his hands. After breakfast, he makes me sit on the toilet while I twiddle with a leaf I found on the floor and then he takes me off and puts another nappy on me and as soon as it's tight around me I feel it getting wet and warm. Then there is a ringing sound that means I'm going to the other place and he grabs my bag and opens the door and she is there smiling and takes my hand and we walk to the bus where I sit in my seat because it is always where I sit. There are others in other seats, but there are not two on a seat. One of them screams and it hurts my ears so I put my fingers in them.

'I know how the bus moves and follow its turns all the way, but it turns the wrong way which makes me confused and anxious because that's not the way the bus goes so I grab the hair of the girl in the seat in front and she cries out and grabs my hand and then he sits next to me and tries to pull my fingers apart but I don't like being touched and the bus is still going the wrong way, but then it's going the right way again, I can see the trees that the bus touches and I'm on the way to the other place again so I sit quietly and then get off the bus and go into my room which is my room because I go there during the light and it has a picture of me on the door.

'I get upset there a lot when someone makes me do something I don't want to do and then I smack my own head and bite my hand until I can feel it properly and when this happens someone carries me into a room by myself and leaves me there with a twiddly until I calm down. Sometimes they let me go outside, which is when I feel best because I can be by myself and find leaves and feathers and feel the wind on my face and this makes me laugh.

'If I want something, I can't just take it, I have to give someone a picture of the thing I want. But if I want it I just want it and I can see it so why can't I just have it? Sometimes I get the right picture but sometimes I get a picture and I still don't get what I want and I have to get another picture and I don't understand why I don't get what I want because I got a picture and then I bite myself again and if someone gets too close I grab them so they will get me what I want. Sometimes I just grab what I want and run away with it and then someone takes it off me and I pull their hair and dig my nails into them because I'm angry now and don't know how to stop being angry because I don't know what anger is or where it comes from and then sometimes water comes out of my eyes and I stop feeling angry and I feel better.

'When I'm very, very hungry I sit at the table and things are put in front of me and if I don't want them because they're the wrong colour or shape, I throw them on the floor and eat what I like but I'm still hungry so take what I like from another plate because it's what I like and I'm hungry and someone takes it away from me and I throw my plate and everything into the air and try to grab all the other food I like because I'm still hungry and when I'm hungry I want to eat so why can't I eat when I'm hungry? Eating makes me happy. Someone puts a fork or spoon in my hand before I can eat but I'm very, very hungry then and want to eat and I can do it quicker with my fingers so I drop the fork or spoon and use my fingers because I'm hungry and this time I get to use my fingers which is good because it's quicker than a fork or spoon and also I like the feel of the food.

'When I'm only a little bit hungry people take me back to my room and make me do more things I don't want to do so I smack my head and bite my hand again. Then I put on my coat, which means I'm going back to see him, and I get on the bus again and sit in my seat because it's where I sit every day and the bus stops and another gets off and I want to get off because I get off when the bus stops because that's where he is, but another gets off and I bite my hand and smack my head until I can feel it and then my legs are hot and wet, which feels nice, and then the bus stops and I get off because I get off when the bus stops and he is outside the bus and I run past him into the house and open the door where all the food is and take an apple and a slice of bread into the garden. Then he comes into the garden and takes my clothes off and wipes my legs and bottom with wet tissues and puts a nappy on me and warm soft trousers and kisses me on the head and the face and lets me run around the garden which I like best because it's quiet and I can pick grass and leaves and flowers to twiddle with and I am on my own and I do this until he calls the name "Jonah" and then I know it is food because that's the way it happens and I run inside and sit at the table and he gives me a plate of food that I like because I eat it all. Sometimes I still want to be in the garden so I grab my food with my hands and run outside with it which is okay because he doesn't stop me, but when I want to be on the sofa and still want to eat and grab my food in my hands and run to the sofa, he shouts at me, but I'm hungry and want to sit on the sofa so that's what I do.

'When I'm not hungry any more I go back out into the garden until the light goes away and then I go inside and he puts the pictures on for me because that's what he does when the light goes away and I sit on the sofa and eat apples and watch the pictures. When it gets very dark he calls the name "Jonah" again and I go upstairs because when it is very dark and he calls "Jonah" it is time for hot water and bubbles and cuddles and squeezes and music and fish-tank light and bed again and that's the best time again.'

I'm instantly aware of the silence. The judge breaks the spell. 'Well then, thank you. I am aware of the lateness of the hour and the necessity for Mr Jewell to attend to his father at this time. Therefore, I will take closing statements in writing from both counsel, if that is acceptable, by three p.m. tomorrow? Good, then I will close this tribunal. Mr and Mrs Jewell, this tribunal will publish its decision within the next three weeks.'

Alien

I have no time to speak to Emma. We just hug, the relief escaping through shaking limbs. The fight is over, the legal fight at least. Out in the fresh air, my thoughts climb out of the Jonah box and take hold of my fading father. Emma says, 'Georg and I have said our goodbyes, but kiss him for me?' And I nod. *Goodbye* – such an inconsequential word. Most of the time it is not a permanent farewell. This is a day that will surely end like any other, I tell myself. It is the only comfort I can find.

The hospice is an oppressive place. Full of the dying and the distraught, where forced conversations with other relatives inevitably turn to the subjects of tumour growth rates, chemotherapy, radiotherapy, experimental drug trials and the relative benefits of cremation and burial.

It is quiet in an irritatingly reverent way that can only remind the residents that they are dying – at least it would if the majority of them weren't already off their tits on morphine.

Dad's in a single room – an honour accorded the really nearly dead, and not something you'd wish to feign just for the privacy. So he truly is near the end. Without hair or eyebrows he looks halfway there, like an alien about to be dissected in Roswell.

His eyes are closed. I pull up a chair and sit close by his chest, watching for the telltale signs of the rise and fall from the thin sheet covering what's left of him. The left side of his neck is a strange reddish purple and so swollen that his head resembles a peach stone balanced on an aubergine.

'It went well?'

The words are barely audible, so little air now makes it through his voice box – the tumour has seen to that – but the morphine seems to allow a few through at a time.

'The barrister is very optimistic; we should get the judgement in three weeks.'

'Three weeks? Go back...'

'Dad...' But he has dropped off again. I stare at the suspended bag of fluid, the contents of which are doing their best to keep him sleepy, calm and pain free.

Three more words escape before he slips deeply under: 'Bring me Jonah.'

Maurice has arrived and is haranguing the doctor when Jonah and I get back from playgroup. I pretend not to know him and lead Jonah into the relatives' lounge where the television is mercifully showing CBeebies. I hand him an apple and he sprawls on a waterproofed turquoise sofa and stares at Mr Tumble.

'Ben,' Maurice calls from the doorway. 'This is no place for the boy.'

'If you're referring to Jonah, Dad wants to see him and, as he's the one who's dying, I think he should be allowed to see who he wishes, don't you?'

Maurice holds up his hand in defeat and squeezes his eyes closed in a vain attempt to trap the tears.

I check Jonah, still mesmerised. 'I'm going to see if he's awake. Watch Jonah for a couple of minutes, Maurice.'

'I don't think...'

But I've already left the lounge. I still need a little time alone with my father.

I don't want to imagine what he has to tell me, don't want to accept that there are certain things I long to hear him say before he goes. When I enter, he's lying slightly propped up with a pen in his left hand and a piece of hospice notepaper resting on a book on his lap. I sit next to him. His eyes are barely open and with so much morphine in his system, the concentration and energy required to drag the pen across the paper is monumental. The pen falls from his hand and he dozes off again. The cancer has ruined his handwriting. That sophisticated cursive artwork that I so admired is now the uncertain, scratchy symbols of a four-year-old forced to write on a bouncing Tube train. It is for me, though:

Ben
Do not forget

Don't forget what? I want to slap his cheeks or throw water on his face to bring him to. I want the rest of the message. I put my hands on the edge of the mattress and my face on my hands and run through all the possible permutations like a Bletchley Park code-breaker, trying to imagine my father mouthing the words to me, examining his strange syntax, running through his lexicon, the things he has so far left unsaid – and the pen begins to scratch again, each letter revealed with unbearable slowness. I turn away, get up and walk to the window. It's raining in Hampstead, which only seems to add to its aura of classy, creative melancholy.

The pen stops scratching and he's drifted off again. I go back to the chair and take the paper from his lap and read and read again and laugh, loudly. It is a genuine spontaneous laugh, without bitterness, because it is a glorious, final punch-line.

Ben
do not forget
tax return due end October

I find Jonah still glued to the TV with his face and shirt now covered in pink yoghurt. Maurice sits uncomfortably in a brown leatherette tub chair, reading.

'Where did he get the yoghurt?'

'Sorry?'

'Maurice, where did he get the yoghurt from?'

'I don't know. The fridge, I think?'

'You think? I asked you to watch him.'

'I did.'

'Then how come he's plastered in yoghurt?'

'I watched him go to the fridge,' he says, without looking up.

I take wet wipes from Jonah's bag and clean him up as best I can.

'How's Georg?' Maurice asks.

'Go and see for yourself.'

'No, I don't want my final memory of him to be this.'

'What? Alive?'

'Mr Jewell.'

Both Maurice and I turn round as the nurse calls.

'Your father is conscious again and asking for Jonah.'

'Be there in a minute,' I say. 'Maurice? Are you coming?' But he doesn't answer.

Jonah baulks at the antiseptic odour, but an apple and a feather disperses his irritation.

'Jonah, Papa wants to see you. Come and sit here next to him.'

He skips to the chair at the near side of the bed and drops into it, bouncing three or four times as the springs give beneath him. I stand at the other side, out of the way, leaning against the cooling window. I study my father. Not much of him still looks alive and what little life remains has – it seems – made its way down his left arm into his grey fingers, which are heroically reaching out for his grandson.

Jonah leans forward and places his head on the mattress next to his papa's hand. The fingers crawl spider-like up Jonah's head, disappearing into his hair as they climb, and then slowly settle into a barely perceptible caressing motion. I know how it feels to run my fingers through Jonah's hair and for him not to resist. It is in these moments that I feel most certain that he loves me back, that every word, like Dad said, is a little lie built for a purpose with an agenda and that the physical, sensory world that Jonah inhabits is the purest form of truth there is.

Lying there, he is as still as I've ever seen him.

An hour passes and no one moves. My father's breathing has become low and erratic; Jonah's eyes have closed and he is snoring softly, his face set in a dreamy grin.

A nurse comes in and smiles at the scene. She checks Dad's breathing, feels his pulse, looks in his eyes.

'Any time now,' she says gently. 'He's peaceful. Would you like me to stay?'

'Yes, please, but could you let Maurice know? He's in the lounge.'

'Certainly,' she says, and leaves, only to return a minute later by herself. 'For some people, it's easier,' she says.

At the very end it happens so quickly, almost with impolite haste. Just a simple 'he's gone' from the nurse, who calls the time of death and leaves us to say our goodbyes. Dad's fingers are still curled round Jonah's hair and I gently stroke his face to rouse him and he sits up bleary-eyed.

'Papa's gone, Jonah.'

Jonah climbs up on to the bed until his face is directly over his papa's and stares into his lifeless eyes – it's enough to burst the dam inside me and I start to blubber and cry. Jonah leaves the bed and bounces up to me, laughing, and I take his hands and bounce with him, also laughing, following him around the room in a crazed dance while my father lies dead on his hospice bed, and I can think of no other ritual that would mark his passing better.

Light bulb

My father leaves instructions for his cremation, and that – ever the humorist – his ashes be dispersed over Margaret Thatcher.

It's a small affair – Jonah, Maurice and I, the rest of the card school, a handful of ancient Trotskyites and a solitary woman hanging back in the shadows. Emma? I'm too anchored to this pew to check, too scared to let my mind go orienteering. A rousing recording of 'The Internationale' blasts as the plain chipboard coffin is conveyor-belted into the furnace like a forgotten prize from the Generation Game.

I am happy not to provide a eulogy because I only have platitudes, and Jonah . . . well, Jonah. So it is left to Maurice – or rather Maurice insists. By his standards, he is dressed for the occasion – a shiny charcoal-grey three-piece that's never seen a dry cleaner – and I close my eyes as he walks down the aisle toward the lectern platform, the trail of sweet pungency that accompanies him turning this redbrick barbecue joint into an Orthodox church, incense swinging.

Jonah sits twiddling foliage; the wreath kindly sent from the bowls club should probably last him a good hour.

The minister helps Maurice on to a box provided for the shorter of the eulogists and quietly explains where to position the microphone. Maurice places his cigar stub next to it, reaches into his cardigan pocket and pulls out a wad of dog-eared notepaper. His amplified throat-clearing is like the roar of the MGM lion.

'Thank you, rabbi.'

The minister talks closely into his ear.

'You're not a rabbi? So what? A trainee?'

The minister returns, though less closely.

Maurice stares directly at me. '*Shnorrer*, I suppose I'll have to say *Kaddish* as well? Anyway . . .

'So, what kind of man was Georg Jewell? Don't worry. This is no quiz, I will tell you the kind of man he was.

'Georg, Georg, Georg – I hated him like a brother, but what can you do? You can't choose your family any more than you can choose the size of your *schlung*. And with Georg, when we first met each other, I instantly hated him because he was bigger and stronger and I was older. We were just two skinny boys, still years from bar mitzvah, speaking two different languages – me, Dutch, he, Hungarian – we were just two boys who'd survived the Nazis, who suddenly found themselves walking side by side down a railway track in 1944.

'Georg offered to share his food with me – and what did I do? So hungry I'd been eating grass? I said yes. And Georg? Georg shrugged and tore his bread and cheese in half, and we sat down in the grass on the side of the road and went to sleep. And for this I loved him, but trust – trust is a different matter altogether. Normally I would have left him by the roadside.

'But two weeks later we're still together – wandering around like a couple of *shtummers* talking in sign-language. I can't leave him. Why can't I go? I ask myself. I hated him for an act of generosity, but I couldn't drag myself away.

'I tried a couple of times, left while he was still asleep, but for some reason I began to dawdle and stop until I saw him striding toward me out of the distance and as he approached we just set off together again without saying a word. He never asked why. I never asked him if he was angry. There were many occasions when other stragglers tried to tag along – maybe for a day, sometimes a week – and when they were with us I experienced horrible jealousy. I would dream of murdering them in their sleep – but they never stayed and we still didn't talk.

'He tried me with Hungarian, I tried him with Dutch; he tried me with Yiddish, but I spoke Ladino – only Jews could invent more than one secret language. Then one day we are wandering through a small French town – the name slips my mind – and it has a library this town and I – a learnt thief through necessity – crept in and stole out with a book, a dictionary, a French–English dictionary, but crucially, a dictionary for children. With pictures. There was just one choice then – French or English, and of course we could have studied both, but we chose English because America was our destination. You may have guessed, we never made it.

'It didn't take us long to learn the basics; we tested each other with words, then sentences as we walked and lay dozing in the evenings.

'Of course, we had no idea if we were speaking it properly, how could we? And we only ever used it to practise what we would say when we arrived in America, because by then we had a language that served us perfectly without the need for words – and it was a language of the heart.'

Maurice pauses and places his head on the lectern. When he looks up again his eyes are full of tears.

'The truth is, Georg saved my life more than once. It was on the seventh night after we'd met, while we sheltered in a barn, that he saved my life for the second time. We thought it was empty, and neither of us expected to be confronted by a German soldier, a deserter, no doubt, but that is what happened. As we lay on the straw, he came from nowhere and suddenly there is a knife at my skinny throat and I am being dragged toward the barn door. I was terrified, but Georg? He just stood up and stared, his hands behind his back, and began to walk towards us. I could feel the German's sweat dripping on to my head. It was murky in that barn, but as we got to the door the moon lit us perfectly from the back and Georg moved so swiftly that the Nazi never saw it coming.

'The German just dropped, like someone had ripped the muscles from his bones. Georg had caught him perfectly between the eyes with a rusty old plough blade.

'I knew that I was a burden to him after that, that he would have a better chance on his own and, many years later, I asked him, "Georg," I said, "why didn't you just leave me?" And his answer? "Any more than one is too many. Losing one is painful, losing two is painful more, losing three and the pain goes. Everyone needs a little pain and you, Mauritz, you are a little pain – so I can't afford to lose you." And he never did lose me. But now I have lost him and Georg, you were wrong, losing one is very, very painful.'

And then he starts to cry, which doesn't suit him, and I am dumbstruck by these revelations, staring at the furnace doors, while the jigsaw of my life with him goes up in flames, unfinished. I stand up as Maurice shuffles back to the pew and attempt to put my arm around him.

'Maurice, when was the first time he saved you? Tell me.'

But he shrugs me off. Then we stand together as he intones the Hebrew prayer for the dead, the *Kaddish*, from a battered old Hebrew prayer book and I try to keep up with my internet-downloaded transliteration:

Yisgadal v'yisgadash sh'mey rabah . . .

With the final Amen, the scant crowd disperses toward the back of the hall. Jonah sits, as he has sat the whole way through, picking the wreath to the wire and littering the floor with leaves and petals.

The handshaking takes an eternal five minutes, but I can't drag myself back to the car and, while Jonah investigates more wreaths, I stroll the length of the blood-red wall, reading the names on the memorial plaques. Each religion has its place, marked out by a gentle change in surnames – Stephenson, Singh, Shah, Stein. I scan from top to bottom looking for the familiar, the Jewish geography of the dead.

'Your cousin went out with Marc Bolan, didn't she?'

Turning from the rock legend's memorial plaque, I reply. 'When he was Marc Feld, yes. But I've told you that a hundred times.'

She's smiling. 'A thousand times, at least.'

I let the silence settle between us, replacing the tension with needles of memory. 'A million.'

'A gazillion,' Emma says.

'You win.'

'No one wins,' she whispers.

We stand together and stare at the plaque.

'I'm so very sorry about Georg, Ben.'

I feel her breath on my ear, it is as close to touching as we've been for nine months.

'It must be hard. The grief, I mean.'

'There's been a lot to grieve for, Emma.'

I hear a sigh, feel a hand in mine. It is small and insistent. It's Jonah. He wants to leave.

'Can we talk, Ben? Now?'

'If he lets us.' The phrase lingers.

The sun has filtered through, so I have an excuse to don my sunglasses. I give in to Jonah's tugging and, as I turn to be led, notice that he has Emma's hand too – a beautiful young boy with his parents, what could be more natural?

'He knows where he's going?' I ask.

'You do, don't you, Jonah? You're going to the park,' she says.

A park I don't know, or at least have never been to with him.

'You're going to Goldstream Park, aren't you?' she says. 'It's where Georg used to take him.' And then, as if to the sky: 'I would meet them there sometimes.'

'Sometimes?' I ask.

'Quite regularly,' she says.

'A chain of extraordinary coincidences?' I smile.

'Exactly.'

Jonah releases his hands and continues four or five paces ahead. He's programmed the SatNav and we're now robotically following its instructions.

Through the gates he picks up speed and begins to trot with arms by his sides. I begin to run after him.

'Leave him, Ben. I know where he's going. He's off to the water garden.' His laughter carries back to us on the breeze, it is high and joyous, disbelieving almost – like he's the luckiest person in the world, like something so stupendous has happened that his whole body has been freed of its own weight, his head thrown back, his legs adjusting from trotting to skipping. All that's left for him to do is fly.

The water garden is a vast circle of brightly coloured rubber bitumen, formed into a mosaic of sea-creatures – sea horses, star fish, dolphins and a giant yellow octopus. Among the wildlife sit child-activated fountains that throw jets of water high and wide. The air is full of spray and the piercing cat-calls of two- and three-year-olds. Around the circle there are benches and grass and Emma and I settle on one, two sets of eyes bonded to the Gulliver-like form of Jonah, skipping circuit after circuit after circuit, carefully weaving in and out of his Lilliputian comrades, who seem totally accepting of this giant among them and his maniacal chuckling.

'I...'

'I... No, you first,' I say.

'I will not apologise, but I'm sorry...'

'That doesn't make any sense.'

'Will you just let me speak, please, this is hard enough without...'

'I'm sorry, go on.'

'Thank you.'

I can sense her gathering herself.

'Ben, you know it's over, don't you? Not just know, but *accept* it?'

I nod assent, while my mind searches for a caveat, the slightest grammatical twist, a tiny semantic get-out clause. Jonah has begun to venture timidly toward the spouting fountains. His face is set in a gentle smile.

'Okay.'

There is relief in her voice, like her planning is working so far.

The conversation-and-response key that she has no doubt used specialist software to produce is proceeding down the correct branch – if 'yes', say this; if 'no', say that.

I try to identify my feelings for her. My emotions are a compass needle, struggling to settle on a fixed point. Is it love? Is it hate? Love-love-hate, or hate-love-hate? Or am I too close to the pole to ever get a true reading?

Jonah has taken off his shoes and left them in the middle of the circle. Now he sits on the grass opposite, picking at some dandelions and waving their gossamer-like seeds into the air. Wherever they land they will grow, but what if they never land?

'I think it's fair to say that our life, together – with Jonah, too – has been excruciating at times.'

'That's a little harsh,' I say.

'But true?'

'I suppose.'

'We are both accountable, Ben.'

'Responsible, you mean?'

'No, I mean accountable. We both have to accept our part in this, but without blame. There is no blame. We did the best we could, what we thought was right, for the best reasons, with the best of intentions. I need to tell you how it was for me, Ben, and how I tried.'

'You've already told me that, at the tribunal, remember?'

'No, Ben, I didn't. That was about Jonah.'

'So go on then. How was it for you? How did you try?'

Emma gets up from the bench and takes a couple of paces toward Jonah, her arms folded tight, her hands in her armpits. When she sits back down she is close to me. For the first time I look openly at her face. Her cheekbones have lost their prominence, her eyes are brighter than I remember and less sunken.

'The break's been kind to you,' I say. Now it's her turn to laugh.

'Yes, it's been like nine months in Barbados.'

'There's no need, I was only saying...'

'I know what you were saying, Ben. So let me put you straight.'

'Yes, please do.'

There is silence.

'Have you any idea how angry you've been? Not just the last couple of years, but ever since I've known you? It was different when we met, it felt like passion, it looked like passion. It made you enigmatic, charismatic, admirable even. But it's not passion, it's simply anger. I've learnt that about you, Ben. The anger holds you back, it's all fear and resentment and frustration. I tried for years to drag you out of it, but you're comfortable there. It's all you've ever known. That and the booze that fuels it. I've watched you quit rather than face the prospect of failure, dismiss something as worthless rather than risk the chance of succeeding at it. I cried inside when you left marketing to join your father in that stinking warehouse.'

I am indignant. 'Hold on, I did that for you.'

'For me? How? It was just another stick to beat yourself and everyone around you with.'

'I did it so we could afford to have Jonah.'

'Did I ever once ask you to do that?'

'No, but it would have meant...'

'Me giving up work? Is that what you were going to say? Did you ever ask what I wanted?'

I look up at Jonah and before I realise it I'm halfway across the water garden – my shoes sloshing through standing water. Jonah is jumping up and down in a puddle, his skin turning browner before my eyes. I reach out for him, but he bats away

257

my hand and skips to another part of the circle where he stands, playing with his hair, while a knot of toddlers splash nonchalantly beside him. Emma is at my shoulder.

'He was a gift for you, wasn't he?'

'Not for you?'

'Yes, of course, but I'm talking about you. He's been a gift to your sense of self-loathing. Because as soon as Jonah arrived, as soon as his autism became apparent, he became your mission. You had the perfect excuse not to look at yourself ever again. Just focus on your son, your poor autistic son and nothing else. Forget about me, I should understand where the priorities lie, shouldn't I? I too should give up on myself. Isn't that right, Ben? I should give my whole life to Jonah too. But I need something back. I know you think I'm selfish, but I want to be loved back. And you just stopped. You always fall back on your devotion to Jonah. But in what sense did your self-piteous drinking help Jonah with his autism?'

'My drinking did not cause Jonah's autism.' There, I've said it out loud, as if the volume will convince me that I completely believe it.

'I didn't mean that,' she says softly. 'But how present were you? How useful could you be, half-cut most of the time? It couldn't all just be cuddles, kisses and laughter. You forced me to be the serious one.'

My daydream of this meeting was one of emotional reunion or, at the very least, a tearful exclamation of eternal love fucked by the fickle finger of fate. I want to find the words, but I am scared they will wreck my fragile equilibrium.

'I just wanted to be his father.'

'Ben, you wanted to be everything to him that didn't involve any thinking ahead. So you made me be Jonah's secretary and press officer.'

'So, what, you thought you'd just dump us? Make up some bullshit story about single fathers being more likely to win a tribunal. I can't believe I fell for it. Throw us out of the house, dump us on my dad, make me ask him – no, beg him – for the money to fight for Jonah. You sent me back there, Emma, and I had to wipe his arse before he died.' My sunglasses are blurring. The tears are hot and burn my shaven cheeks.

'I was desperate, Ben.' She's digging at her cuticles with her thumbnails; the ends of her fingers are bitten and sore.

'You couldn't have been that desperate if you made it to Hong Kong! Emma, I...' Her face has turned strawberry-mark crimson. 'You weren't in Hong Kong, were you? My God, you weren't! Well, Emma, Jesus...'

'I had to, Ben. I had to go away, I had to find a way, it was all I could think of. Georg, he...'

'He knew? My dad knew?'

'I was ill, Ben! I'd been sick for years.'

'What the fuck are you talking about, ill? You've never taken a sick day from your precious job in your life. No, I would have noticed. You looked fine. If you were ill you would have told me.'

'I couldn't even admit it to myself. So how could I have told you? It was all I had left that was mine. You'd stolen my peace of mind, I thought it was keeping me alive...'

'You've lost me.'

'Pills, Ben, bloody pills.'

'I couldn't sleep,' she says, stirring her coffee and picking at a blueberry muffin. We are alone, for now, in the park café.

'I remember, but didn't the doctor give you something that helped?'

'Yes, it solved *all* my problems.'

'But the doctor gave them to you, it's not like you were snorting cocaine. If you were taking that many, wouldn't you have been asleep all the time?'

She holds her mug with two hands and lets the steam creep through her eyelashes. 'Zopiclone. A feeling of well-being, followed by a yummy drift into sleep. I liked the feeling, more than the sleep...' She sips from her mug. 'Especially in the mornings. I'd wake up with a feeling of impending doom. The prospect of Jonah, his moods, the smell, the rush, what I hadn't managed to do the night before, the day ahead, you – and I found the tablets helped. Just the one, as I woke up, got me over the hump. And it was fine, for a long time, but I'd begin to run out before the end of the month and the edginess I felt before I could get another prescription – God, I can't tell you.'

'I didn't know,' I say, as much to myself as to her. She waves it away.

'Then I had the bright idea of ordering some more from the internet, just in case, to cover the shortfall. But as soon as they arrived, I took two. I'd never done that before, but it felt good – and it was something for me, you know?'

I knew.

'It felt risky and naughty and I just thought: fuck it! If this is what it takes to live my life then so be it.'

'How long?' I ask, and her face changes. The bravado that heralded this revelation has dissolved, the anger she expressed in the water garden has passed and now I have this alter-Emma opposite me, vulnerable, diminished and a mirror for my shame.

'Five years, give or take.'

'Five years!' I'm stunned. How could I have spotted nothing? Five fucking years. 'And work? Did they not notice?'

'I hid it from you, didn't I?'

She drinks some more coffee and opens a bag of mini cookies that Jonah has purloined from the café counter. I spy the café owner jotting it down in a notebook.

'I began to make mistakes. Nothing serious, but it made me paranoid. I wanted to sleep all the time. So I made the decision that I had to give them up, when the last batch ran out I wouldn't order any more. The first day without was unimaginable. It was like waking up in a hurricane, I could hear every sound in hi-definition and at full volume, I was hopelessly paranoid, thought I was going to die. So I told work I had flu.'

'I remember now.' And I did. A week of dirty nappies, take-aways and curses. I couldn't get to the pub or sneak booze back into the house and I resented every day of it.

'I couldn't bear it. I couldn't bear the anxiety. Couldn't take the reality. Getting the prescription from the doctor was like winning the lottery and I was off and running again, only worse.'

My hands are over my face, my sunglasses over my hands.

Her voice is faltering. 'The week before you left, I almost killed Jonah. You were out and I'd just bathed him and washed his hair and I only left him for two minutes, to turn the oven off, and I could smell him before I saw him and it was everywhere, Ben. In his hair, down his legs, on the carpet, his mattress, the walls. His handprints were on the walls, Ben, and he just laughed at me and I found myself throwing things at him, anything I could find – toys, clothes, CDs – and he began biting his hand and jumping angrily and I just couldn't stop swearing at him. I was out of control and I looked down and I had the glass vase in my hand and...'

I have never seen her cry like this, with her whole body.

'And I took two pills and showered him – which he hated – and filled him full of Calpol and gave him melatonin to knock him out and stuck him on the sofa while I scrubbed and scrubbed and scrubbed and struggled to pick him up and put him to bed and hoped he wouldn't wake in the morning and then you came in and all you had to say when I told you was *you should have put a nappy on him.* A fucking nappy, Ben.

'And the saddest part of all was that I felt guilty. While you polished off half a bottle of whisky, I sat in my drug-induced stupor full of guilt and shame and planned the least disruptive way to kill myself – to unburden you and Jonah of the weight of my hatred and incompetence. I wasn't even going to end my life for *me*, I was planning to do it for the men in my life – neither of whom even spoke to me.'

I need to get up and walk. 'Give me a second,' I say. Jonah has his back to me, he is gripping the green playground railings. I quietly walk up behind him and lean down to kiss his brown neck. He doesn't flinch. The sun has warmed the air and the children's cries have dampened in the rising humidity. I take my glasses off and turn my closed eyes skyward. But a vision of my father in his hospice bed forms on the inside of my eyelids and I reach for my son and bathe his cheek and his neck with their torrent. He stands rigid.

My tear ducts have acted as pressure valves and I feel calmer as I walk back to her and sit down.

'They call it a moment of clarity. It was after I spoke to Georg about you and Jonah moving in with him. It was something he said that triggered it. I'll never forget it,' she says.

'What was it? Ben's a *shmock*?'

She smiles. 'No, he said I shouldn't make the same mistake as him. He said that I must love myself and forgive myself, or life will get stuck, like a record, in a groove. That same day, I made an appointment to see a psychiatrist and told her everything. Three days later, instead of checking in for a flight, I checked myself into rehab.'

'Rehab,' I repeat. 'With heroin and cocaine addicts?'

'Yes. And alcoholics.'

I change the subject. 'What did work say?'

'I signed off with stress. They all know about Jonah, but I didn't want them to know about the drugs and I didn't want it on my medical record either. I didn't use the company health insurance, I paid for it myself.'

'So that's why you couldn't pay for the tribunal upfront? Dad knew all this, too?'

'He had to, Ben. I needed him to look after both of you and I needed him to lend us the money for the tribunal.'

'He agreed to lend us the money? Before? But he put me through hell.' I shake my head. 'At least he was consistent.' I stare at the floor; honesty begets honesty. 'I didn't leave marketing, I was sacked. They caught me drinking. Dad, as ever, was my last hope.'

'No, Ben, I should have been your last hope. Why didn't you confide in me?'

'I thought you'd leave me. And you? Why didn't you tell *me*?'

'I didn't think you cared.'

We look closely at each other and embrace. It's miserable and summons up the grief like a catalyst. In the end it isn't words – either written or spoken – that convince me my marriage is over – it's the feeling of being embraced by a stranger.

'I should really get back to the house,' I say.

'Do you want me to come with you?'

'No, no need.'

'Well then, can I take Jonah? It would make life easier for you.'

'Yes, thank you.'

So we arrange ourselves, pick up phones and keys, finish off our drinks and linger, both in contemplation and – in my case – huge regret.

'Ben, look at Jonah!'

A blond boy, no taller than Jonah's knee, has caught his attention. We watch as Jonah drops to his haunches, looks the child directly in the eye and treats him to a glowing, sparkly-eyed grin.

'I've never seen him do that before. Have you ever seen him do that before?'

'No,' I nod in wonder, 'I never have.'

Summer

Dad leaves me the house – which is more than I expected. If I thought he had no idea what was going on at the warehouse, I was wrong. He left it to Valentine, it turns out – who has postponed his Caribbean return – and I'm glad for him. I offered my help and he laughed at me. There was a private pension and life insurance that leaves me debt free, and with a little in reserve and with Emma's promised half of the tribunal cost, the house can be properly childproofed and Johnny's cheque torn up.

The summer holidays are in full swing now. It's late August and I'm simply biding time. Jonah and I are in a rhythm. The council grudgingly agreed to three days' a week holiday club for him – which he is enjoying. And on the other days, we hit the park, McDonald's, then the park again – we do what he wants to do, life is easier like that. His mood is eerily calm, a calm before the storm, but who knows? I don't know if he misses Dad, whether he remembers him, even. Maybe he was just another adult there to meet his needs, which are and will remain – in material and social terms – very simple. Although it's strange that Jonah has made a unilateral decision to sleep in

Dad's bed. He may find the remaining scent comforting, or he may just like the bed, or the shadows in the darkness. Again, it's a mystery. But he wakes less often.

Maurice has been round regularly and I haven't had the heart to ask for his key back, so he just arrives. He has taken some mementos – wrapped them in oil-cloth like precious gems.

Emma and I have agreed an informal, workable arrangement around Jonah and she's back in his life on a regular basis. He saw the sea for the first time this summer and I can imagine him, in later life, tanned and carefree, wandering along the sand pulling seaweed and shells and twiddling to his heart's content.

I am beginning to accept my part in all these troubles, to find some compassion, to think about making amends, to think about starting again. Still, in the forefront of my mind is the outcome of the tribunal and I can't begin to think of a life ahead until then. So I'm on hold a bit.

Currently, I'm listening to Radio 4 on my back on the sofa, having given up the *Guardian* crossword with just one clue solved. Jonah is off at club – they picked him up an hour ago and he skipped to the bus with a smile.

I can feel my eyes closing as the doorbell rings.

'Maurice, use your key.'

But the bell rings a second, third, fourth time.

'Fucking hell.' I slide from the sofa and head to the front door. I see his shape through the stained-glass window and open the door.

'Maurice, why didn't...'

It's not Maurice.

It is the postman with a recorded delivery letter.

It's arrived.

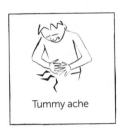

Tummy ache

M y stomach fights for independence as I open the envelope.
I try to read every word but then start scanning, madly.
My eyes racing after my finger, pulling words from the text,
tallying pluses and minuses as the phrases leap at me.

First Tier Tribunal Special Educational Needs and Disability

DECISION

Appeal by: Mrs Emma Jewell and
                    Mr Benjamin Jewell
Against decision of: London Borough of Wynchgate

Concerning: Jonah (born 11 May 2000)

Hearing date: 28 July 2011

Tribunal panel: Lianne Wyatt (Tribunal Judge)
                         Peter Greeling (Specialist Member)
                         Nigel Prior (Specialist Member)

Appeal

Mrs Jewell and Mr Jewell appeal under section 326 of the Education Act 1996 against the contents of a statement of special educational needs made by the London Borough of Wynchgate (LA) for their son, Jonah.

Tribunal's conclusions with reasons

We carefully considered the written evidence submitted to the tribunal in advance and the evidence given to us at the hearing. We also took account of the Code of Practice and the relevant sections of the Education Act 1996 and the Special Educational Needs and Disability Act 2001.

Our Conclusions are:

1.   We are pleased that the parties maintained a dialogue about the issues in the appeal up to the date of the hearing and include their agreed amendments as part of our order.

2.   In relation to the issues in Part 2 of the statement, there is evidence to support a view that even when Jonah demonstrates appropriate behaviour, this undoubtedly reflects the level of individual professional input available to him. Furthermore,

without this support, Jonah's behaviour presents a risk to himself and to others. Therefore, we agree that the requested parental amendments should be inserted.

3. In Part 3 it seemed to us that the parties were working on different definitions of a total communication approach. We agree that a consistent method for use in all contexts should be identified. PECS is Jonah's preferred method of communication and this needs to be described in his statement as such, but equally this should be placed in the context of a range of other communication approaches as advised. Jonah needs access to a range of choices based on identification of a specific principal method to be provided

4. There was little dispute between the respective speech and language therapists and we concur that the amendments sought in relation to the language programme and direct speech and language therapy should be inserted save for the changes we have made to ensure that Jonah's communication preference is recognised in the provision of a specific method, but that he also has a range of choices as agreed are necessary in a total communication approach.

5. We note the LA's comments about the evidence from Ms Smart and we accept that Jonah has had regular indirect therapy. But we also note that Ms McDonald said the last joint work by the therapeutic team was in October 2010. In the absence of evidence to counter Ms Smart's specific recommendations about the provision of occupational therapy, we accept that the amendments sought by the parents should be inserted in the statement.

6. There is no necessity to insert the requested reference to a specified professional to carry out the functional behavioural analysis. This can readily be done by a teacher experienced in behaviour management techniques.

7. Regarding the central question of an extended or waking day, a delicate line must be trodden between examining the full picture of a child's needs and limiting our decision to a careful assessment of his educational needs within that full picture and deciding what is appropriate to meet those particular needs.

8. **The fact a child has a need for a consistency of approach does not necessarily mean this is an educational need** that needs to be met with educational provision beyond the school day. Similarly, the fact that the well-being of a child and/ or his family may benefit from social care input does not make that provision educational. It is undoubtedly the case that there is only a small group of children whose needs are so complex and significant that a curriculum beyond the normal school day is required.

9. However, it is a matter of fact and degree and judgement in each case and it is the individual needs of the child in question that is determinative. Our task does not include identifying what might be an optimum or ideal provision for the full range of Jonah's educational and other needs. Both consistency and a behavioural programme appear to be features of Jonah's educational needs.

10.   Jonah's combined and complex ASD and *severe* learning difficulties require a change of approach. For this child, his behavioural and related needs are integral to the complexity of his educational needs and are obstacles to his learning.

11.   The LA's claim that the current package was working and producing both progress and consistency did not stand up to close scrutiny.

12.   All the recommended therapies need to be delivered throughout the day across a range of settings by a multidisciplinary team of staff focused consistently on that task and able to plan and communicate effectively

13.   Therefore, given the complexity and interplay of his severe needs and the stage of his education, Jonah requires a level of consistency that inevitably points to a waking-day curriculum.

14.   Clearly, the most important aspect of the appeal for both parties was the identification of the school to be named in Part 4.

15.   Maureen Mitchell School is not suitable to meet Jonah's special educational needs. Therefore, we turn to consider the LA's alternative option of a residential placement at The Sunrise Academy School. However, taking into account all that we were told about The Sunrise Academy, we do not believe it can meet Jonah's needs at this stage of his education.

16.   Taken as a whole, placement at **Highgrove Manor** is the only viable option in the particular circumstances of this case.

Order

Appeal allowed.

Signed: *Ms Liz Goldthorpe*

                 Lianne Wyatt   Tribunal Judge

Amended under Rule 44 Health Education and Social Care Chamber Rules 2008
<u>*21 September 2011.*</u>

I re-read the last sentence over and over again. Jonah won. And my excitement is for him, for the future he is now assured of, for the expanse of green fields and trees, for the chance he will have to exist without the stresses laid upon him by the unpredictability of a non-autistic world. For me? The revelation that I've finally finished something fills me with pride and relief and it is, I reflect – after a string of losses – the first thing I've ever won.

For the first time in months – possibly years – I phone Emma with good news.

'The nightmare is over,' I say. 'We won.'
She cries.

So this is victory. I can allow myself that. Dad's expression of pride, finally finishing something, something life-changing – the realisation that without loving myself, I cannot hope to love another. Emma knew and felt this for herself. She prioritised herself over Jonah; it was what she needed to do. We both screwed up, but at least we're starting to fix it.

I want to sleep for the remaining week. Emma has posted the news about Jonah on her Facebook page, but all I feel is a sincere bitterness that none of these well-wishers were around to help Emma and me when things were at their toughest. Yet now that we've split up and Jonah's going and the chance to invite us over as a family has evaporated, they're full of ebullience. I'm affronted by their shortsighted belief that it's perfectly fine for your eleven-year-old to leave home, probably for good. I feel like sending them all a response, but they wouldn't get the irony. So I ignore them all, while secretly wishing them many happy years of rehab fees and unwanted pregnancies for their proto-delinquent offspring. Their children's words will hurt them more than my son's silence, that I can guarantee them. I need to let these feelings go, I know. They are a cover for my fear and a short-term antidote to my self-loathing, both of which I need to tackle if I want to live a happy life. At least, for the first time, I recognise this fact – which is a good place to start this new journey.

My mood swings between hope and a dull kind of nihilism. If only I could win this for Jonah, I had thought, everything would be good from now on. But feelings are more complicated than that.

Emma arrives to take Jonah for the day and it feels wrong, the three of us in this house, sitting at the kitchen table without Dad. And it occurs to me that this could be the final time around this old table. A full stop for the Jewell family. Maybe I couldn't admit it to myself before, but they are all leaving me. Soon and for good.

'Ben, why do you look sad?' Emma asks.

'Don't I always?'

'It's time to move on.'

I baulk at this familiar sentiment. 'Easier said than done.'

Silence.

'So where do we go from here, Emma?'

'We have Jonah. We will always be his mum and dad.'

'Will you have more children?' The question is out.

'God, Ben, give me a chance to recover from this first. I don't know. Part of me feels that I need another go at this, that I need the chance to be a different mother to a different child. To give Jonah another person that loves him. Another part of me is shit scared that it will happen again. You?'

'No, that's it for me. I couldn't deal with the sense of betrayal.'

'Betrayal of Jonah?'

I nod.

'Someone told me this last week: if you have one foot in the past and the other in the future, you piss on the present,' she says.

'Who was that, the Dalai Lama?'

'But it's true, isn't it? We only really have today,' she says.

'Jonah only really cares about the moment,' I add.

'Even better. Maybe it's time we both accepted that he's an individual, with his own life, to be lived in his way. Maybe we should concede that we've learnt more from him than he has from us?'

It rings true for me. 'I think I recognised that a long time ago, but fought it. Even if he doesn't understand it, or is never able to recall it or put it into words – even in his head – I want him to feel that I love him. I need to know that I've done everything in my power to be a good father. Does that make sense?'

'Yes. You have and he does. You can see it in his eyes, Ben. He adores you.'

I watch them walk away hand in hand.

Wrench

'How hard has this been on you, eh?'

Jonah is lying in my father's bed twiddling a leaf he picked up from the garden at lunchtime. It even made it through bath time.

'Nobody actually asked you what you wanted, did they? We just dragged you around like a show pony, stuck you in front of strangers and they decided for you. Well, this is the deal. Do you remember the place that Papa and I took you to visit? Highgrove Manor? With the nice people and the wood, the animals, your lovely big room, the swimming pool and all that space? The lovely people there thought you were so gorgeous that they want you to go and live with them. They think they can help you learn and have lots of fun and you'll never be bored. You'll still come home for holidays and – of course – I'll come up every weekend or so and see you. Does that sound okay with you?'

The school has sent me some photos and I lay them out on the duvet in front of him. He carries on twiddling. So I pick them up to show him.

'Look, this is the house that you're going to live in, it's called Bell House and this is your classroom and...'

He has a photo in his hand and is holding it up to his face, staring intently at something.

'That's it sweetboy, what can you see? Do you remember something?'

I try to make out the shot from the side, I think it is his bedroom. 'Can I see?'

He hands it to me without blinking and begins twiddling again. It is his bedroom, with its big picture window. I look at it closely. It's pretty bare, as yet undecorated or festooned with his bits and pieces. Is it the tree through the window? I study it carefully and in the background, seemingly running from the tree's upper branches to the window frame, is a rainbow, faint but recognisable.

'There's gold at the end of that, Jonah. A pot full of gold coins. Maybe one day we'll go and hunt for it, what do you say?'

I lie down beside him and watch the fish swim across the ceiling, too tired to move.

'You know, Jonah, you are the world's best listener. You never judge or contradict and I know that whatever I tell you remains sacred. Telling you my secrets and fears helps me to deal with them. Your grandfather admired that in you as well. Are you going to miss Papa? I am – stupid old sod.

'You'd think it was impossible, wouldn't you, not to know the first thing about your own father. I don't mean his name – although even that was a fraud. Apparently, we're Friedmans, but you know that already. Yes, I know, I prefer Jewell too.' I look at him for some kind of reaction, but, of course, there is none. He's just Jonah; surnames are superfluous in his world.

'No, I mean who Papa was as a person. He knew me, knew who I was. He was so accurate, it hurt sometimes, Jonah. But him? He was always somehow just out of reach. You can't not miss a man, a father like that, you see, because you're forever running after him trying to do something that will provide the key to unlock him. Something to make him so proud that he'd trust you enough to let you in.

'Pretty pointless in your book, I would have thought. You're the most discreet person I know. What's it like? I'd love to know. You seem to be so completely emotionally self-reliant. I hope you don't mind me laying my crap on you some nights, but you're the only person I can truly trust.' I rub his back and squeeze his thighs, which loosens his nappy. 'Oh! And you appear to have laid your crap on me this evening too. Let's get you changed.'

I leave him clean, fresh and twiddling happily in the bed that just weeks before my own father lay dying in. Downstairs, I can't even sit in his armchair. Is DNA really passed on? I can imagine a straight line descending directly from Dad to Jonah, but I can't see where it would pierce me on its way down. I envision myself hanging on to that line by my teeth – extreme flossing. I must be full of shit from my mother's mitochondria, there's no other explanation.

So where do I go from here? Well, I'll start with Highgrove Manor and take it one step at a time. I've existed as part of a trio for a decade now, two very different trios, granted, but very soon I'll be a solo act again. Maybe I'll go back and study; my brain has been so full of fantasy it would do me good to fill it with some hard, clear facts and well-constructed arguments. And maybe I should seek some help with the drinking. I panic at the thought of being told to stop completely, but the prospect of living alone and being left alone with the freedom to drink with impunity fills me with greater dread.

As I lie on the sofa, I toy with the idea of selling this house and moving close to Jonah's school. There's nothing to keep me here, after all. Solitude, with the received knowledge and understanding of what being totally alone means, is the opposite of where I saw myself less than a year ago. The trouble is, I comprehend that in my own way I've been a carer and a care-taker for a large part of my life and now – on a daily basis, at least – it's only me, and it's never only been me. I feel a certain responsibility to Maurice. Dad's death is as great a loss to him as to me. But he's somehow phlegmatic about death. I suppose at his age, it becomes a more natural part of living – and I'm too young for bowls. I hear the sound of feet slapping on stairs. Jonah is standing in the doorway.

'Okay, you can have some more toast.'

School

Given Jonah's propensity for strangulation, it's safer to give him the back seat to himself, with Emma riding shotgun next to me. Yet he is strangely subdued – maybe serene – as we set off around the M25 toward the M40. Emma spends the journey with her eyes closed and her hands clasped tightly on her lap. Neither of us feels like talking, the silence less awkward than forced conversation.

It's the second week of September, two weeks since the verdict arrived, and we've made acclimatisation visits since then; one for a day and one overnight for Jonah, when they had to wake him up at nine the following morning for breakfast – he's becoming a proper teenager.

But today is the day.

Today.

Is.

The.

Day.

How do I feel? How will I feel?

I think the answer is straightforward. If he feels good, I'll feel good. Anything less, I cannot contemplate right now.

Only two more miles.

He knows, I think. No, I'm sure he does. I can see in the rearview mirror that he is bouncing and the outside of his mouth has creased. He does know.

We pull on to the long driveway and stop in front of the wrought-iron gates for the fourth time and I press the entry button.

'I have Jonah Jewell.'

'Great, come through the gates and drive down to the big house where we'll meet you and take Jonah's stuff.'

'Okay.' We drive through and I'm ready to do a handbrake and spin away. Thank you for all your efforts on Jonah's behalf but he's all right now, really he is, look, watch, he can talk, he can read, dance, swim, sing, poo on the toilet, we'll just go home, it's fine.

I pull up outside the grand Georgian former manor house, gently wake Emma, turn round and watch him staring out the window. I get out of the car. It's warm.

Emma follows and stands beside me, she's biting her top lip.

The boot is already open and his belongings are being carried to his room in Bell House, when out steps the man himself – hair adorned with dayglo feathers, one apple in his right hand, another in his mouth.

Emma approaches him gently and crouches down, taking his left hand between both of hers. 'I love you, Jonah.'

He takes his hand from hers and replaces it with a chewed-up apple, then leans his whole body back in the car until only his arse and legs are visible. When he reappears, it's with a piece of silver tinsel. Emma walks to reception and I gently coax him toward the house's open door.

Inside is a welcoming committee. The arrival of a new child

in a school of only fifty is an exciting event and Jonah seems to sense it. At least twenty staff stand in a semi-circle smiling and calling his name and he stands very still, surveying the throng before beaming at them, with his half-eaten apple thrust in the air like an Oscar statuette.

'Shall I take him?'

'Sorry?'

'Shall I take Jonah now? He can have lunch while his room's being sorted out. He's got school this afternoon.'

He's going.

'Yes, but I might need to . . .' I pull Jonah to me and breathe in his smell, squeezing him until he pushes me away. 'I love you so much.'

The keyworker has Jonah's hand already and they are strolling towards a door on the left of the entrance way. My arm is in the air – a farewell, a salute. It won't move, I can't move it. Stuck, as in a plaster cast, joined to my waist by a metal support.

'Ben,' Emma says, softly. 'We'll see him very soon.'

This is too much loss, I have to force myself to remain still and repeat the mantra that has held me up throughout this painful process: *this is for Jonah, this is for Jonah, this is for . . .*

'JONAH!'

He turns as they reach the door and I catch up to them fumbling in my pocket.

'I forgot this.'

I hold the crystal paperweight to his face. A rainbow of colours cuts across his forehead and I kiss it there and run my hands through his hair.

He takes it from me, smiles and skips away without looking back.

*

The ride home is deathly. Everything aches by the time I pull up to drop Emma off and we acknowledge our parting with a raised hand. Is that it? All I want to do is duvet dive. Johnny has arranged a night out of the house for me tomorrow, to 'take my mind off things'. Short of a lobotomy, I see no solution. But tonight I intend to wallow, inebriated, in Lake Solitude.

I lie on the sofa all night, swapping texts with Maria and dozing, and only left the lounge to have a shower an hour ago. The passenger door is already open when I walk out of the house.

'Up for it?'

'No.'

'Oh, you're not going to be a miserable git, are you?'

'You know me better than that.'

'I know you.'

Johnny pulls away with a screech. His driving style diametrically opposed to the way he lives the rest of his life.

'You all right for dosh?'

'Yes, surviving. So where are we going?'

'Amanda's making dinner and she's invited a friend along.'

I inwardly cringe. Not because of the quality of Amanda's cooking, but on behalf of whichever poor singleton is going to be traumatised by the first night of my comeback tour.

'Come on, Ben, crank it up a couple of notches. She's a lovely girl.'

'I'm really not in the mood for this, Johnny. Not yet.'

'Look, it's just dinner.'

We're bumper to bumper down Heath Street, until he turns right and pulls up outside a four-storey Victorian villa – the bottom two floors are theirs. Amanda meets us at the door.

She hugs me gently and whispers 'sorry' in my ear. Johnny has already passed us.

I can make out the back of a head through the lounge door as I take off my coat in the hall. The hair is dark and curly and cascades over the back of the leather sofa.

'Uncle Ben!'

Tom flies down the stairs in a Superdry t-shirt and sweat-shorts and almost knocks me over as we hug.

'He's missed you,' says Amanda.

'How's Jonah?'

'Jonah is . . . good.'

When he finally stops laughing, he asks: 'When can I see him?'

'We'll meet in the park when Jonah comes home at half term,' Johnny chips in. 'I'll arrange it with Uncle Ben. Now, go back upstairs and play on your Xbox.'

'Will you save me some dessert?'

'Yes, if you go up now,' says Amanda.

He smiles at me as he scrambles back up the stairs.

'Come and meet Rachel.' Amanda grabs my hand.

I feel bizarrely unfaithful just being here and take her hand without looking. But they have sat us opposite one another and I realise as I take in the face beneath the hair that if I was still my fifteen-year-old self, she'd be the perfect identikit. She seems not remotely shy, in fact, she is staring at me. Johnny and Amanda are fiddling in the kitchen and I know that my earlobes are burning red.

'Do we know each other?' she asks.

This classic opener is a bastard. It means I have to look up and study her face and run through all the possible locations in which we may have met or conversed. Also, it requires me to say *possibly*.

'You do look familiar. Where were you brought up?' she asks.

'Willesden, then Muswell Hill, you?'

'The Suburb.'

I resist the temptation to ask which suburb. She uses the definite article, assuming I know she means Hampstead Garden *Suburb* and, of course, I do know she means Hampstead Garden Suburb, it just irritates me that she assumes I know and therefore can now draw all the conclusions necessary based on that one simple fact. I have drawn a conclusion, despite this. I don't like her. This irritates me too. It continues unabated.

'School?' she asks.

'Alexandra Palace, you?'

'Henrietta Barnett.'

Of course. 'Wouldn't be from school then,' I say, wanting it to stop.

But she evidently doesn't. 'University?'

'Didn't go. You?'

'Oh, it doesn't matter.' She blushes.

This brief romance is over, it appears, I have fallen at the third hurdle – badly. Shoot me. 'No, tell me, I may have had friends there who weren't fuck-ups like me.' I can't help myself.

'I never meant . . .' she says.

'No, of course not.'

'Cambridge,' she admits.

'Nuh, got me there.'

Johnny rescues us with a bottle of fifteen per cent New World white.

'Where were you at university, Johnny?' she asks, as if

checking she hasn't walked into a rough pub in the wrong part of town.

'Manchester. So was Ben. We shared a flat for three years. He was just testing your intellectual snob quotient!'

She squints at me and purses her lips. 'Don't tell me, you did Psychology?' she says, smiling through her wine glass.

Johnny answers for me. 'Politics.'

'At the Polytechnic,' I add.

'Down with the proles, then?'

'It's where I'm most comfortable.'

'Comfort's underrated.'

'As is sobriety. Johnny, refill, please.'

Am I being charming by mistake? She laughs at my anecdotes and smiles at me in between sips of the tomato and red pepper soup. I hear Johnny and Amanda giggle and catch their conspiratorial winks. I need to stop drinking before I succumb to enjoyment. Rachel saves me from such drastic and, frankly, impossible action.

'Amanda has told me you've been having a bit of a hard time. I'm sorry to hear that.'

I don't know how to respond, so I don't.

'Jonah sounds fascinating and he's such a pretty boy.'

There is a photo of Jonah and Tom together and smiling, on the mantelpiece. It's a rare image and I find myself searching it out. Melancholy invades.

'Does he have a special skill?'

I know she means Jonah. 'Sorry?'

'Jonah's autistic, isn't he? Does he have something he's amazing at?'

This is the question that always strikes me down, sobers me

up and is asked by people who think Dustin Hoffman's *Rain Man* is a textbook representation.

'He rolls over when I tickle his tummy.'

'Ben!' Amanda scolds.

'I'm sorry. No, he has no special skills to speak of, he's not at that end of the Autistic Spectrum.' I know she wants a detailed infomercial on the ins and outs of autism but the level of ignorance always leaves me shocked and determined to shock.

'Not unless you count crapping in his pants, of course.'

She laughs at me. 'This is going well, Amanda, don't you think?'

And now, do I fancy her? Or am I just pissed and horny?

'Sounds like he's a character, your son?'

'Yes, he certainly is. He's completely non-verbal, no words at all.'

'What, never?' Rachel asks.

'Well, he occasionally speaks to *very* pretty girls.' Pissed, horny and flirting, it would seem.

'I think I might like to meet this son of yours.'

Within moments of the cab pulling over, I feel the loneliness course through me like a sickness – sick at the thought of being touched by someone else, sick at the thought of never being touched again. It is a weird night, one of those high summer evenings that never quite go dark.

I sit on the low front garden wall and smoke a cigarette. And then another, dangling my keys from my little finger. Suddenly, I don't want to go in, not to this house. Everybody leaves this house and now it is left to me. I drag myself to the front door and slip the key in the Yale lock. A rush of fetid memories assails me and the dark oppresses me. Tonight will be a night of whisky, television and sofa sleep – lights on. I need the noise, I need the voices. I need the company. I want my wife. I want my son.

'I made you coffee. You shouldn't *zarf* so much.'

'Dad. What time is it?'

My eyes focus, and it's Maurice. Not Dad. He and I stare at each other awkwardly and turn away again, in unison. 'Eleven. Drink your coffee,' he says.

I am coming to with a sense of unease, like there's something crucial I forgot to do, that and a headache.

'Jonah!'

'The boy's at school, remember? You took him up yesterday.'

I take a sip. My throat feels like a gorilla's armpit. 'Maurice, I appreciate the gesture, but you really don't have to check on me every day.'

Maurice grunts. 'Your father, he wrote stuff down.'

'Stuff? What kind of stuff?'

'Stuff. Stuff! Here.'

He passes me a mangled sheaf of flimsies, stained and ragged.

'My tea is brewing,' he says, making for the kitchen.

'Maurice, what the fuck is this?'

He shouts from the hallway, 'Read, just read already. I'll explain later.'

For the eyes of Benjamin Jewell <u>ONLY</u>. March 1976

We had lived for hundreds of years — although
nobody knows for certain — in Hungary, a place
far away from here, to the east, in a city
called Budapest — well two cities actually: Buda
and Pest, divided by the River Danube but united
by a great bridge. Well, the Friedmans were
not unhappy there. We were a good family, a big
family, your grandfather — my father — Louis,
was a physician. He had many patients and we
lived well.

When I was born in 1934 it seemed to be very
good to be a Jew. My father and my mother, Edit,
loved me very much and they loved my brother,
Jonatan — your uncle — too. I worshipped my
brother, he was three years older than me, tall
and dark with a beaming smile that was always
shining on me. But in other ways he was different. He would or could not speak and seemed to
float through life. If I didn't watch over him
carefully, he could just disappear, and when he
lost his temper? Oh my God! Even I could not
calm him.

On three occasions the police returned him
to the house after he'd slipped away from Mamma
during shopping trips. There had been com-
plaints, they said. Jonatan apparently had been

wandering the fruit market helping himself to whatever he fancied, taking a single bite and then tossing the apple, orange, plum or pear over his shoulder without a second thought.

Now, in 1939 the Germans and that bastard Hitler invaded Poland — which was next door to Hungary — and they had already marched into Czechoslovakia. Then, the following year, Hungary became allies with Germany and the atmosphere changed for us. Suddenly, people stopped visiting Father's surgery and Mamma began to cry every day. I was too young to know this at the time, of course, I wasn't much more than a baby — but it is important for you, Benjamin, to know because you are the youngest Jewell, you must keep this story alive for your own son or daughter.

In January 1944, I was nine and Jonatan was twelve. He still wasn't talking and had not started school. My father employed a tutor for him, but he would not learn. By then, also, I was talking non-stop and was reading like a grown-up. I don't know if I was any cleverer than the next nine-year-old but, compared to Jonatan, I was a child prodigy and quickly I became the older brother. Jonatan couldn't learn, couldn't sit still and the tutor resigned in frustration — there was nothing he could do — Jonatan, he said, was an imbecile.

During the following weeks, as I had not started school yet, I became my brother's keeper. It was impossible to keep him in the house, he was physically strong and would become aggressive to everybody but me if he was locked up. So, as a compromise, I would go walking with him every day, firing back the taunts of the neighbourhood children and returning stones with equal venom. I loved my brother and would have killed anyone who tried to harm him.

We celebrated his thirteenth birthday on February 18 that year with a party for family and friends — Jonatan didn't seem to notice or care. That night, when I was in bed, my father came to visit me. 'Georg,' he said, 'Jonni is going away tomorrow.' I sat up, panicking. 'Why, Father?' I asked. 'I can look after him.' He smiled at me and lay next to me on my bed — something he'd never done. 'He is going to a place where he cannot hurt himself or be hurt and hopefully where he can learn to look after himself. Where he will be safe from whatever happens here.' 'But I'll look after him,' I appealed. 'It is agreed,' he said, shaking his head, and even at that young age I could hear the pain in his voice, Ben. And then I heard my father cry, huge gasps and sobs, and the wetness on my cheek I can feel to this day.

When you see your father cry for the first time it is like someone cuts your legs from you, the world changes in an instant and everywhere you look you see dangers, threats. When I heard my father cry that night I suddenly knew that I had to take care of myself from then on. Seeing your father cry is a terrible thing.

The following morning, Jonatan was gone. I could see Mamma had been crying — her eyes were ringed with red — and my father seemed to have shrunk into his reading chair, his newspaper covering his face. I grabbed some bread and jam and slipped out of the house and — day after day — I repeated the walk that Jonatan and I had taken before he left. I didn't know if I hoped to see him or some of the boys who had taunted him then so I could get my revenge. I was a man now, I knew, and would never back down.

I walked like this for a month, Ben, until the streets became full of people running in all directions like a lion had escaped from the zoo and was rampaging through the city looking for dinner. But it wasn't a lion, Ben, it was those bastard Nazis, their boots cracking on the cobblestones, their eyes identical and black as their uniforms, silver bolts of lightning on their shoulders and skulls on their lapels. I'd heard of these Nazis — the very worst, Ben, the SS. My Uncle Piotr had warned me of these; like the evil aliens in my American comic books, their arrival meant death, our death, the Jews' death.

I ran home so fast I thought my chest would explode and found my father sunken in his chair with his newspaper just as I'd left him the month before. 'The SS, the SS are here!' I screamed, but he didn't move. 'Father, the Nazis are in Budapest!'

'It was inevitable. Now go and clean up, your hands are filthy.'

By October, they were everywhere, tanks and soldiers marching and rumbling down the streets; German blaring from megaphones — and that's when they started taking people away. They were in a hurry, because the war by then was going badly for them. They were in a hurry to send all the Jews off to the camps, to Auschwitz. We all had to wear yellow stars so they could round us up easily and they had lists of names and addresses of important Jews — like my father.

I wasn't there when they took him and Mamma. My last memory of him was in that chair with his newspaper. And my last memory of her? In bed, my lovely boy, red-rimmed eyes and smelling of Palinka. I tore off my yellow star and ran through the streets for hours looking for them, but as dusk fell I knew I was in danger and crawled beneath a wooden porch for the night. All I had were the clothes I wore and a piece of paper taken from Father's study with the address of Jonatan's sanatorium written on it. I decided to rescue him.

If only Dad had talked to me about Jonatan. Surely he could see that autism was something in our family? How much heartache could he have saved me from, the guilt over my drinking, the thought that I was responsible for Jonah's autism. But then,

I hadn't shared those fears with my father. We had hereditary speech and language problems of our own, it would seem, just less obvious than Jonatan's or Jonah's.

Maurice is standing sheepishly by the door.

'How long have you had this?'

He comes and sits beside me on the sofa. 'Maybe thirty years, give or take. It is all true, Ben, every word,' Maurice says. 'There's a lot more of it, too.'

Icing

The ride to Lake Balaton from Budapest is forty-five minutes, but with Maurice beside me it feels like days. In Budapest, I register a claim for my grandfather's property and look into reparations for my father. The authorities are polite, the forms constructed to deter. I make a mental note to make use of Emma's legal brilliance. It's not really about the money, or the belated justice, I think that with Jonah's help I have warmed to the prospect of the fight. Almost seventy years ago it may be, but my indignation is new and raw and Jonah's adult life is not yet secure. He has been at Highgrove Manor for a year now. The time has flown and I am looking forward to his first fortnight-long stay at home.

Norah, our guide, meets us from the train. Early twenties and socially optimistic, she's of a generation that is not embarrassed by a mission such as ours. Her white VW Golf zips us from Balatonfured toward the lakeside town of Tihany, along a flawless tarmacked road.

'The building is still there,' she says to me over her shoulder – the car has only three doors, so I'm in the back. 'I checked. There has been no major development there.'

'What's it used for now?'

'A private school of some sort, they're expecting us.'

'And the lake house?'

'Redeveloped.'

Tihany is swish. Oversized villas, disguised with logs and planks to resemble simple cabins. Norah takes a road to the right as we enter the village and we lose sight of the lake. We drive through pines until the road narrows into a drive and – at its end – a grand house.

'There, did I tell you, Ben, *nu?*'

But I am staring at a painted wooden sign above the entrance: JEWELLY ISKOLA AUSTIST GYERMEKEK.

'Norah?'

'It says the Jewelly School for Children with Autism.'

I need to sit down, there is a bench just inside the building's portico. So this is where our name comes from, where my identity was forged also. Then I spot the PECS and Makaton symbols stuck to Velcro on the door's glass panels. I don't need Norah to translate these.

The director speaks perfect English and entertains us with coffee and cake.

'The Government gave us the property in 1993, no claim had been filed.'

'But you kept the original name from when it was operating?'

'Yes, it seemed fitting. Here are the photos you asked about. I think this one you will find most interesting.'

It is black and white, a postcard of the house taken from outside what appears to have been a perimeter wall – now gone – and taking in the foreground. On the far left of the image, in the shadow of a pine tree, stands a shed.

'The shed, is it still there?'

'No, it was falling to pieces when we arrived. Nothing had been touched for fifty years and it was hazardous for the children.'

'And the wall?'

'This is not a prison. It was the first thing to go.'

I'm anxious to search the grounds. 'May we go outside?'

'Of course, I will accompany you.'

The area is overgrown with woodland plants and grasses. It's thick and anonymous, no noticeable undulations or clearings. Maurice and I walk figure of eights, kicking away small plants, weeds and bracken. After half an hour I'm hot, tired, frustrated and drop to my haunches to smoke a cigarette. It must be here somewhere.

'Maybe we should ...'

'No, Maurice. I need to find this.'

I drop my cigarette butt and grind it out with the toe of my boot and it catches on something solid. I fall to my belly and scrape through the undergrowth with my fingers – it is the corner of a brick.

'Maurice, here.'

Maurice stands and lights a cigar, while I clear away the plant life and soil from the brick. Gradually more emerge, like a rusty mountain range. I feel like an Egyptian tomb raider, carefully digging out blocks of the pyramid. There are dozens of them. They have toppled over time, so I brush them off and lay them flat, running my hand over their surfaces, turning them over. Three stand out. They create an almost perfect square and the engraving, although weathered, is clear.

JONATAN, TIZENKET

BATYAM

NAGYON SAJNALOM

GEORG

I look to Norah.

'It says: Jonatan, thirteen. My brother. I am very sorry. Georg.'

'My uncle, my uncle is buried here. My Uncle Jonatan.'

Maurice begins the *Kaddish*.

I look at the school director and Norah. 'Could we have a moment, please?'

The two women head back to the building as Maurice finishes the prayer for the dead and I unzip my rucksack and remove a trowel and the container – both smuggled through customs. I dig and the earth comes away easily, it takes me no time to create a hole large enough for the urn. I feel Maurice's hand on my shoulder as I place the urn in the hole and refill it with my hand, patting it down.

'You want it now?'

'Yes, if you haven't accidentally blown your nose on it.'

Maurice passes me the ragged onion skins of paper – the secret of my father – and I begin to re-read, out loud.

```
...I decided to rescue him. I had a roll of
pengo notes stolen from my father's bureau,
tied with a purple ribbon and hidden inside the
lining of my coat, and his gun, a Luger.

    The morning was bright and cold, the sunlight
slanting off the Danube warmed my frozen fingers
and toes and dried my tears of grief to dirty
smudges.

    Kelleti Station was my destination, across
the bridge in Pest. Before the fighting we had
summered at Balaton every year; my father had a
surgery there, which he held in the front room
of our lake house. I would swim, while Jonatan
```

paddled his feet in the cool waters from the
jetty, laughing and splashing as I disappeared
beneath the water, rising again to blow mouth-
fuls of water over him as though from the
blowhole of a whale. He never learnt to swim and
Anton, Father's assistant, would sit with him,
holding his shoulders in case he should slip in
and drown.

After my swim, we would walk the shore,
tossing stones and shingles into the lake and
watching the boats bobbing and zipping around
each other. There was always warm chocolate when
we returned and a sip of Bull's Blood at dinner.
Then we would sit by the picture window as the
summer sun bid us goodnight — waiting until the
last orange glow tucked itself beneath the blanket of shallow hills opposite. I slept dream-
lessly. Jonatan slept little.

Life was gentler than in the city, Jonatan
was calmer, Mother was happier; Father smiled
more.

A small blond boy in an oversized coat can
wander invisibly beneath the frantic stares of
adults and the walk to the station was surprisingly uneventful. The Nazis were edgy and
unprepared, leaving the checkpoints to Hungarian
sympathisers who themselves were terrified of
the rumours of the advancing Red Army.

The station was heaving with people. I wound
my way in and out of lines of queuing escapees,

crawling sometimes, ignoring curses and flailing
arms until I reached the ticket office.

'Balaton,' I said.

The ticket master laughed at me, patted me on
the head and turned his gaze to a man standing
behind me.

'Balaton,' I said, louder. 'A ticket for
Balaton, now, please. I have money.' I could
feel the agitation of the crowds behind and my
resolve began to dissolve into tears.

'How much to Balaton?'

'Go home, sonny.'

'I need to go to Balaton.'

The ticket master reached across the counter
and grabbed me by the collar.

'Go home now, boy, before...'

'Sell the boy a ticket.'

I turned to see where the voice had come
from. A tall man, blond-haired and bespectacled.
The rest of the queue began to join in, chanting
at the window.

'All right, all right, Balaton. Four pengo.'

I dug into my coat and pulled four notes from
my bundle and handed them over in exchange for a
ticket.

'The train, there, front two coaches. You'd
better run, it leaves in three minutes.'

The train began to move as I closed the heavy
door and stumbled down the corridor looking
for an empty compartment. There were none, so I
chose one with a single spare seat, next to the

window, amid a family of five — grey-looking and nervous. I wrapped my fingers around the butt of the Luger and fought against the rocking train's invitation to sleep.

I was shaken awake by the guard. 'Boy, you can't live on this train. Get up now and get off — and be careful — there are still Germans near the oilfields to the north.'

I rubbed my eyes and felt for the gun and money in the lining of my jacket — both safe. 'Is this Balaton?'

'You are by the lake. Balatonfured. Where are you heading by yourself?'

'Tihany, I'm going to meet my brother.'

'Come, climb down.'

It seemed by luck that I was on the right side of the lake. Balaton is huge and it could easily have been an eight-hour trek around the shore, but the guard said if I walked quickly and took care I should reach Aszotto in an hour — where I could eat — and Tihany another two hours later.

'Why Tihany, boy? There's nothing there but some old lake houses and the sanatorium where they keep the lunatics.'

'He's in our lake house waiting for me.' I could tell he didn't believe me, but he told me to go carefully and remounted the train. I watched it build steam and disappear and began walking in the direction of Aszotto. I was starving, having not eaten for several hours,

and the early autumn chill cooled me as I began
at a trot.

But Aszotto was a ghost town, smouldering
in places, windows were smashed and cartridge
cases littered the floor. I searched three abandoned houses for food and found little but the
remains of a hastily abandoned meal of pork and
potatoes — too mouldy to eat. I drew some water
from a well and drank and left as quickly as I
could. Bad things had happened there, I knew, so
I took the Luger out of my pocket and held it by
my side as I left Aszotto behind and continued
down the road to Tihany, talking in my head to
Jonatan, planning adventures and games and trips
to faraway places.

It was so silent that I heard the car
approaching a full five minutes before it
arrived and was safely behind a pine tree as it
drew level and passed me. It was not a car, but
a German truck, green and canvas-covered with
Swastikas on the doors and the shadows of soldiers visible from its open back. It was heading
where I was heading and where I was heading
was to rescue Jonatan. Once it was out of sight
I ran and ran until I thought my heart would
burst.

It took me another thirty minutes before the
roofs came into view, the roofs of Tihany, and
ten minutes later I was crouching behind a tool
shed, outside the walls of the Tihany Jewelly
Sanatorium, Luger in hand, watching as about a

dozen black-clad SS laughed and chatted in the
fading light, passed cigarettes among themselves
and urinated against the wheels of the truck.

There were five bursts — not the bang of my
father's handgun I now clutched in my hand, but
something far bigger, something that sounded of
death. I felt my heart split in two.

A few minutes later, two SS came out of the
sanatorium and climbed into the driver and passenger seat. The others threw their cigarettes
to the gravel and stubbed them out with fury
before jumping into the back of the truck.
It then swung round and sped off back toward
Aszotto.

By now only the faintest glow outlined the
horizon and the silence had returned — all but
the pumping of my heart. I left my hiding place
and ran, crouching, into the darkness of the
sanatorium. My footsteps echoed off the marble
floor. I could just make out a wide central
staircase with a corridor either side — I went
left, holding the gun in front of me.

There were five rooms off to the left of the
corridor, offices, and as my eyes grew accus-
tomed to the darkness, I saw that they were like
my father's with medical cabinets and charts and
strange instruments. The first four rooms were
vacant, but from the fifth came a light — dim
and orange — and a whiff of tobacco smoke. I
crept in slowly. It was the dying ember of a
cigarette hanging limply from the lips of a man,

his white doctor's coat polka-dotted with red. Next to him, lined up like a little girl's collection of dolls, lay four women in nurse's uniforms — similarly polka-dotted — and to my young mind, playing dead.

'Jonatan!' I sprinted from the room, frantically calculating the burst of gunfire I had heard less than ten minutes before. Five bursts, five dead.

'Jonatan!' I searched the offices off the right corridor — all empty — then I took the stairs two at a time, all caution gone.

'Jonatan!' At the top, a large double door with the lock shot through stood open. Inside, beds sat either side like a hospital ward and on each lay a person, perfectly still, on their backs with their hands by their sides.

'Jonatan!' I found him in the last bed on the right-hand side of the row, tucked beneath a crisp white sheet, his eyes closed, his guileless smile fixed on me. 'Oh Jonatan, Jonatan. It's all right now, they've gone. I've come to rescue you, to take you home.'

I touched his cheek, but its chill stung my finger, I kissed him and shook him and cried on him but my tears froze to crystals. I climbed on to the bed with him and held him and spoke of our future into his deafened ear and then I slept.

I was young, but I had seen enough to know that he had been rescued by those with the polka-dots before I arrived and that they had died for their kindness. He was whole and he was smiling and whatever they gave him sent him off to be with Mamma and Papa in peace and with happy thoughts. They had saved him from a Nazi bullet.

He was bigger than me, of course, he was three years older, but the next morning, using the mattress as a sled, I dragged him from the ward, down the stairs and to the shade of a pine tree outside the walls of the sanatorium and — with a spade from the tool shed I had hidden behind the previous day — I dug a grave and buried my brother and marked it with a brick and earth headstone, bashed from the wall with a sledgehammer.

But there was one thing I couldn't bury with him, couldn't bear to part with — Father's paperweight. His crystal paperweight that split the light and shone a rainbow over Jonatan's innocent face — for that was all I had left of my family. 'Jonatan's Jewel', my father called it. It had made its way there with Jonatan, a gift of parting. And I was now parted from everything I had known and loved. I was somebody else, so I should change my name and what else could it be? From the hospital in whose grounds I buried him, to the paperweight I now clutched in my hand: both told me this was now my beginning and from then my name was Jewell.

I stayed one more night, collected up as much food as I could carry and set off back toward

Balatonfured and the train — making sure to
stick to the trees.

The platform was deserted. Scraps of news-
papers blew in the breeze. I stood scanning
the horizon and it occurred to me that the only
people I had encountered since arriving the
day before were either dead or Nazi soldiers.
I walked over to the station master's office.
The door hung off its hinges, the desk inside
covered with coffee-stained papers and the
telegraph box torn from the wall. The railway
map remained, however, so I carefully unpinned
it from its cork board and folded it so that it
would fit in my jacket pocket.

It felt as if everyone was dead. Not just my
parents — as I discovered later — and Jonatan,
but the whole world. Maybe I was the last alive.
At first, the thought exhilarated me. So childish, I know, but all I could think of were the
empty stores, full of goods and food and all
for free, all for me. I would live in the biggest house in Budapest and crown myself king,
drive a different motor car every day and never,
ever go to school again. But there is only so
much silence one small boy can take, only so
many solo games he can play before boredom sets
in and then loneliness and finally fear. If I
became ill, who would treat me? And if I became
so ill that I lay dying, who would comfort me
the way the nurse who sent Jonatan to sleep no
doubt comforted him?

So what should I do? Return to Budapest, follow the track I had rolled down the day before, or walk the other way — west, I guessed, although I was not sure. I had to make a decision. I could have waited for ever for a train and one may never have arrived, but I knew that the tracks led to stations and stations belonged to towns and in towns there may be people. So I jumped down on to the dusty tracks, my shoulders already aching with the weight of the provisions I had removed from the sanatorium, and turned away from Budapest, my home and, as it turned out, a home I would never return to.

People always imagine that railway lines are straight, but they are not, they follow contours, they swish through valleys, burrow through hills and bridge rivers and they go on and on. I passed three deserted towns before the sun beat down on my uncovered head and there, about an hour outside the last, stood an unmanned junction box and the track split in two like an undone zip. I sat in the box to find some shade, drank some water and carefully unfolded the map.

North-west, or south-west? Either way meant Austria. I flipped a pengo coin — on such simple acts lives are won or lost — and headed north-west where I knew that I would eventually reach the Danube again and where the map showed more lines through more towns, although how long it would take me on foot, I did not know.

I walked those tracks for three days taking
shelter where I could find it, but even in my
sleep I was riding those rails. I began to talk
to myself, just to check that I still had the
power to talk. Solitude does that to a person.
I also had conversations with Mamma and Papa
and Jonatan, with the family whose carriage I
had shared on the way from Budapest to Balaton,
with Comrade Stalin — pleading with him to hurry
— and even with Adolf Hitler, in language I had
heard used in some of the seamier neighbour-
hoods of Budapest but had never had the courage
to use, even among my closest friends — or even
with Jonatan, who could not have repeated it
anyway.

And then, on the fourth day, as I sat on the
rails nursing my aching feet, I felt the slightest vibration creep from my backside and up my
spine. The sensation grew stronger until I was
almost bouncing like on a fairground ride.

It was a train. A train! But I was nowhere
near a station, in truth I had no idea how far
I was from the nearest town. For two days I had
counted my steps, trying to measure the distance
I had travelled. Should I run back? Should I run
forward? Would it stop for me anyway? Trains
move faster than nine-year-old boys, this I
knew as a fact, so I jumped from the line and
ran to the highest ground I could see — a small
hillock, overgrown and verdant — and stared
into the distance, squinting against the sun,

trying to separate steam from wispy cloud until
I gained a sharpened view of the locomotive's
face. It grew larger and larger, so quickly that
I thought it must have been travelling at a hundred miles an hour. I began to wave, first with
one arm, then with both, my rucksack flung to
the floor, and, yes! It was a Hungarian train,
the insignia was clear to me and my waving was
joined by jumping. I grabbed my bag and sprinted
back toward the track, praying it had slowed
enough for me to jump on and see a face, hear a
voice, grab a hand.

I was right, it had slowed, but only to negotiate the growing incline, and the locomotive,
so smiling and familiar as it approached through
the sun-soaked rays, turned demon as it reached
me, each open door of the steam-breathing mon-
ster a cobra's eye, with lids of black iron and
gunmetal eyelashes spitting bullets at me as it
passed.

I hit the floor, instinctively, flattening
myself against the grit and weeds beside the
rails until the firing stopped and the cattle
wagons whumped and whumped and whumped past
me; wooden and numbered and Swastikaed. The
train did not slow; the only ride available it
appeared would have been to Hell and I didn't
want to go, not then, at least.

I lay on my stomach looking up as the last
wagon drew up to me and — as it did — one plank
lifted at its rear, and as the train hit the

brow of the hill, this final carriage gave
birth, from a gap no larger than a school exercise book. A bundle squeezed out, fell to the
track and rolled like a balloon — so light it
was — until it settled at my feet.

The bundle had a face, not much of a face,
so prominent were its bones — but a face nevertheless. A boy's face with relief shining like
torch beams from his sunken eyes.

I pointed to my chest. 'Georg,' I said,
while he took his hand and mimed the action of a
drink.

An age later, after I had fed him water drip
by drip and he had slept and then revived a
little, I tried again. 'Georg,' and held up nine
fingers. 'Nine years, Magyar.'

With effort he held his skeletal child's hand
out to me and I took it. So thin it was, I swear
I could feel my own thumb through its width.

'Mauritz. Nederland.' Two fives and a two. He
was twelve, but reached just to my shoulder. His
forearm bore the Jewish tattoo, so there was no
need to ask.

'Maurice, I want to take the bricks with me, before the writing
weathers away. They're tactile, Jonah can read them. I'll put
another stone in their place.'

I have thought about this moment constantly since Maurice's
revelation, written and rubbed out, rehearsed and re-rehearsed.
Maurice promises to fill me in about their time together before
arriving in England, but it is enough – for now – and I plan

310

to type it up as soon as I get back, before the pages become unreadable.

This forced solitude, as unwanted and painful as it is, will stretch as far into the future as I allow it. So, I must try to acknowledge the situation as an opportunity to accept optimism without guilt – my life is valuable enough for me to care about it and, dare I think it, maybe Emma won't be the last woman in my life.

I have so much time now. I don't want to waste it on drunken days and daytime TV – years can pass that way. No. I will return to England and begin my journey and listen to *my* voice, trust what it has to say.

But for now, as I stand here, beneath a sun-dappled pine, beside my family's lake, thinking of my father and finishing a postcard to my son, I am suddenly voiceless. Suddenly, perfectly *shtum*.

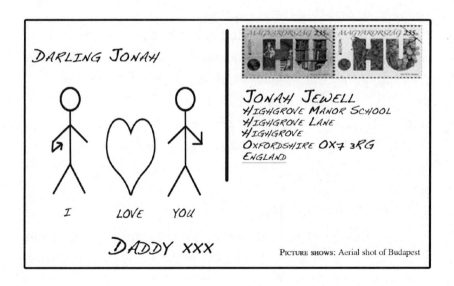

DARLING JONAH

I   LOVE   YOU

DADDY xxx

JONAH JEWELL
HIGHGROVE MANOR SCHOOL
HIGHGROVE LANE
HIGHGROVE
OXFORDSHIRE OX7 3RG
ENGLAND

PICTURE SHOWS: Aerial shot of Budapest

Why I Wrote *Shtum*

The day after I took my own autistic son to begin a new life at a wonderful residential school in the country, I began the MA in Novel Writing at City University. Having just emerged from a year-long battle with the powers that be to get him there, it seemed serendipitous. After all, it had been more than a decade since I'd truly had the time to concentrate on writing – such was the level of dedication he required.

To be frank, I was exhausted and emotionally raw and the last subject I wanted to write about was autism. However, after frustrating my tutor, Jonathan Myerson, with adamant refusals to do so, I went home for the weekend and pondered long and hard, and came up with a list of pros and cons.

When I returned to City the following week, my conclusions were the following:

1. It would have to be funny – because autistic children can be joyously hilarious. As an example, when my son was six or seven, he developed an aversion to my mum. If she entered a room he was in, he'd physically push her out and close the door after her!

2. Honest – I was truly fed up with being asked what my son's 'special talent' was.
3. How would I feel if someone else wrote this story?

And then there was the ironic realisation – long held – that my son, with no language, was far better at communicating his wants and needs than I was.

After all the soul searching and prevaricating, it was number two that kept hammering at me. I wanted to be honest, even if revealing the brutality of the reality was counter-intuitive.

Before my son was born, I read *The Curious Incident of the Dog in the Night-Time* and loved it. Over the years since his birth, I have witnessed the elevation of autism – especially Asperger's – to something almost fashionable. I'd heard autism used as excuses for shoddy behaviour, as an insult, and seen it adopted as a badge of honour.

This was galling to me and, no doubt, to the countless other families dealing with the day-to-day misunderstandings and devastation it could bring. So I found myself in a challenging and (again counter-intuitively) responsible position – how could I write a novel that had a mute central character? How could I write a novel that was about autism yet, at the same time, dealt with so much more?

Shtum is the result.

I hope you enjoy it.

Jem

Acknowledgements

My partner, Catherine Ercilla, who fell for me because of my writing, and – despite my uselessness in most other areas – is still here and is my best friend and reader.

Noah Lester, who will never read this book, but who may – if the mood takes him – throw it out of the window.

Eloise Lester, whose psychology degree will, I hope, save me a fortune in therapy in the coming years.

Karen Ferberman, to whom I owe thirty-four birthday presents, innumerable cigarette lighters, a hundred explanations and, crucially, a bearable youth.

Mitchell Ross, for forty-six years of laughter, ludicrous antics and many shared sorrows.

My amazing agent, Laura Williams, and all at PFD who backed *Shtum* after hearing a badly-read 1,500 words above a pub in March 2013.

My brilliant Orion editor, Jemima Forrester, and publicist/ force of nature, Sam Eades.

Jonathan Myerson, Lucy Caldwell and Clare Allan of City University.

My anti-insanity squad: Dr Claudia Bernat, Dorit Dror, Mel Davis and Wendy Davis.

Dame Stephanie Shirley, the founder of Priors Court School, Berkshire, and all the dedicated staff therein.

The bionic Tracey Fenton and all at TBC for their enthusiasm and support.

The late JC deputy-editor and theatre critic, David Nathan, for accepting my post-lunch filing cabinet violence as completely appropriate behaviour.